James Bond and Moonraker

Also by Christopher Wood in Triad/Panther Books

James Bond, The Spy Who Loved Me

Christopher Wood

James Bond and Moonraker

TRIAD PANTHER

Published in 1979 by Triad/Panther Books
Frogmore, St Albans, Herts AL2 2NF

ISBN 0 586 05034 5

Triad Paperbacks Ltd is an imprint of
Chatto, Bodley Head & Jonathan Cape Ltd
and Granada Publishing Ltd

First published in Great Britain by
Jonathan Cape Ltd 1979
Copyright © Glidrose Publications as Trustee 1979

Made and printed in Great Britain by
Richard Clay (The Chaucer Press) Ltd
Bungay, Suffolk
Set in Linotype Plantin

Contents

To Vernon Harris,
with affectionate gratitude

1

THE END – AND THE BEGINNING

The 747 was flying high, nosing aside wisps of cloud as a celebrity might brush past eager reporters. It was not alone. On its back was the squat outline of the space shuttle it was transporting, the word MOONRAKER distinctively lettered on its sides. Seen from afar, the shuttle looked like a giant fish riding on the back of a cruising whale.

Inside the control cabin the captain's eyes flickered over the panels of instruments, the wavering needles, the banks of coloured lights. There was nothing abnormal. The 747 was flying itself. There appeared to be no adverse reaction to the unaccustomed load. The captain was surprised and relieved. It proved what a hell of a good aeroplane the 747 was. The captain indulged a twinge of patriotic pride and wondered, not for the first time, why the space shuttle was being lent to the British. Was it just for an air show? It seemed a gesture both expansive and expensive at a time when the Administration was cutting back savagely on overseas spending and when the space programme itself was being starved of funds to the point where there had been accusations in the Senate that space was being abandoned to the Russians.

Maybe the British boffins had come up with something that NASA could use. That seemed the most likely explanation. While the shuttle was in England, the British scientists could run their own tests and confer with their American colleagues. Despite limited resources it was difficult to believe that the British had not come up with something since Bluestreak, if only at the drawing board stage.

Beside the captain, the first officer glanced at his watch

and moistened his lips. He was thinking of pleasure, not business; of an apartment off the Bayswater Road in London where a lady of his acquaintance would be checking that there was still enough Jack Daniels left in the bottle and that an extra towel hung in the bathroom. She would do this before she went to work in a library so that she could get home by six with any extra supplies that were necessary and take a bath and scent herself, and wait for him. He knew she would be waiting because he had telephoned her in the middle of the night before the trip. She was always waiting. Always glad to see him. She was a passionate girl but, like many English girls, ashamed of her carnality and inclined to cloak it in coyness. She would open the door to him in the most provocative underwear she possessed and complain that she had been expecting him an hour later. He would back her into the bedroom and make love to her and she would protest at the same instant as the dry nail varnish flaked off against his punctured back and her well-cleaned teeth bit into his shoulder.

He wondered what shape the evening would take. She did not always open the door in a négligé. Normally she would be waiting to receive him in a dress of becoming simplicity, perhaps adorned with a large antique brooch. She would take the flowers he proffered with small cries of joy and stand on tiptoe to push forward her cheek for a kiss. Then it would be into the small sitting room and a vase for the flowers and a Jack Daniels on the rocks for him. And all the time a constant flow of questions that never waited for answers, and reminiscences about people he had never met. 'You know, it was frightfully funny, but ...' It never was funny, or even interesting, but he would listen with a good-humoured expression on his face and sip his drink and let his eyes enjoy the breasts and the curve of the skilfully aligned legs that the rest of his body would be savouring in good time.

After a second drink, a gin and Schweppes' Bitter Lemon for her, he would suggest dinner and they would go round the corner to a small Italian restaurant where the lights were low and the prices high and the clientèle leant across the tables to hold hands and looked round quickly every time somebody entered in case it was their wife, husband or established lover.

Once at the restaurant he would transfer his allegiance to a bottle of Valpolicella and listen to her talk about her job; or rather, the man she worked for. He surmised that this man had once been a lover although this had never been explicitly stated. There was resentment but at the same time grudging respect and a kind of fascination. The man was married but he was not happy with his wife. He would have been happier with her, if she would have him, was the inference.

Whilst the saga of the library unfolded the *prosciutto e melone* would give way to the *petto di pollo* and the girl's face become even more desirable in animation. She was probably trying to make him jealous but he did not care who else had her as long as she was always available on demand. As he debated whether they needed another bottle of wine his legs would stretch out to find hers and immediately feel the pressure of her calf against his and her hand upon his thigh. Her lips would start to stay apart temptingly and glisten in the candlelight. He would forget about the second bottle of wine and suggest that they drank their coffee back at the apartment. He smiled. They had never had that coffee yet.

'What are you sniggering about, Joe?' The captain's voice cut in on his reverie.

'Nothing in particular.'

'Some broad you're going to lay in London?'

'I'm too much of a gentleman to answer that question.' The first officer spoke over his shoulder. 'How are we doing for time, Dick?'

The navigation officer, who was Britain's contribution to the ferrying of the Moonraker, looked up from his plotter. Close inspection would have revealed a faint blush on his pink cheeks. He was not used to exchanges of the kind he had just heard between the captain and his first officer. 'Not bad at all, sir. We're fifteen minutes up on our E.T.A. already. If this tail wind keeps up we could be at Heathrow forty minutes ahead of schedule.'

'Excellent,' said the captain.

The navigation officer looked down at his charts. Somewhere, far below in the strange half-light between night and day, was the town of Champagne. What a name for a town at the northern end of the Rockies in the Yukon Territory of Canada. Perhaps there actually was champagne there once when the gold rush was in full spate and the word Yukon was synonymous with twenty-four carats. He thought of men wrapped in furs staggering out of a blizzard and kicking their snow shoes against the hitching rail of a saloon. The swing doors bursting open, the gust of warm air, the honky-tonk music in the background, the slaps on the back, the fire of the first shot of whisky hitting the back of the throat, the satisfying pressure of the bag of gold dust wedged solidly against the underbelly.

Now the saloon had probably given way to Frank's Fast Food Dinette, catering for truck drivers climbing down from the air-conditioned comfort of their cabs on the Alaska Highway. Half an ear on the local radio, half an eye on the girl behind the counter. The sizzling hot plate appearing through the hatch. Three eggs, sunny-side-up on rashers of bacon that overlapped the plate and were further anchored by a small mountain of crusty hash brown potatoes, the whole accompanied by a mug of steaming black coffee. The navigation officer could taste the saliva building up inside his mouth. He could almost feel the invisible knife in his hand breaking through the delicious, fatty, fried crust of the hash browns. With any luck, if there were no stacking problems at Heathrow and the Kingston By-pass was not throttled by returning commuters, he would be home in time to help the children with their homework and eat supper with the family. He had tried to ring Louise and let her know when he was likely to be back but there had been no reply. She must have been out at one of her yoga classes or helping clear up after a War on Want lunch. It did not really matter. It would be more of a surprise for them when they saw him.

Inside the lower deck of the Moonraker a trained ear could have heard a faint vibration. All was in darkness. The whole structure of the craft trembled. Then there was another sound. A muffled, fizzing noise like a firework in a tin can about to explode. But the noise went on and on and there was no explosion. The noise did not get louder but there slowly came a faint glow of light that showed itself like a tiny slit mouth at the extremity of one of the wall lockers. The glow concentrated itself about the locked securing catch, which slowly began to turn red and then white hot. A thin column of black smoke rose in the air and the metal began to buckle. Fifteen seconds passed and then there was a sharp crack and the locker burst open. Immediately the bright light that was revealed extinguished itself and the glowing metal faded rapidly until it lost its identity in the darkness. The shuttle continued to vibrate through space and there was a rustle of clothing as a man's legs swung from the locker. A thin torch beam probed the darkness and a laser welder was tossed on to one of the bunks. The light probed like an impatient finger and found what it wanted: the opening device on the opposite locker. This was swiftly pressed open and a second pair of legs swung into view.

The two figures that were revealed looked like hobgoblins in the quarter-light. Their tight-fitting black uniforms covered them from head to toe and were melded into pressurized oxygen masks with tubes that led from beneath the reinforced glass panels at eye level to two thin cylinders on their backs. They did not hesitate but moved instantly towards the foot of a spiral stairway. The first man to emerge led the way and began to climb. Above him was the control cabin of the Moonraker space shuttle.

In the cabin of the 747 the first officer rubbed his hands together ruminatively. 'How we doing now, Dick?'

'We just passed over Fairbanks.'

'On schedule?'

'Twenty minutes ahead.'

The first officer rubbed his hands some more and thought of how in a few hours' time he would be walking his date back from the Italian restaurant. The winter fog would be fuzzing up the street lamps. He could hear their footsteps and see the breath in the cold air. He liked London in the winter. Most of all he liked the thought of what was going to happen once the prim counterpane had been stripped off the bed that was too small for sleeping but just the right size for everything else.

He felt the captain's eyes on him.

'I can read you like a book, Joe. I don't think I ever flew with a –'

He broke off as he saw the first officer start forward in his seat.

'What the –'

A light was flashing on the right-hand extremity of the control panel.

'The shuttle ignition!'

'There must be a fault in the system. Check the circuits!'

Before the first officer could obey the order there was a deafening roar and the 747 lurched as if swatted in mid-air by an invisible hand. The cabin trembled and the roar in-

14

creased in intensity.

'What the hell's happening?'

'The shuttle's taking off!'

'It can't –' The voice broke off as it was overtaken by the terrible reality. An eldritch wail nearly split their eardrums and a blinding light burned their staring eyes as if the door of a blast furnace had suddenly been wrenched open before their faces. The orbital engines of the Moonraker achieved full combustion and a ball of flame engulfed the cabin, scorching the screams out of the crew's throats. Like an insect poised after delivering its deadly sting, the Moonraker shuddered in mid-air and the fiery exhaust from its tail continued to play on the cabin of the stricken 747. Almost simultaneously it roared away in a steep climb. The nose of the 747 drooped and flames raced the length of the fuselage. Like a heavy cinder it started to fall out of the sky.

Admiral Sir Miles Messervy, K.C.M.G., alias M, gazed thoughtfully out of the window of his eighth floor office overlooking Regent's Park. The office belonged to Transworld Consortium but this was also an alias for an adjunct of the British Ministry of Defence which might have been termed the Secret Service. 'Might have been' if M had nothing to do with the appellation. He would have found such terminology too showy and dramatic for his puritan, sea dog tastes. He preferred the obscurantism of Transworld Consortium and had even regretted, though accepted the wisdom of, the change from the organization's original title of Universal Export. He reached out across the red-leather-topped desk and helped himself to a pipeful of tobacco from the polished brass fourteen-pounder shell base that served him as a memento of his naval days and a tobacco jar, in that order.

There was an atmosphere of brooding menace in the air

that perhaps communicated itself from the clouds lowering over the park. Perhaps not. M was uneasy. He felt his eye drawn to the telephone on his desk as if receiving some telepathic message that it was about to ring. Just below the receiver was a light that glowed red when a top secret call was being placed from the upper echelons of the Ministry of Defence. The light came on when kings died and presidents were assassinated.

As M watched, the telephone rang and the light glowed red.

M's pulse did not change an iota. He held his half-filled pipe in his left hand and picked up the receiver. 'M here.' He listened to the urgent, harassed voice on the end of the telephone and the lines at the corner of his clear, grey eyes deepened. 'Very well, Minister,' he said finally. 'We'll get on to it.' He replaced the receiver and paused to reflect for an instant before flicking up the switch on the intercom that connected him to his secretary.

Her voice came through immediately. 'Yes, sir?'

M took a deep breath and spoke with a voice long since purged of all emotion. 'Moneypenny. I want 007. As fast as you can get him.'

2

'ENJOY YOUR FLIGHT'

The face was dark and clean-cut with a three-inch scar showing whitely down the right cheek. The eyes were wide and level under straight, rather long black brows. The hair was black, parted on the left, and brushed so that a thick black comma fell over the right eyebrow. The longish straight nose ran down to a narrow upper lip below which was a wide and finely drawn but cruel mouth. The line of the jaw was firm and ruthless.

The man was wearing a dark blue alpaca suit, a Sea Island cotton shirt and plain black shoes made for him by John Lobb of St James's Street, London. His tie was black and hand-knitted and a trifle thinner than contemporary fashion dictated. But James Bond was impervious to the transient fads of the male fashion world. Such details were of no interest to him. He pulled out a gunmetal cigarette case and considered his fiftieth cigarette of the day. As he looked down at the scuffed metal he could almost see the report of his last medical check-up which M had slid across the desk, one eyebrow raised above those damnably clear grey eyes:

The officer admits to a daily consumption of alcohol in excess of half a bottle of spirits of seventy proof or above. He also smokes an average of sixty non-filter cigarettes per day. These cigarettes are specially made for him from a mixture of Turkish and Balkan tobaccos with a higher nicotine content than ordinary brands. On examination, this regimen [Bond smiled at the recollection of the word 'regimen'] is beginning to have the expected effect. The

17

tongue is furred. The blood pressure raised at 180/100. The liver is becoming palpable. There is no diminution in the frequency or severity of the occipital headaches referred to in a previous report. The spasm in the trapezius muscles has increased in intensity and the 'fibrositis' nodules are becoming more manifest.

It is difficult to avoid the conclusion that the health of the officer is being systematically undermined by his *mode de vivre*. ['Fancifully put,' thought Bond. 'What is happening in Harley Street these days?'] It is strongly recommended that if his working efficiency is not to be seriously impaired he cease smoking immediately and cut down his intake of spirits. A change to wine would be preferential and total abstinence ideal.

Unequivocal. That was the least that could be said of the report. M had made no strictures but suggested that Bond consider the implications of his check-up. Seriously.

James Bond decided to do so as he smoked his fiftieth cigarette of the day. He slid it between his lips, snapped the gunmetal case shut and reached for his battered Ronson. The small, orgasmic flame flickered and he drew the smoke in greedily. He felt in perfect shape, and when he did not he would take whatever action he felt necessary of his own accord. Medicals were for overweight men who sat behind desks telling other people to do things. He wondered how most doctors would make out under their own stethoscopes.

Smoking was also, for Bond, part of the ritual of flying, and he enjoyed rituals. He enjoyed a well-made vodka martini too. He looked round the cabin of the eight-seater private jet that had been sent to speed him back from Dakar and located a small refrigerator that looked promising. It was tucked just behind the entrance to the cramped pilot's cabin and below a rack of glossy magazines that Bond had already flicked through. With an intuition that Bond found wholly admirable the stewardess appeared through the opening and slid the door closed behind her. She was a tall girl with a wide, sensuous mouth and well-shaped breasts. Her smile had not been over-used flying the routes followed by the commercial airlines and it came across as a genuine expression of a desire to please. Her clothing was simple. A beautifully cut grey woollen skirt and a white silk shirt with matching stock.

'Would you like a drink?' she said.

Bond returned her smile. 'I knew you were a mind reader. Do we have any Gordon's gin or a grain-based vodka?'

'I don't know about the grain-based.' She bent down to open the refrigerator and Bond enjoyed the firm rounding of her haunches. 'I thought vodka was made from potatoes.'

'A lot of it is.'

The girl stood up with a bottle of Gordon's in her hand. 'That's all we have, I'm afraid. Unless you'd like whisky?'

'No, thank you. I'll take four measures of Gordon's with a smidgin of dry martini, shaken till it's ice cold. If you can lay your hands on a long shave of lemon peel, my happiness will be complete.'

The girl looked down at him approvingly. 'You know what you like.'

'I think that makes it easier for everybody,' said Bond. He held her glance for a second longer than was necessary and expelled two dragon's breaths of smoke through his nostrils. 'How long have you been working for Transcontinental?'

The girl went about mixing the drink. 'Only a few weeks. It took so long to get through security clearance.'

'I thought I hadn't seen you,' said Bond thoughtfully. 'I didn't recognize the crew either.'

'They're like me,' she said. 'Recent arrivals.' She flashed her bewitching smile and advanced towards him with the drink on a circular silver tray.

Bond took it and felt the satisfying coldness of the glass against his fingertips. 'Thank you.' He turned his head and smiled as the girl slipped into the seat beside him. She leant back and drew up a knee provocatively. 'Delicious,' said Bond.

'You haven't tasted it yet,' said the girl.

'I wasn't talking about the drink.' Bond raised the glass to his lips and drunk. As a substitute it was exceptionally good. He turned to the girl again. 'I may never travel with anyone else.'

'You're so right, Mr Bond.' A small automatic had appeared from beneath the silver tray and was pointing at the pit of his stomach. The blunt muzzle did not flinch.

Bond sighed. 'You're a grave disappointment to me. I was hoping for a look of surprise when I mentioned Transcontinental.' He shook his head sadly. 'You're supposed to be employed by Transworld.'

'It doesn't matter.' The girl's voice was brittle, within a decibel of breaking. She was under strain. Big strain. She had been given a job at the very limit of her capabilities. It was doubtful whether she could carry it through. Bond realized that she was supposed to kill him. The skilfully executed ground-level hijack at Dakar Airport, the substitution of the crews. It had all been leading up to this moment. The girl's lips were pressed tight together. She was trying to find the courage to pull the trigger.

Bond jerked the glass away from his mouth and the muzzle of the automatic tilted defensively. At the exact instant that the gun moved, Bond lashed out with the back of his fist and struck solidly against the hand that was holding it. The girl let out a cry of pain and surprise and the automatic spun across to the other side of the cabin. Bond clipped the girl smartly against the jaw and was launching himself for the gun when the door to the pilot's cabin slid open. The co-pilot took in the situation at a glance and hurled himself forward to grapple with Bond. Bond was temporarily crushed against one of the seats and then broke free to unleash a right cross that bludgeoned the side of the man's cheek. There was a sharp crack and a grunt of annoyance rather than pain, and the co-pilot came forward again. He was a big man with a parachute strapped to his back and it occurred to Bond that this was an adjunct well worth having in his present situation. He feinted to dive for the gun and as the co-pilot tried to intercept lashed out with his foot for the man's groin. The aeroplane lurched and Bond's blow was diverted by the thigh. He fell back, hitting the wall of the plane. Before he could move again, the co-pilot was on him, grappling for his throat. One hand made contact and the other reached above Bond's head. There was a grinding noise and a rush of air that threatened to suck Bond from the cabin. The co-pilot had opened the emergency door that Bond was leaning against. Bond could feel himself poised on the brink of space with the terrifying void behind him. His hands stretched out to grip the sides of the door opening and the screaming wind tried to tear the clothes from his back. It was taking every ounce of strength that he possessed to stay where he was. The co-pilot saw that Bond was at his mercy and took a step back to deliver the blow that would launch him into space. It was at this instant that the plane entered an area of turbulence, and the floor tilted up towards Bond. He jerked himself sideways and as the plane twitched again, braced his right shoulder against the edge of the door opening. His adversary was launched forward and Bond did no more than guide him into the space he himself had so recently vacated. There was hardly time for a scream of realization and fear to form itself in the man's throat before he was hurtling earthwards, his arms and legs flailing against empty air.

Bond stood braced in the open doorway and looked down, feeling that the wind was pulling his hair out by the roots. Beneath him the co-pilot had conquered his initial panic and was planing down with arms and legs outspread in the classic free-fall position. Bond ground his teeth and prepared to pull away from the terrifying suction that was bent on prising free his grip. At that instant two powerful hands smote him on the shoulders and thrust him into space.

In a nightmare there is a horrible moment when the victim suddenly finds himself suspended in mid-air, his heart seeming to fall faster than the rest of his body. For Bond this was terrifying reality as he plunged earthwards. Far below him was a distant patch of brown which could be mountain or desert. It made no difference. Either would serve equally well as a graveyard. Bond fought panic and forced his arms and legs apart to try to achieve some stability in the air. One chance meeting with the crack Red Devils free-fall parachuting team when on a refresher course with the Parachute Brigade at Aldershot had hardly prepared him for the situation he now found himself in. There was a million miles between principle, no matter how well explained, and reality. This was not the moment he would have chosen to find out how good a pupil he had been.

Bond jerked back his head and felt himself planing through the air. His rate of descent had definitely been slowed. He was like a flat stone wavering from side to side as it sinks through water. He glanced down and saw the unsuspecting co-pilot beneath him. The man had still not opened his parachute. Bond felt a stab of hope. Could he possibly manoeuvre himself close enough to take the man by surprise? He screwed up his eyes against the whiplash of the wind and tried to remember the conversation he had had in the mess at Aldershot. Below him the peaks of mountains were clearly visible. He tilted his body sideways and felt himself starting to slide faster, like a Spitfire peeling off to attack. Not only the cold and the force of the wind were numbing: at every second he expected to lose control and find himself tumbling over and over until the force of impact dashed him to pieces on some jagged, sun-scorched peak of the Atlas Mountains. He folded in his arms and legs and started to drop vertically without the sideways motion. A breast stroke motion of the arms and legs, and he actually felt himself moving forward. It was possible to claw one's way through the air like some clumsy wounded bird.

He glanced sideways and saw the co-pilot fifty yards below him and to the right. One of the man's hands was reaching towards his shoulder. He must be about to pull the ripcord. Bond flung his arms and legs wide and tilted his hands like the wing flaps of an aeroplane. He felt himself slicing through air, and the co-pilot loomed up beside him. The man's head turned and Bond saw his teeth flash white as his mouth opened in surprise. He had no time to react before Bond was on him, feeling the life-sustaining bulk of the parachute against his chest. That was what he wanted. Clinging to the man's shoulder, he unleashed a crippling blow with the flat edge of his hand and felt the force transmit itself to the vulnerable area behind the ear. The man twitched like a stunned rabbit and offered no resistance as Bond fought against the sickening speed of their descent and the metal clasp that secured the parachute. After what seemed like minutes rather than seconds, he prized it open and pulled one of the straps away from an arm barely capable of resistance. He thrust his own arm through the loop and then kicked clear, dragging the rest of the parachute with him. This was the moment of ultimate despair. With both hands struggling to pull on the parachute and fasten the clasp it was impossible to keep stable in space. He felt himself spinning over and over, the ground beneath him and the sky above becoming a crazy kaleidoscope as the wind tore through his clothing and dizzy pain whirred through his tortured brain as if stirring it with a white-hot spoon. And then the clasp clicked home and his fingers tore at the ripcord. For a terrible second it seemed that nothing was going to happen, and then the parachute broke open with a crackle like the spinnaker of an ocean-going yacht bursting forth to steal the wind. Bond's headlong descent shuddered to a near halt and suddenly he was alone and drifting earthwards. To his right were khaki mountains with a distant impression of snow-capped peaks. Directly below him a dusty plain was bisected by a long straight road.

Bond raised his hands to his shoulders and prepared to steer himself towards the road. Marrakesh should not be too far away. It was a pity he did not have time for a night on the town. He thought back to his medical report and smiled grimly. There was clearly life in the old dog yet.

3

a.m. WITH M AND Q

'Ah, James. There you are.' There was relief as well as a glow of welcome in the eyes of M's private secretary.

Bond responded with pleasure to the bowl of winter roses on the desk and the faint upper-class fragrance of some scent he could not place. It was good to be home.

'My flight was diverted, Moneypenny. What's going on?'

There was no immediate response as Miss Moneypenny's head was bent forward announcing his arrival. She flicked up the switch. 'I don't know. He's got the Minister of Defence coming in at any minute. You're to go straight in.' She called after him as he moved towards the door and the telephone on her desk started ringing. 'Does the Chief-of-Staff know you're back?'

Bond turned to nod towards the telephone. 'That'll be him telling you.'

He went through the door and closed it softly behind him. The layout of the room had not changed. The dark green carpet stretching like a putting green to the heavy, polished wood desk with M behind it. Only the big twin-bladed tropical fan, now stationary in the ceiling above the desk, added an incongruous note. Bond wondered how many times M had needed it during the previous summer.

M waved an impatient hand at the chair opposite his desk. 'You've taken a damnably long time getting here.'

Bond sat down and gave a quick description of recent events. M's jawline hardened. 'Somebody obviously doesn't like you. There was that business at Chamonix before your last mission, wasn't there?'

'Yes, sir. I don't think it was the Russians this time.

After the Stromberg affair, I believe they'll give me a few months' respite.'

'You could hardly expect an Order of Lenin,' said M drily. 'Whom do you suspect?'

'Somebody with an old score to settle. There are a number of candidates.'

'Yes.' M nodded his agreement. 'I hope you can steer clear of them for the duration of your next assignment.'

Bond pricked up his ears. 'Yes, sir.'

'Have you had a moment to glance at the station reports?' M picked his pipe out of the heavy copper ash tray.

'No, sir. I came straight to you via the Chief-of-Staff.'

'What do you know about the Moonraker?'

Bond flicked through the card index in his mind. 'It's an American space shuttle. Capable of being launched into space by rocket, orbiting the earth and re-entering the atmosphere to land like a conventional aircraft. They can be used to service permanently manned space stations.'

'And the Americans are just about to phase them into use in the next stage of their space programme. Did you know that we had one coming over so that Q Branch could take a look at it?'

'Absolutely not,' said Bond, the surprise showing on his face.

'Good,' said M grimly. 'You weren't supposed to know. Nobody was.'

'May I ask why the mountain was coming to Mohamed?' inquired Bond.

'In these particular circumstances you may,' said M, kneading the soft tobacco into the bowl of his pipe. 'Q's boys have come up with something they call S.H.I.E.L.D. – Space Heat Identification and Early Liquidation Device.' His expression registered his disapproval of the title. 'Damned if I know why. Everything has to have a brand name like a packet of soapsuds these days. Anyway, as the name implies, once installed in a spacecraft this system will ensure that no intercepting missile can get within miles of it without being destroyed. Apparently it's infallible and the government refuses to let any details out of the country. The Americans are interested in it for their shuttle programme and that's why they've come to us –' M's face grew grim. 'Or rather –' he broke off as the telephone rang, and put down his unlit pipe. 'Very well. Yes. We'll come immediately.' He replaced the receiver and turned to Bond. 'Right, 007. You can hear the rest in the Operations Room.' He moved purposefully round his desk and Bond crossed to the door and opened it. Not for the first time, he wondered whether there was any limit to the diverse range of projects that Q masterminded in his quartermaster's department.

M looked down sternly at Miss Moneypenny as he went past her desk.

'We'll be in the Operations Room. I don't want to be disturbed unless it's critical.'

'Yes, sir.' She smiled at Bond as if grateful to find someone she could exchange a gesture of human warmth with. It had often occurred to Bond to ask himself what particular brand of loyalty bound Moneypenny to M. To be his personal amanuensis could not be the easiest job in the world. It was rumoured that M had once given Moneypenny a bottle of Harvey's Bristol Cream sherry at Christmas, but this rumour was never substantiated. It was more likely that he had wished her the compliments of the season with a grave nod that counselled caution against taking advantage of any opportunity for profligacy or licence. Bond also wondered why Moneypenny had never got married. She was a handsome girl and could never have lacked for suitors. Perhaps, like him, she had decided that she was irrevocably wedded to the service. Perhaps for both of them M represented a stern father figure who commanded all their respect and attention.

M led the way down the long corridor and turned left opposite the lift. Bond knew better than to expect him to say anything while they were walking. A gruff nod to a colleague was the only incident on the journey. M paused at the second door along the corridor and turned the handle briskly. The Operations Room was like a small cinema with rows of seats sloping down to a screen. There was a lectern and a blackboard taking up the space not occupied by the screen. Maps and other visual aids could be lowered like backdrops and controlled from the projection booth, which was independent of the main room.

Bond recognized the two men waiting in the room. One was Frederick Gray, the Minister of Defence, who was just being relieved of his Cromby overcoat by one of the ushers who vigilantly escorted all visitors to Transworld Consortium from the moment they crossed the threshold. He shook M's hand without much warmth and nodded at Bond. The men had met before. The second man in the room was Q, wearing a tweed suit that looked as if it had been borrowed from a gillie after a particularly energetic day's deer stalking. He, too, nodded at Bond, and raised his arm in an awkward gesture of greeting. The usher withdrew discreetly.

'Thank you for coming, Minister,' said M. '007 knows the background to the Moonraker visit but not the immediate cause for our concern. I'd be grateful if you would recapitulate, Q.'

Q nodded and was quickly at the rostrum. The others took seats in the back rows of the theatre. Bond sat apart from M and the minister, feeling the tingle of expectation that always arrived at the start of a new job. He was keyed up, waiting for the words to emerge from Q's mouth.

'The Moonraker was being transported from California on the back of a 747. The 747 has crashed in Alaska.'

Bond's expression bore witness to the gravity of the

news. 'Accident?'

M did not turn his head. 'Listen to what Q has to say and form your own opinion.'

Q pressed a button on the lectern and the lights dimmed. He pressed a second time and a picture flashed up on the screen. It showed the wreckage of what was apparently an air disaster strewn over the side of a rocky, snow-covered mountain side.

'No survivors,' said Bond. It was not a question.

Frederick Gray turned and looked Bond straight in the eyes. 'No Moonraker,' he said.

Q continued before Bond could say anything. 'NASA experts have been over every inch of wreckage with a fine toothcomb.' He broke off as more photographs of twisted, scorched metal appeared on the screen. 'There is no trace of the space shuttle.'

Bond could hardly believe what he was hearing. 'Are you suggesting that the Moonraker was hijacked in mid-air?'

'There seems to be no other explanation,' said M. 'The Moonraker was on the 747 when it left California.'

'There was no wireless communication before the crash?'

'None.'

'And the crew of the 747?'

'All the bodies have been recovered. A positive identification will probably not be possible in every case, but there's no reason to believe that any of them were involved in what happened to the shuttle.'

'It looks like the Russians,' said Bond. He thought of his statement in M's office. Not much of a respite. 'What better place for them to pull off a hijack? Five hundred miles and they're over the Bering Strait and home and dry.'

'The American early-warning systems are particularly sensitive in that part of the world,' said M. 'They picked up nothing.'

'They must have taken a risk and flown low.'

'Quite a risk,' said M. 'A space shuttle is hardly designed for hopping icebergs.'

'Do you think there's somebody else involved, sir?' asked Bond.

'It's a possibility,' said M. 'Though I agree with you. The Russians must remain the prime suspects.'

'The whole situation is exceptionally embarrassing,' said Gray stiffly. 'The Moonraker was coming to us because H.M.G. didn't want to let our technical know-how out of the country. I don't think the Pentagon took very kindly to that. Now this happens. To make matters worse, the navigator in the 747 was an R.A.F. chap. It all adds up to something approaching an international incident.'

'You don't think the Americans believe we had anything to do with it?' asked Bond incredulously.

There was an awkward silence. 'No,' said Gray, 'I don't really think so. But sometimes things are said in the heat of the moment –' he broke off and performed an agitated movement with his hands as if finding the subject almost too painful to discuss.

M's voice rode in firmly. 'The point is that the Americans hold us partially responsible for the loss of their shuttle. There's a strong onus on us to find out what happened.' He looked deep into Bond's unflinching eyes. 'That's going to be your job.'

Bond nodded. 'Yes, sir.' He turned to Q. 'The wreckage of the 747 yielded no clues?'

'Nothing. Laboratory tests are still being conducted but I doubt if they'll come up with anything.'

'Where was the shuttle made?'

'In California. By the Drax Corporation.'

'Hugo Drax? The multi-millionaire? I didn't know he was involved in the American space programme.'

'It's both an obsession and a philanthropic gesture,' said M. 'With NASA starved for funds, they can hardly refuse the money that Drax is prepared to pump in. He has a complex in California that has been turned over completely to the manufacture and testing of the Moonraker shuttle.'

'With technical assistance from NASA, of course,' said Gray.

Bond grappled with his incredulity. The funds that Drax must have at his disposal to shore up the American space programme could be nothing less than astronomical. 'I think it might be politic if I paid Hugo Drax a visit. It would be an indication of our concern, and it would give me a chance to sketch in some background. I might be able to pick up a lead.'

'Agreed,' said M. 'I want you to leave immediately. We'll inform Drax of your arrival, and I'll make a courtesy call to the C.I.A. We don't want any more noses put out of joint.' He turned to Gray to see if the minister had anything to add.

Gray stood up briskly as if eager to be on his way. 'Thank you, Sir Miles. You will, of course, keep me in touch with all developments.' He turned to Bond with an 'England expects ...' expression on his face. 'Good luck, Bond. I don't have to reiterate how important this business is. We don't want Anglo-American relations to take a pounding.'

'No, sir.' Bond inclined his head respectfully to the representative of Her Majesty's Government, who turned to find that the usher had magically materialized with his overcoat. He was shown out and Bond imagined that the meeting was over. A glance from M stayed him in his tracks.

'There's one other thing, 007. Q Branch have come up with a new – er – item for you.' The word 'item' was spoken without great warmth or respect. Bond had the impression that M would have preferred to say 'gadget'. As the survivor of a number of naval engagements, M found it difficult to take seriously any weapon smaller than a twelve-inch gun.

31

Q was impervious to any intonation that M chose to employ. He removed a small box from his pocket and withdrew what at first glance appeared to be a narrow leather strap for a wrist watch. 'Extend your arm please, 007.'

Bond did as he was asked, and the strap was fastened round his wrist. On closer inspection he noticed that it was made like a miniature cartridge holder. Some objects were tucked into the small leather slots. Sartorially it was not something he would have chosen to wear, and he looked at Q questioningly.

'We're shortly going to be issuing this as standard equipment,' said Q. 'Standard, that is, to double-0 prefixes. It's activated by nerve impulses from the wrist muscles.' He positioned Bond to face one of the cork panels on the other side of the room. 'Extend your arm and jerk your wrist back.'

Bond did as he was told and there was a sharp crack like a twig breaking. A small dart was embedded in the cork so as to be almost invisible.

Q held the lid of the box up to Bond. 'There are ten darts in here. Five blue-tipped, with armour-piercing heads, and five red-tipped. They have a cyanide coating that causes death in less than thirty seconds.'

Bond looked at his wrist and shook his head. 'Very novel, Q. You really must make an effort to get them into the stores for Christmas.'

4

HUGO DRAX AT HOME

Bond came down the corridor from the 747 at Los Angeles
Airport feeling a familiar sense of jet-lagged irritation that
he had to relive half a day of his life. Still, at least nobody
had pushed him out of the aeroplane this time, and the cold
buffet in first class had been a welcome change from the
usual overheated plastic food made particularly unbearable
by the bestowal of fatuous titles in gastronomic French.
There had even been a well-chilled bottle of Puligny-
Montrachet rejoicing the eye with the 1971 printed on its
damp label.

'Will James Bond, passenger from London, please make
himself known at the British Airways desk.' Bond heard
the message as he came out into the open concourse. and
stepped aside from the mass of passengers streaming like
lemmings to see if their baggage had accompanied them on
the flight. A clean-cut young man wearing a short-sleeved
shirt and a button bearing the legend 'I'm happy when
you're happy' was waiting behind the British Airways desk
with an upturned pencil poised for action. Beside the desk
stood a girl of surpassing beauty who could only have been
American. Her two rows of perfect teeth were not only
white but reflected enough light into the eyes of the be-
holder to dazzle. The large blue eyes were widely spaced
and balanced the longish, straight nose and the warm,
generous mouth. The blonde hair which shone like spun
silk bounced as if animated by the aura of good health that
radiated from every chromosome of her body. As Venus
rose off Paphos on the island of Cyprus, so could this girl
have appeared out of the sea off Malibu and stalked ashore

to take her natural place as a Californian beach goddess. She was wearing a white one-piece uniform that looked like a mechanic's overall and accentuated her copper tan. From a distance Bond was not certain whether the uniform was worn for fashion or expediency. When he got nearer he saw the word Drax emblazoned on one of the pockets beside an insignia which appeared as a double spire within intersecting orbits. Bond's interest quickened. The girl looked at him expectantly.

'Mr Bond?' There was a faint but discernible edge of hope in her voice that was not unflattering.

'That's right.'

'Hi. I'm Trudi Parker. Mr Drax sent me to fetch you.' Her manner was relaxed and friendly. There was none of the obsequious formality that Bond was used to receiving when being met at airports.

'That's very thoughtful of him,' said Bond. He prepared to follow the last of the departing passengers from his flight but Trudi held out a slim hand. 'If you give me your baggage tags I'll have your stuff sent on. We're not going that way.'

The young man behind the counter twisted his pencil through his fingers and received the tags as if they were precious gifts. Bond decided that the name Drax clearly stood for something in this part of the world.

'Follow me.' Bond did as he was told and found it no hardship. Trudi moved beautifully, rising on to the balls of her feet as if she was about to launch into a dance routine with each step. Her shoulders were broad and well muscled, with one arm slightly more developed than the other. Bond surmised that she did a lot of swimming and probably played a club-standard game of tennis. She led the way into one of the satellite corridors that bore no letter or flight number, and they descended a ramp and emerged into bright sunshine. At a few hundred yards' distance were the banks of commercial aircraft nuzzling by their satellite corridors like calves at a bulk feeder. Directly ahead, across the runway, was a helicopter of a gyrodyne design that Bond did not recognize. Proudly emblazoned along the side were the words DRAX AIRLINES and the symbol that adorned Trudi's uniform.

'Are you my guide and mentor?' asked Bond.

'I'm your pilot.'

Bond made a good job of conquering his surprise. California was no place to be accused of sexism. 'I don't recognize the helicopter.'

'There's no reason why you should. It's the prototype of a model that Mr Drax is developing.'

'I didn't know he owned an airline.'

'He's big in communications,' said Trudi casually. 'He owns a couple of railways in South America. Then there's the steamship company in Japan and his trucking business. I don't really know the half of it. I should think only Mr Drax and maybe some of his accountants do.' She nodded to another helicopter that was standing by with a Drax pilot in the cockpit. 'He'll be along with your bags in a few minutes.'

'I feel very well looked after,' said Bond.

'That's the idea.' She gestured towards the helicopter. 'I guess you've flown in one of these before?'

'Quite a few times,' said Bond.

'Good, then I don't have to give you the reassurance bit.'

'You mean, we're just going to take off?' asked Bond. 'What about passport formalities? I've just flown in from England.'

'When you're a guest of Mr Drax, things become very informal.' Trudi smiled engagingly. 'Mr Drax wouldn't invite anybody if it wasn't in the best interests of the U.S.A.'

'He seems a law unto himself,' said Bond.

Trudi climbed into the cockpit. 'He's a very successful man. Americans respect success. Not only that, they trust it.' She waited until Bond was strapped in beside her and then spoke swiftly into the radio, asking for permission to take off. Seconds later they were climbing steeply and spinning away towards the north. Bond looked about him for signs of the much-trumpeted Los Angeles smog and wondered if it was as difficult to run down as a genuine London pea-souper. Below him was an impression of long straight streets running across each other like latticework, whilst broad freeways curved to the horizon. It was like the layout of a giant snakes and ladders board.

'How far have we got to go?' asked Bond.

'A couple of hours. Is this your first time in California?'

Bond admired the relaxed skill with which Trudi controlled the helicopter. As a man who liked nothing better than to be behind the wheel of a fast car, he had always responded to an attractive woman who knew how to handle a machine.

'I've been here a few times,' said Bond. 'I know the East Coast better.'

'You look kinda Ivy League,' smiled Trudi.

'You don't make it sound like a compliment,' said Bond.

'I didn't mean to make it sound like an insult either.' Trudi pointed down through the perspex. 'That's Hollywood.'

'So there is the big sign on the hill,' said Bond. 'It's a shame nobody gives it a coat of paint.'

'I'm certain they'd be real grateful for any volunteers.' Trudi applied fingertip pressure to the controls and the helicopter shifted direction towards the north-east.

Bond smiled to himself. He liked Trudi. She was self-assured and she had a sense of humour. There was no trace of pretension about her. She was also a damned good pilot. Not for the first time, he considered how beauty can almost be a disadvantage to a woman. Most men believe that women purchase beauty from the gods at the price of intelligence. When he had first seen Trudi he had thought that she must be a cover-girl much sought after by tooth-paste advertisers. If she had been plain, round-shouldered and dressed in a calf-length smock he would have been prepared to believe that she was a Nobel prize winner.

'San Fernando on our left,' indicated Trudi.

Bond scolded himself. Trudi was absorbing too much of his attention. She was a beautiful girl but she was not the reason he was in California. 'I expect you know why I'm here?' he said.

Trudi shook her head. 'Nope. We get a lot of visitors. I don't know everything that goes on. I'm just a humble pilot in the service of the Drax Corporation.'

'You know about the crash in Alaska though?'

Trudi's face grew serious. 'Yes, I heard about that. The 747 coming down with the Moonraker. They were on their way to England, weren't they?'

'That's right.' Bond was interested to hear the official version of the crash repeated back to him. The disappearance of the space shuttle had not been made common knowledge. 'I'm investigating the crash.'

'So you've been to Alaska?'

'That's right.'

'Gee. You must have moved fast.'

Bond studied the girl out of the corner of his eye. There was nothing in her expression to confirm that she knew he had been lying about visiting Alaska.

Los Angeles and its satellite towns had now been left behind and the gyrodyne was flying with impressive speed and smoothness over a flat desert-like plain with a range of mountains in the distance. Bond calculated that they must be on the outer fringes of the Mojave Desert. It was an inhospitable region bisected by long ravines and dried-up river beds. The ground was reddish-brown and peppered with scrub, and the hot desert wind was throwing up miniature dust storms that cast a fine film against the perspex canopy. Bond was surprised by the direction they were taking. He had anticipated that Drax's space venture would be situated near his main California installation, in the San Joaquin valley north of Bakersfield.

'We're over the Drax estate now,' said Trudi. She performed a creditable rendition of the old Western cliché: 'As far as your eye can see, that's Drax country.'

'He owns a lot, doesn't he?' said Bond.

Trudi turned her head and there was no humour in her eyes.

'What he doesn't own, he doesn't want.'

Bond let silence reign and watched the sage brush drifting across the plain. Almost imperceptibly the outline of the distant mountains slowly began to harden and the desert give way to more fertile grazing ground browsed over by long-horn cattle that hardly bothered to raise their heads as the helicopter flew over. Ahead, the grass was greener still and there was a sprawling collection of buildings that looked like a small town.

'This is the main complex,' said Trudi matter of factly. Bond looked down, impressed. There was a railway line and a small marshalling yard, what appeared to be a medium-sized power station and five enormous hangars, one bearing the word MOONRAKER painted on its roof. Bond thought back to the Hollywood sign. This one was larger. A landing strip and control tower lay adjacent to the hangars and there was a large semi-circular building that Bond guessed must be a wind tunnel.

'So this is where the Moonraker shuttle is made?' he asked.

'That's right. Workshops, hangars, design and experimental blocks, test centre – the whole caboodle.'

Trudi had taken the chopper down low and Bond could see men in overalls operating fork-lift trucks in the deep valleys between the hangars. Apart from the sign on the roof there was nothing to tell the visitor that this place was not a large factory tucked away in the desert. Just as, perhaps, an ammunition factory might be.

Bond looked ahead and was puzzled to see a line of tall poplar trees. Even more so when he caught a glimpse of what lay beyond them. A French Renaissance château scarcely smaller than Chambord, its turrets gleaming in the sun like something out of a fairy story. Bond refused to believe what he was seeing. It must be a façade. Some remnant from a long forgotten film shot in the desert that had been left standing because of its amusement value. Look behind it and there would be an untidy framework of scaffolding to keep the thing upright. But the stones looked real enough, as did the formal French gardens with their box hedges, shingle paths and orderly battalions of identical flowers. Bond turned to Trudi and saw the amused expression on her face.

'Every stone brought from the Loire Valley,' she said.

'By Hugo Drax?'

'Who else?'

Bond looked again at the majestic sweep of the white stone and the recessed windows twinkling like rows of scales on a fish's back. 'Magnificent. Why didn't he buy the Eiffel Tower as well?'

Trudi smiled. 'He did, but the French government refused him an export permit.'

Bond grinned back at her. 'Oh well, I suppose if you have to live next to your work you might as well do it in comfort.'

He returned his gaze to the gardens. They were almost over-generously endowed with marble statues of athletes and goddesses reaching from their plinths as if desperately trying to attract attention. Their very number suggested that they were genuine and that Hugo Drax was a man who could never have enough of a good thing. The gyro-dyne swept around the corner of the building and Bond looked in vain for the scaffolding. A formal lawn fronted the long expanse of the building and on it fifty young men and women lay on their backs in five rows of ten. As Bond focussed on the scene they sprang to their feet, raised their arms above their heads and began to rotate their upper bodies on the fulcrum of their hips. They were dressed in black leotards and at first glance appeared like a ballet class undergoing a programme of loosening-up calisthenics. What was immediately obvious to Bond as they stretched their arms upwards and tilted back their heads was that they were the most beautiful group of people he had ever seen. He looked at Trudi questioningly.

'They're the astronaut trainees. They're part of a project very close to Mr Drax's heart. The Drax Corporation Astronaut Training Scheme.'

'I thought all that was handled by the National Aero-nautics and Space Administration?' said Bond.

'It used to be, but Mr Drax offered a scholarship if it could be open to people from all over the world.' She shrugged. 'You know, like space belongs to everybody. It was an offer NASA could hardly refuse. They provide a lot of the teaching staff, the Drax Corporation has paid for the installation.'

Bond looked back admiringly. 'They're more like the finalists in a Mr and Miss Universe contest.'

Trudi smiled. 'Mr Drax went out of his way to select the finest physical specimens.'

Bond looked at Trudi appreciatively. 'I gathered that back at the airport.'

Trudi's fingers tightened on the handle of the control column.

'You're trying to turn a young girl's head, Mr Bond.' She moved her arm and the helicopter dipped earthwards.

When the rotor blades had almost stopped turning and the banshee wail of the engine died away to the shudder of a sewing machine shuttle, the canopy was drawn back and Bond unclipped his belt and climbed down to the small take-off pad on which they had landed. 'Thanks for the ride,' he said.

Trudi's smile challenged sunlight. 'Any time,' she said. She gestured towards a flight of stone steps and Bond climbed out, feeling the warm desert air on his face. So incongruous were his surroundings that he found it difficult to know exactly where he was. It was as if he had suddenly arrived inside a dream that had taken on the trappings of reality. A man in the black jacket and striped grey trousers of an English manservant hurried forward as they came to the top of the steps.

'Mr Bond's bags will be arriving in a few minutes, Gilbert,' said Trudi. 'I'll show him his room.'

'Yes, miss.' The man was English. He spoke with a faint trace of a cockney accent. He lowered his head to Bond by way of respectful greeting and remained at the top of the steps with his hands clasped across the front of his body, scanning the sky like a hunter's dog waiting for the first duck.

Trudi led the way across the terrace past poker-shaped shrubs in wrought iron tubs and through french windows that reached up three times Bond's height and still fell twelve feet short of the sculpted ceiling of the interior. The drawing room stretched away like a picture gallery and was a furniture repository of antiques gleaming under a turtle-shell thickness of polish. Bond glanced about him as he crossed the Persian rugs and tried to equate his surroundings with his recollections of Randolph Hearst's castle at San Simeon. He had never seen it in its heyday, but first

41

impressions suggested that Hugo Drax had made progress in the realm of twenty-four carat gold eccentricity. Two great doors allowed access to a marble hallway with more busts in niches and alcoves and a wide staircase dividing into two beneath a large oil painting which must have been either a Rembrandt or a masterly imitation. Bond felt ill-equipped to judge but his inclination was towards the former. There may have been something slightly vulgar about the display of so much wealth, but it was a very genuine vulgarity.

Trudi moved gracefully up the stairs and turned right at the painting.

'We're along here,' she said. Bond permitted himself a raised eyebrow. 'I mean of course that both our bedrooms happen to be in this wing. There's no shortage of them.'

'What a shame.' Bond looked at the suits of armour that lined the walls at intervals of ten paces. They were mostly French, with the face-pieces protruding forward in cruel spikes. The corridor was wide and the roof criss-crossed with painted timbers. The ceiling plaster between was an intricate tapestry of beautifully painted flowers. Even the leaded panes of the windows appeared genuine, an occasional yellow or blue diamond appearing amongst the thin ice-like slivers of antique glass.

Trudi stopped by a door and threw it open. 'This is your apartment. I'm next door.'

'Very handy,' said Bond. 'I'll remember that if I need a glass of water.'

'I'll make sure my toothmug is clean.' Trudi glanced at her watch and became businesslike again. 'I'll let Mr Drax know you've arrived. Your bags should be up right away. Will you be through cleaning up in half an hour?'

'I can be.'

'Good. Cavendish, Mr Drax's butler, will come and collect you. I'll see you later.'

'I hope so,' said Bond. He looked after Trudi as she walked away down the corridor and then entered the room. It was dominated by a large four-poster bed with a silk canopy bearing a fleur-de-lis motif. Bond wondered how many kings and queens of France – and their lovers – had slept in it before he was accorded the privilege. The ceiling was high and painted with a scene representing heavenly activity that involved cupids with trumpets, old men with long beards and plump, pink ladies who were having difficulty in disguising their private parts behind the insubstantial swirls of diaphanous material that they chose to wear in preference to clothing.

There was a discreet tap on the door, and Gilbert entered to place Bond's battered Vuiton suitcases on a carved oak settle which stood at the end of the bed. Bond thanked him and walked into the bathroom, which might have been moved in its entirety from a Paris hotel *de grande classe*. Tiles from floor to ceiling, a deep bath with taps like golden trumpets and a Heath Robinson shower attachment constructed like an antique flame thrower; black and white tiles on the floor and more mirrors than in a whore's bedroom; a bidet with a light blue pictorial design that was practically willow-pattern. A comfortable, white towelling ankle-length robe hung sensibly next to the bath.

Bond stripped off, took a long cold shower and selected fresh underwear and a clean Sea Island shirt from one of his bags. Not only did he feel the desire to eradicate all traces of the journey from England but he wanted also to perform a spiritual absolution. To feel again like a well-primed machine when he advanced to come under Drax's scrutiny. He knotted his tie, knowing that one part of his preparation was lacking. He wanted a drink. A glance round the room led him to a small Louis Quinze cabinet standing on four squat bulldog legs. He pulled at one of the drawers and found what he was looking for. The whole façade of the piece had been skilfully transformed into a door which swung open to reveal a refrigerator well stocked with all the spirits that an international traveller might have acquired a taste for. It was an act of artistic vandalism and might just as well have concealed a television set. Bond was glad that it did not. He could develop a migraine by merely glancing at the lists of television channels in an American newspaper – or advertising catalogue, as he was wont to think of those publications. He bombarded the bottom of a tumbler with ice cubes and poured a generous measure of Virginia Gentleman over the glistening rocks. For his money it was the best Bourbon made outside Kentucky. The rich, brown liquid swirled enticingly and the ice danced and chinked as if engaged in some private celebration.

Bond let a first, generous mouthful of the liquor bite him in the back of the throat and then drank more slowly. There were still ten minutes before Drax's butler was due to appear. He looked round the room, and his eye was attracted by the headboard of the bed. It was splendidly carved and the centrepiece showed two mermen in the act of besting a sea monster. The mouth of the monster was open and its head stood forward in relief from the rest of the carving. As an incitement to violent passion the piece perhaps had something to recommend it, though Bond thought it more likely that any occupants of the bed would be intimidated by the beast a couple of feet above their heads. There was something very life-like about its bulging eyes and rapacious rows of teeth. Bond remembered his childhood, and how he had screwed up his courage to dart his fingers into the open mouth of a stuffed alligator. In a gesture that was pure nostalgia, he crossed to the bed and pushed his fingers into the opening between the two rows of wooden teeth. He was surprised to feel something move.

Curiosity immediately aroused, he withdrew a thin metal

pick from the lining of one of the Vuiton suitcases and after a few minutes' probing succeeded in hooking out the object he had felt. It was a miniature microphone fastened to a lead that appeared to stretch down behind the bed. Bond looked at the appliance thoughtfully and then slipped it back into its hiding place. If it had been switched on, the sound of his probing would have been picked up and whoever was listening would guess that the microphone had been discovered. He wondered if Hugo Drax liked listening to people talking in their sleep or whether there were more voyeuristic reasons for the presence of the mike. Perhaps it was the accompaniment to some hidden camera positioned in the opposite wall. Whatever the explanation, it made Bond more eager than ever to be brought face to face with his host.

Bond had been examining the contents of the room for several minutes without finding anything when there came a second discreet tap at his door. He opened it to find himself face to face with a grey-haired man whose expression was knowing without being presumptuous, deferential without being humble, and dignified without being patrician. He wore black trousers, a black frock-coat and a dark grey waistcoat with horizontal stripes. His black bow tie was hand-knotted. He could only be Drax's butler.

'My name is Cavendish, sir. Mr Drax is awaiting you in his study.'

Bond nodded and followed the butler into the corridor. Cavendish led the way along the wide corridor and down a different but scarcely less imposing flight of steps to the one by which Bond had mounted. The sound of someone playing a Chopin waltz wafted up to meet them. Bond wondered who the pianist was. The technique was nearly flawless. Only in the matter of expression did the pianist leave something to be desired. There was an involuntary holding back; an inability to surrender completely to the liberated spirit of the music.

Cavendish crossed a hallway and the sound of the music grew louder. It was coming from the room they were approaching and stopped dramatically an instant before Cavendish swung open the door. 'Mr Bond, sir.'

Bond stepped forward as a bearded figure rose from a distant piano. His first impression was of the size of the room. The word study suggested somewhere small and snug. Perhaps it was a residue of his schooldays but he had expected to find himself in a smallish room littered with open books and work in progress. A room that reflected something of a multi-millionaire's myriad business activities. The only books in this room were the leather-bound volumes climbing to the ceiling in tiers. The room itself was the size of a small concert hall, but anything smaller would have been no match for the man who was now threading his way ponderously through the antique furniture.

Hugo Drax was a large man with shoulders like an American footballer. He had a big square head and carrot red hair parted in the middle and flopping down awkwardly on each temple. His skin was pink and blotchy and this was particularly noticeable around the area of his right temple and cheek, which had clearly undergone plastic surgery. The skin was puckered, and shone unpleasantly like plastic that had started to melt. What could be seen of the right ear beneath the thatch of hair suggested that it had been badly mangled. The face had a lopsided look because one eye was larger than the other and Bond guessed that this was due to the contraction of skin that had been borrowed to build up the upper and lower eyelids.

Drax's mouth was almost invisible behind a large bushy moustache and his side whiskers grew down to the level of his ear lobes. There were irregular tufts of hair on his cheeks, and the whole appearance of his head was like that of an underwater object which has accumulated accretions of weed and vegetation.

By no standards could the work that had been done on Drax's face be deemed a success, and Bond decided that the plastic surgery must have been undertaken a long time ago. Probably when Drax was a young man and certainly before he could have afforded the finest treatment in the world. Perhaps the circumstances of the injury had precluded any treatment at all. Drax was probably in his late fifties. It was very feasible that he had been injured in the Second World War on a battle front where men were lucky to receive any medical attention, let alone have their faces rebuilt. Hugo Drax. Bond idly wondered which side he had been fighting on.

'James Bond.' The voice was a warm growl with the merest trace of an accent. 'Forgive the immediate use of your Christian name but your reputation precedes you to the point where I feel I know you already.'

'How do you do?' Bond felt a huge, blunt hand close about his. He thought of these hands playing the Chopin and rejected once and for all the myth that artistic fingers are always long and sensitive.

'I'm honoured that your government should have sent you on so delicate a mission.' The tone had a mocking edge to it that made Bond's hackles rise.

'Delicate?'

'To apologize in person for the loss of my space shuttle.' The word 'my' was underlined. Drax turned aside peremptorily in a manner that was almost an affront, showing Bond his back as he picked up a pair of silver tongs and reached towards a silver tureen of the kind that Bond would have expected to hold devilled kidneys on a breakfast sideboard. Something stirred at the far end of the room and two enormous Dobermann pinschers followed the route their master had taken from the concert grand. They paused before Bond and looked at him as if wondering what he tasted like. Drax opened the tureen and removed two gobbets of raw meat, which he tossed in front of the dogs. They looked down at them and then up, expectantly, at Drax. He turned back to Bond, his face twisting into the shape of an ironic smile.

'How would Oscar Wilde have put it? To lose one aircraft may be regarded as a misfortune. To lose two seems like carelessness.'

He snapped his fingers and the two dogs fell on the meat and were almost immediately licking the spot on the carpet where it had lain. Bond found the speed with which he was growing to dislike Hugo Drax almost alarming. There was a refined vulgarity about the gesture with the tongs which offended him almost as much as the mocking, condescending tone and the desire to impress with the Wildean quotation. Bond's voice was steely as he replied.

'Any apology will be made to the American government, Mr Drax – when we've discovered why there was no trace of the Moonraker in that wreckage.'

Drax spread his huge hands wide. 'Your loyalty commands respect, Mr Bond.' The tone was overtly sarcastic.

Bond made up his mind that he must press on before he said something that he would later regret. 'I imagine that you must have your own suspicions regarding the disappearance of the Moonraker?'

'I think you only have to look five hundred miles further west than the site of its disappearance. Russia, Mr Bond!' The false joviality dropped from Drax's voice. A tiny pinpoint of red appeared in his distorted eyes to complement the scarlet flush on his cheek. 'Thanks to our pusillanimous government, we have surrendered space to them. Do you realize that I, a private individual, am responsible for nearly forty per cent of the American space programme? It is scandalous, is it not?'

'It sounds a very patriotic gesture,' observed Bond.

'It is not really patriotism,' said Drax nobly. 'I do not believe that one country should be in a position to occupy space as in the old days a colonial nation might have acquired new territory. That is what the Americans are in danger of allowing to happen.' He smiled his ugly smile. 'With their experience of the British, you would think that they would know better.'

Bond's expression gave no indication that he was offended by the jibe. 'If the American space programme is lagging behind the Russians', why should they want to steal your Moonraker?'

'Because the Russians take no chances. They know what I am doing here. They know that I am the one dynamic force capable of galvanizing this country into an awareness of its responsibilities. They want to see what I'm up to. The Russians never sleep, Mr Bond. Only when they are dead!'

Bond saw the xenophobia in the eyes and heard the voice reveal traces of its Teutonic ancestry as it surrendered control to passion. He wondered if Drax had been one of the young Germans who fought on the Russian front and was left with more than physical scars from the experience. It might explain his obvious hatred of the Russians.

The door clicked open and suddenly there was a new presence in the room: a man, small in stature, but built like a giant spinning top. He had no recognizable neck and his swelling girth appeared to have put such a strain on his flesh as to have pulled the skin of his face tight and reduced the eyes to faint scar-like slits descending towards the lobes of his ears. His hair was dragged back from his face in a pigtail and he waddled across the room carrying a large silver tray on which were arranged a Georgian silver tea service, Rockingham china and a plate of daintily cut sandwiches. The contents of the tray and its bearer made an incongruous combination. Bond looked at the man's tiny mouth and found it smaller than his eye slits. These glistened to show that somewhere behind the folds of skin Bond was being subjected to close and perhaps unflattering scrutiny.

'On the table, Chang,' said Drax, indicating the positioning of the tray with a wave of his hand. He turned back to Bond. 'You have arrived at a propitious moment. One in which I pay homage to your country's sole, indisputable contribution to the advancement of Western civilization.' He extended an arm towards the Georgian tea pot. 'Afternoon tea.'

Bond smiled despite himself. It occurred to him that in the space of a short conversation Drax had revealed a sufficient love–hate relationship with things British to mark him out as one of those who secretly resented his draw in the lottery of birth. A stroke of fortune that no amount of money could ever correct. Bond guessed that Hugo Drax would have liked to have been born an Englishman. He had not been and therefore he set out to ridicule that which he could not have. Unlike Groucho Marx, who did not want to be a member of a club that would have someone like him in it, Drax did want to be a member of a club that could never have him as a member.

'I'm not a great tea drinker,' said Bond.

Drax's eyes mimed regret. 'You disappoint me. Surely I can press you to a cucumber sandwich?'

'No thank you.' Bond held up a hand as Chang proffered the plate and once again saw the glistening slits sizing him up. The man's upper arms were the size of an ordinary man's thighs. He was like a compressed Sumo wrestler. The destructive force that he would be capable of releasing must be terrifying. 'The Moonraker. Is it made entirely in California?'

Drax swallowed a cucumber sandwich at a gulp before answering Bond's question. 'Assembled, yes. Made, no. I own a number of subsidiaries throughout the world producing components.' He slurped noisily at a cup of tea. 'As I have intimated, the conquest of space represents an investment on behalf of the entire human race. It is therefore logical to seek out the best that each nation has to offer.'

Bond found his gaze drifting beyond the mullioned windows. The astronaut trainees could be glimpsed, still at their exercises. Perhaps it was a new batch. 'Are you referring to people or skills, Mr Drax?'

Drax appeared to be surprised by the question. 'Why both, Mr Bond.' He pressed a button set into the corner of the writing area of an antique desk. 'I have taken the liberty of arranging a tour of the installation for you. I think it advisable that you see how we go about things. We can discuss the matter of the Moonraker over dinner. I will expect to see you in the Orleans Room at seven-thirty.' As he finished speaking, the door opened and Trudi came in. 'Miss Parker will escort you to Dr Goodhead, who will show you round. Please feel free to ask any questions that enter your head.' The intimation was that the entry of questions into Bond's head might well be a haphazard process with no guarantee that Dr Goodhead would have a particularly taxing afternoon.

'Thank you for being so co-operative,' said Bond, numbing his already cold mouth with a glacial smile.

'A pleasure.' Drax took a step towards the door as if to show his guest the way and then stood his ground until he was alone with Chang. He held out his empty cup and looked into the concentrating face as the tea was poured. 'I want you to look after Mr Bond, Chang,' he said slowly. 'See that some harm comes to him.'

5

A WHIP-ROUND FOR MR BOND

Trudi escorted Bond to a small vehicle like a golf buggy and they drove away down the gravel drive. Bond had the impression that eyes were watching him from behind the tall windows, but he could see nothing. Trudi remained silent and he sensed that she had been able to read his expression and knew that the interview with Drax had not gone well. He considered questioning her about her relationship with her employer but decided that this was not the moment to invite such confidences. Later perhaps.

The buggy crossed a bridge at the frontier of the poplars and left the French Renaissance behind. Across a stretch of open ground planted with shrubs that had not yet reached maturity was the first of the enormous hangars. Trudi skirted it and arrived at a glass-fronted building that looked as if it housed offices. It reminded Bond of a three-storey mouse cage he had owned when a boy. He almost expected to see a giant exercise treadmill beside the filing cabinets.

'This is where I leave you,' said Trudi. 'You'll find Dr Goodhead at the end of the passage past the reception desk.'

'I'll see you tonight,' said Bond.

'This evening, you mean.' Trudi raised a hand in farewell and glided away towards the château without looking back.

Bond conquered a sigh and wondered what Dr Goodhead would be like. Probably some dry-as-dust scientist talking incomprehensibly in technical jargon. The kind of man who could split the atom without discovering how to stop the dandruff that built up on the shoulders of his white coat.

Bond entered the building and walked past the empty reception desk and the inevitable iced water dispenser. As he advanced down the corridor, a beautiful girl in a black leotard approached him. Her skin matched the colour of the leotard and she had a woollen jacket around her shoulders. There were two small beads of perspiration above her wickedly curved upper lip and Bond guessed that she had just returned from a physical work-out with the astronaut trainees. She smiled winsomely and moved on her way, the muscles rippling beneath the leotard. Bond felt again a strange sense of unreality. It was difficult to reconcile Renaissance châteaux and beautiful girls with mannequin proportions with the ultra-modern technology of a space laboratory. He continued down the corridor and stopped before a door with the name Dr H. Goodhead neatly printed in black letters on a white card. Bond knocked; there was no answer. He opened the door and found himself in an outer office with a secretary's desk, filing cabinets and wall charts. The room was empty. The door to the inner office was ajar and Bond pushed it open.

Standing with her back to him was a slim girl wearing a light grey jumpsuit. The back was promising. It was long and ended in a slim waist giving way to tight, well-rounded buttocks and legs that covered many graceful inches before they reached the floor. The shoulders sloped gently and the white flesh on the neck was visible because the hair had been combed up and piled in a business-like fashion on top of the head. A few errant wisps sprouted out attractively like the spread tail feathers of a bird. The girl was studying a flow chart as Bond came in, but she turned swiftly and fixed him with a piercing blue eye. Her forehead was high, her nose straight and her mouth wide and faintly super-cilious. There was an authoritative set to her jaw and the whole face had a stern wariness about it that was at odds with the soft, feminine curves of her well-shaped breasts. The impression that Bond got was that here was a woman who wanted to be treated like a man – or thought she did. He had met the type before in male-dominated societies. As personal assistants they began to take on the characteristics of their bosses.

'Good afternoon,' said Bond. 'I'm looking for Dr Goodhead.'

The girl advanced towards him. 'You've just found her.' The smile was a formality.

'A woman.' Bond reflected that he could have made more effort to keep the surprise out of his voice.

The girl inclined her head graciously. 'Your powers of observation do you credit, Mr Bond. It is Mr Bond, isn't it?'

'James to my friends,' said Bond.

The girl extended her hand briskly. 'Holly Goodhead.' The hand was firm and dry, but the pressure it exerted minimal. It was a very formal handshake.

'Are you one of the astronaut trainees?' asked Bond.

Holly parted her lips slightly as if she had experienced a twinge of pain. 'I'm fully trained. By NASA, the Space Administration. They assigned me here.' She looked at Bond levelly for an instant and then moved towards the door. 'Come, Mr Bond. I'll show you round. You don't want to lose time as well as a space shuttle, do you?'

Bond shook his head ruefully as he followed his guide. It seemed that a good friend was hard to find at the Drax Corporation. His acquaintance with Dr Holly Goodhead had not started off memorably.

The first hangar they visited was where a Moonraker was being assembled. Holly showed a pass and after two sound-proof doors had been opened they were in a gigantic workshop with the air full of the smell of welding equipment and the output of the light sources accentuated by the

54

blaze of torches. The framework of the shuttle rose in the air like a rocket and at all levels men were working on the scaffolding that surrounded it, like bees crawling over a honeycomb.

'Each of these men is a specialist technician,' explained Holly above the noise. 'They could be teaching at M.I.T. if they weren't here.'

'There seems to be an enormous amount of activity,' said Bond. 'Do they always work at this rate?'

'Mr Drax has set some pretty tough completion dates. He wants to get a test programme into space by the end of next month.'

Bond gazed upwards and felt awe as he realized what he was looking at. A craft that when finished would be able to perform an almost limitless number of orbits of the earth and yet return to base and land like a conventional aircraft. No parachutes. No spheres plummeting into the ocean and relying on a fast destroyer to retrieve them. He watched a Medusa of coloured wires being hauled aloft and marvelled at man's ingenuity. What he was seeing made him resolve to temper his dislike of Hugo Drax with respect for what he was doing. To place his resources at the service of mankind was an act of supreme generosity. It far outweighed any personal mannerisms that Bond might find objectionable. Bond thought again and frowned. There was the question of the bugging device in the bedroom. That he did find difficult to reconcile.

Holly recited a list of statistics that Bond tried to absorb and then led the way through another set of connecting doors to another vast hangar. An elevator took them up to a catwalk, and from there they could look down on a group of trainee astronauts clustered around what seemed like the cockpit of an aeroplane affixed to a transfusion system of wires and jointed rods. As Bond watched a trainee climbed into the cockpit and seated himself at the controls, which represented, Holly informed him, those of a Moonraker. Hardly was he in position than the cockpit began to buck and rock. Bond looked at Holly anxiously. She brushed a wisp of hair behind an ear calmly. 'You're watching a flight simulator,' she told him. 'It can replicate every possible problem contingency that might arise under actual flying conditions.' The simulator suddenly shot forward and rose steeply into the air, with the metal rods bending grotesquely like the limbs of a stick-insect. A television camera moved in synchronism over a nearby panorama of the Earth's surface. The fuselage slipped backwards and lurched sideways like the chamber of a revolver turning as the gun was fired. Bond was not sorry to be standing where he was. He looked across at the opposite catwalk and saw the oval bulk of Chang observing him balefully. The figure folded its arms as if in contemplation and then turned and disappeared through a shadowy doorway.

'Technical competence is of course vital,' said Holly, as if repeating a lecture she had given many times. 'However, no subject can perform at optimum unless he or she is in a state of peak physical fitness.' She looked at Bond pointedly as she said the last words and for a moment he wondered if she had read his medical report. 'What we are going to see next covers this aspect of preparation.'

Bond said nothing but moved with Holly into the nearest elevator, which deposited them before a door with the word 'Gymnasium' emblazoned on it. Beyond the open door was a space which could have contained a football pitch and still left plenty of room for a couple of thousand spectators. It was equipped with vaulting horses, ropes, wooden bars and all the paraphernalia that Bond remembered from his schooldays. Half a dozen very pretty girls in the now familiar black leotards were working out on the parallel bars under the tuition of a barrel-chested instructor.

Bond looked at them appreciatively. 'Astronaut trainees?'

Holly looked at him sharply. 'Do I detect a note of disapproval?'

'It was certainly not intentional,' said Bond honestly. 'Perhaps in the past I might have been guilty of thinking that there were enough heavenly bodies in space.'

The corners of Holly's mouth pinched together disapprovingly. 'Forgive me saying so, but I find that kind of schoolboy humour particularly obnoxious, Mr Bond. There is more to being an astronaut than the ability to wear heavy boots.'

'Of course,' said Bond.

Holly had not finished. 'There are many ways in which women are better suited for space than men. They are more patient. Their ability to rationalize a situation is often far more highly developed than a man's. Their aural-visual senses are in no way inferior. In the matter of smell –'

'I know,' said Bond. 'Women smell better than men.'

Holly looked at him coldly. 'I think your persistent recourse to bad jokes is a kind of defence mechanism. Let's test *your* eyesight, Mr James Bond, 007, licensed to kill.'

Before Bond could reply, she had turned her back and was stalking towards a long narrow chamber not unlike a shooting gallery. At the far end Bond could see a number of charts bearing rows of letters in diminishing sizes. He sighed and walked towards the gallery.

Holly was waiting for him, bustling with eagerness. It was the first emotion she had shown since their meeting. 'Let's take the chart in the middle,' she said. 'I don't suppose you have any trouble reading the top line?'

Bond tilted his head to one side. 'X-H-Y –'

'Good,' said Holly briskly. 'If you couldn't read that you wouldn't qualify for a driving licence. Now, read me out the bottom line of letters on that card.'

'The bottom line?' said Bond. His tone suggested that

57

the task would be a challenge for any man.

'That's what I said.' Holly's eyes threw down the gauntlet.

Bond took a deep breath and leant forward, narrowing his eyes to slits. There was a long pause.

'It's not easy, is it?' said Holly bossily.

Bond's eyes screwed up some more and his neck imitated that of a tortoise tempted by a particularly succulent morsel of lettuce.

'P-R-I –' he began.

'No!' Holly's cry of triumph was almost a shout. 'You must be guessing, Mr Bond.' She screwed up her eyes eagerly and started jotting letters down on a pad. 'Now, let's see how we compare.' She advanced to the chart and looked back over her shoulder. 'I'm sorry. The last line reads O-C – B-H-A-X.'

'You amaze me,' said Bond. His tone had suddenly thrown away its mantle of deference. He stalked down the aisle and plucked the card out of its holder. 'I'm afraid you're wrong, Holly. The last line on this chart says "Printed in Des Moines".' He pointed to the small print on the bottom right-hand corner of the chart. 'I think you'll find that makes the first three letters P-R-I.' He looked into Holly's eyes and after a couple of seconds allowed his arrogant face to relapse into a smile. 'You look very pretty when you blush, Dr Goodhead,' he said. 'Now, what are you going to show me next?'

Holly said little until they had passed into the next chamber, and Bond enjoyed the silence. He reckoned that he was just ahead in the game but that Holly Goodhead was not a girl who gave up easily. She looked up at him calmly and indicated the structure they were facing. 'This is the centrifuge trainer. It simulates the acceleration you have to withstand on being shot into space.' Bond looked at the futuristic fuselage on the end of the long arm and was reminded of something from the fairground. 'The Whip', it had been called; capable of spinning faster and faster with the jointed end performing body-breaking contortions. He looked up and saw the broad expanse of glass that formed the front of what must obviously be the control room. With a slight start of surprise he saw the diagonal slits that masked Chang's eyes looking down on him.

'Perhaps you'd like to try it?' Holly was looking at him with a fresh challenge in her eyes.

'I'd be delighted.' Bond's statement was hyperbole but there was no way in which he was going to concede ground to Holly Goodhead.

A technician stepped forward and the front of the fuse-lage snapped back like a dragon's mouth. Bond found himself settling into a claustrophobically small space, with his knees pushed up towards his chest. Holly leant forward and there was a certain relish in the way in which she secured a safety strap across his shoulders. Bond sniffed her scent with obvious appreciation.

'Joy?'

Her reply, if it could be deemed a reply, was un-equivocal. 'Put your arms on the seat rests.'

In a short time these too were securely anchored. Like any man denied the use of his arms, Bond began to feel un-easy. 'What's that for?'

Holly smiled at him. It occurred to Bond that she prob-ably enjoyed tying knots about men as much as she enjoyed tying them in knots. 'To stop you knocking yourself out.'

Bond's apprehensions were in no way diminished. 'How fast does this thing go?'

Holly stepped back and dusted her hands. 'Three Gs is equivalent to take-off acceleration.' She smiled kittenishly. 'It can go up to twenty Gs but that would be fatal. Most people pass out at seven.'

Bond tested the strength of the straps that bound him.

'You'd make a great saleswoman.'

For the first time, Holly's features relaxed into the ghost of a genuine smile. 'You don't have to worry. There's what we call a chicken switch.' She indicated a column rising from the floor to stop within reach of Bond's right hand. There was a button set in the end of it. 'Start off by holding that column with your finger pressed down on the button. The moment the pressure gets too much for you, release the button. The power will be cut off immediately.'

Bond looked sceptically into Holly's clear blue eyes. 'Immediately?'

Her jaw tilted scornfully. 'Surely you're not nervous, Mr Bond? A seventy-year-old can withstand three Gs.'

Bonded twisted his head and tried to look up to the control room.

'Trouble is, there's never a seventy-year-old about when you want one.'

Holly interpreted Bond's glance as one that sought reassurance. 'Don't worry, Mr Bond. You're in good hands.'

A telephone rang and a technician answered it and called Holly over. She spoke for a few seconds and then returned to Bond. 'Mr Drax wants to see me. I'll be right back.' She transmitted a brief, sardonic smile like a flash of semaphore. 'Enjoy yourself.'

Bond watched her and the technician leave the room and felt doubt deepen into unease. He had felt less than entirely welcome since his arrival at Drax's isolated desert estate. If an accident was to befall him, what better moment for it to happen? He tried to reach the straps that were securing his arms but his fingers could only reach the chicken switch. He pumped it in time with his accelerating heartbeat, waiting warily for the power to be switched on. A low humming noise vibrated through the fuselage and, slowly at first, the rotor arm began to turn on its central axis. Bond braced himself and watched the walls of the room disappear into a continuous blur. The G-force spread him against his seat like putty and he gritted his teeth as a piercing whining noise orchestrated the top-like spinning of the fuselage. This was it, 'The Whip' of his childhood days, but revolving at a speed that would have torn the original from its moorings and hurled it half-way across the fairground. He forced himself to look down and saw on the counter that he had already passed four Gs. The rate of build-up surprised him. The pulverizing pace was increasing with every second. There was a frenzied singing in Bond's ears and the piercing shriek of the centrifuge was like a nail being driven into his brain. Past five Gs now. Honour was satisfied. Not without an effort, Bond lifted his thumb from the button.

Nothing happened.

Bond waited an instant and saw that the button had indeed risen. He cried out but was unable to hear his own voice. The centrifugal force was holding him in an invisible vice. Only pain had freedom of movement through his body. His tortured, throbbing eyes looked down. Six Gs. Now he knew what was happening. They were going to kill him. Holly Goodhead had been opportunely called away. The brutal slab of menace that was Chang had done the rest. No doubt there would be mutual recriminations and many regrets. Terror, rage and desperation burned through Bond like a forest fire. He fought to apply pressure against the straps that held him but the centrifugal force made the raising of an eyebrow a labour of Hercules. Seven Gs. 'Most people pass out at seven.' He remembered Holly's words and the mocking look in her eyes. Was he going to be like most people? Like hell he was!

The noise of the centrifuge was now a high-pitched screech that broke the mind apart like an ice-pick. The blur before Bond's eyes was grey tinged with red. He felt as if every drop of blood was draining from his face. As if his eyeballs themselves were being pushed into his head. He opened his mouth to scream and felt his lips being pulled across his paralysed cheeks as if smeared by a giant hand. No sound emerged. Eight Gs. His head was going to explode and a shock wave of nausea and dizziness churned through his stomach. Bond knew that he had seconds before he lost consciousness, and with it his life. He must do something! He must not give up the fight! His eyes, glued to the counter, suddenly saw the strap around his wrist. The strap that Q had given him in the Operations Room. The sleeve of his jacket had ridden half-way up his forearm and now clung like a second skin. Bond felt a stab of hope. If he could somehow jerk back his wrist ...

Finger by finger, Bond broke apart his clenched fist and extended his hand along the arm of the seat. Every movement required a force that was borrowed from the will to survive rather than any strength that could escape the death hug of the centrifuge. If he could fire down the rotor arm it would be like striking at the head of the octopus. His teeth ground together so that he expected to feel slivers of enamel in his mouth. He fought the pain and the mind-splitting wail and strove to prize his fingers from the seat arm. As if held by adhesive, the fingers trembled and then snapped clear to rise half an inch in the air. The thumb lagged behind. Bond summoned up all his remaining strength of spirit and will for the supreme effort. The black curtain flecked with red was being drawn for the last time. He dragged down his eyelids and his wrist arched, fingers spread, like a maimed spider making its death stand.

Crack!

Bond's eyes were closed, but the flash shone through the lids like torchlight playing on a blind. There was a deafening explosion and a crazed grinding noise that faded with the imperishable resonance of a steel heel being dragged across asphalt. As quickly as it had taken hold, Bond felt the grip loosening. His body detached itself from the seat and he came away like a sticky sweet from its wrapping. Sweat lathered his aching body. He was within half a breath of voiding the contents of his stomach. The hatch snapped open and hands tore at the straps that stopped him from slumping forward. He heard Holly's voice above the others and pulled up his head to open his eyes.

Holly was looking at him, aghast. 'What happened?' It was difficult to doubt the concern on her face.

Difficult but not impossible. Bond opened his dry mouth and tried to find some saliva to lubricate his words.

'Something must have gone wrong with the controls.' Holly's voice was incredulous. She stretched out a supporting hand as Bond started to pull himself out of the seat. 'Let me help you.'

Bond brushed the hand aside. 'No thanks, Doctor. I think I've had enough treatment for one day.'

6

BED AND BORED

Trudi Parker rested her beautiful blonde head against the pillow and sighed. It was eleven o'clock at night and the novel, closed, with Trudi's finger inserted between pages 64 and 65, had long since failed to maintain its initial slender promise. It lay against the silk sheets with the author's face on the back cover looking up at her sadly and reproachfully. In real life it was difficult to believe that any man finding himself where the author was would have had reason for either sadness or reproach. The sight of Trudi's breasts inadequately concealed behind the fabric of her flesh-coloured silk nightdress might indeed have provided that vital fillip to the style which the book so desperately needed.

Trudi sighed again and wished that she did so because she was tired rather than bored. The writer's style, though plodding, laboured and tortuous, fell just short of that exquisite tedium which can produce a printed soporific. On the contrary, it lumbered into the category of work that asks questions it cannot answer, raises expectations it can never fulfil and leaves the reader asking not for more, but something; in other words, unsatisfied.

Trudi stuck her tongue out at the lugubrious author and placed him face downwards on the marble-topped bedside table. What the hero's philandering wife did when she found out that her philandering husband had fallen in love with his philandering secretary would never be revealed to her. The prospect of not sharing any more of their overlapping lives, which seemed to commute between Madison Avenue and the Adirondacks, came almost as a relief.

Trudi studied her even, white nails and reached idly for an emery board. Somewhere in the distance came the mournful cry of a coyote. A warm desert wind stirred the curtains. Outside, the night was clear, and needle-points of stars shone with uneven degrees of brightness. Trudi put down the emery board unused and stretched out a hand for the bedside lamp.

There was a light tap on the door.

Trudi withdrew her hand and sat up. The door opened and James Bond came in. He closed the door behind him and leant against it, surveying her. He wore a navy blue polo-neck pullover and a pair of similarly coloured tropical worsted trousers. Trudi wondered where he had been and, with more immediate interest, where he was going. She pulled a sheet up before her demurely.

'Mother gave me a comprehensive list of things not to do on a first date.'

Bond smiled his thin, hard smile and crossed to the bed. 'Maybe you won't need it. That's not what I came here for.'

Trudi conquered her disappointment and hoped that no trace of it showed in her voice. 'What do you want then?'

Bond sat on the bed and looked at her levelly. This time there was more warmth in his smile. 'Would your feelings be shattered if I said information?'

Trudi forgot about the sheet that slipped down about her waist. 'Why should I tell you anything?'

Bond leant forward and kissed her hard on the mouth. 'Because you like me.'

Trudi shook her head in amazement. 'Who are you?' She suddenly remembered how good his mouth had tasted. 'Do that again.' She leant forward and Bond's head tilted obligingly. This time the kiss was long and deep. Delicious premonitions of pleasure stirred through her with the touch of warm fingertips. 'What do you want to know? Is it to do with what happened this afternoon?' News of the accident on the centrifuge trainer had quickly spread through the installation. Apparently, by some million-to-one chance, two circuit break-offs had been transposed when a simple electrical fault was being repaired.

The corner of Bond's mouth twisted down ruefully. 'No. Mr Drax has been very generous with his explanations and apologies. It's what he hasn't told me that I'm most interested in.'

Trudi was puzzled. 'What do you want to know?'

'What goes on here besides the manufacture of the Moonraker and the astronaut training programme?'

'I still don't know who you are.'

Bond took a deep breath and decided to make the lie elaborate.

'I work for the British Aircraft Corporation. Investigating air crashes is my speciality, I'm afraid. There are a few puzzling features about this one and we can't rule out the possibility that sabotage was involved. It's mere supposition at the moment and I don't want to make Mr Drax alarmed.'

Trudi put her hand on Bond's arm. 'You mean, what happened to you this afternoon might not have been an accident?'

Bond tried to look grave. 'That's a possibility too. It would help me to get an idea of why someone should want to strike at the Drax Corporation if I knew exactly what they're developing here. I think Mr Drax might misconstrue my interest and, at the moment, I have no definite evidence to put before him. I'm still waiting on our own lab reports of the Alaska wreckage.'

Bond was glad to see Trudi nodding sympathetically. She would clearly like to help. 'It's pretty difficult for me to tell you anything,' she said. 'Like I said, I'm just Mr Drax's personal pilot. I know there was a very "top secret" project in one of the laboratories, but everything has been moved now.'

Bond's pulse quickened. 'Where to?'

Trudi shook her head. 'I don't know. One morning it had gone. All the technicians too. I was surprised nobody told me about it. I'm normally involved with all the flights that come in and out of here. They must have left from the railhead.'

Bond frowned. 'Where was the laboratory?'

'If you're thinking of going and looking at it, you can forget it,' said Trudi. 'It was burned out just after the move.'

Bond's smile was grim. 'Accidents do happen around here.'

Trudi folded her arms beneath her bosom and leant back against the pillow. 'It's most unusual. Normally, nothing very much happens around here.'

Bond raised an eyebrow. 'Really?'

'Absolutely. That's why your visit to my room was such an event.'

Bond looked down at the lambent curve of the soft, sensual mouth. It was difficult not to be aroused by the beauty of this girl. There was a need in her eyes too.

'What about that list of your mother's?'

Trudi's arms uncrossed and reached out to slide round his neck. Her lips parted to receive anything that he might wish to give. 'What mother?' she breathed.

7

BEHIND THE CLOCK

An hour later Bond was moving silently along the route he had followed with Drax's butler. He had left Trudi asleep with a seraphic smile plucking at the corner of her mouth and a sheet pulled tight about her naked body. In that pose she had looked like a small child tucked up snug in its cot. It gave a false impression of what she had been like in her waking moments.

Bond paused at the foot of the stairway and listened. He could hear a clock ticking, but nothing else. The hall was lit by moonlight and the busts in the niches peered out like spies. Bond crossed to the door of Drax's study. No light shone from beneath it. No sound came from within. Bond closed his fingers around the handle and pushed down. There was a soft click and the door opened. Bond paused for a moment and listened again. If by some chance the Dobermann pinschers were still in residence he wanted to give them time to announce their presence. Satisfied that there was no one there, Bond slipped into the room and closed the door behind him. The task before him was daunting. He had no idea what he was looking for and there was enough furniture there to stock an auction room. He crossed to a Louis Quinze escritoire and found it locked. This was not surprising. Neither, after what he had discovered in his room, were the two thin wires running down its back and along the top of the skirting board. The piece was either booby-trapped or attached to an alarm which would go off if anybody tampered with it.

Bond was pondering the alternatives when the door opened quickly behind him. He had hardly sunk to the floor when Trudi came in wearing a long white silk robe and a worried expression. 'James?'

Bond rose to his feet and Trudi shrank back. Bond quickly placed a finger to his lips. 'You whetted my appetite.' She looked puzzled. 'For information. Is there a safe in here?'

Trudi's eyes widened. 'You must be nuts!'

'Possibly.' Bond glanced round the room. A handsome gilt wall clock was flanked by two lights. Their position seemed incongruous in terms of the total layout of the room. The clock was not a work of art that cried out for illumination. Bond approached the clock and listened. It was not working.

Trudi watched him like someone who has hidden the object in a game of hunt the thimble. Her face was drawn with anxiety. 'James –'

'Would you say I was getting warm?'

'James! You've got to leave.'

Bond reached up and opened the glass front of the face. The face swung with it to reveal that it was no more than a façade. Behind lay the round door of a small safe with a combination dial in the middle of it.

'So far, so promising,' said Bond. 'I don't imagine you know the combination?'

Trudi shook her head slowly. She was almost hypnotized by fear. 'I wouldn't tell you if I did.'

Bond looked at the graceful figure silhouetted against the moonlight and felt a quick pang of sexual hunger. What was it that made a frightened woman so desirable? Psychologists would probably be able to furnish an unflattering reason. He slipped his hand into the pocket of his trousers. 'All right. I won't press you.' A slim rectangular shape had appeared in his right hand and was positioned against the side of the face next to the dial. Trudi saw something glowing and had an impression of superimposed fluorescent lines. It was like looking at an X-ray plate. Bond began to manipulate the dial with his fingertips and the pattern changed. Trudi looked round the room trying to establish that she really was in Hugo Drax's study and not asleep in her bed dreaming some strange dream. There was a click and the safe door jumped open. Trudi did not wake up. She was still in Drax's study. She looked at the object in Bond's hand. 'That's amazing.'

Bond pressed it against her left breast and narrowed his eyes as the rectangle glowed. 'You have a heart of gold.'

Trudi smiled nervously. 'You won't need an X-ray machine to see it if Mr Drax catches us here.'

Bond thought that she was probably right. He swung open the door of the safe and peered inside. At first glance it appeared to be empty and his heart sank. Then his probing fingers felt the back wall give and he exerted sideways pressure. The back of the safe slid open to reveal another space behind. It was a clever ruse reminiscent of the secret compartments built into the backs of drawers in period furniture. Bond extended his arm and withdrew a sheet of design paper folded into four.

Trudi was now trembling. 'For God's sake, James!'

'All right.' Bond's voice was cold and hard as he shouldered her aside. It was the expression his face had worn at the most passionate moments of their lovemaking. She felt again that there was something frightening about the way in which his mood could suddenly change. To cross this man would be dangerous.

Bond quickly spread the engineering drawing on the nearest flat surface and his eyes sped over it. It showed a sectionalized drawing of a globe with a complicated section around its equator. Alongside was a drawing of a small cylindrical object with a glass phial enclosed in it. 'Do you know what this is?'

Trudi shook her head. 'No.'

Bond believed her. He quickly raised something to his eye, and there was a click and a small flash. Almost before Trudi had finished blinking, the drawing was being returned to the safe and the front of the clock swung shut. Bond returned the miniature camera to his pocket. 'Right. Let's go.'

'You go first,' said Trudi.

Bond hesitated for a moment and then kissed her lightly on the cheek.

'All right. Look after yourself.'

'And you.'

Bond moved swiftly to the door and opened it a couple of inches. He paused, listening, and then slipped out. Trudi waited for the sound of his footsteps but heard nothing. Behind her, a clock wound itself up to strike and her heart jumped at the unexpected noise. She looked warily round the moonlit room and crossed to the door. Bond had left it slightly ajar. Taking a deep breath and hearing her pulse thumping, she stepped outside and reached behind her to close the door. She was more frightened than she had ever been in her life. The door clicked to and the sound seemed to echo through the vast vaulted hall like a pistol shot. Trudi waited for a reciprocal sound, a light to come on, but there was nothing. She stepped away from the incriminating door and almost ran to the foot of the stairs. Like a child playing a game, she told herself that everything would be all right if she could reach the first landing without being seen. She climbed two steps at a time, the weight on her heart lifting with every step. Ahead of her, like a timekeeper on the finishing line, stood a suit of armour, a mace clasped in one of its mailed fists. Trudi swept past it and moved down the long corridor.

Beneath the stairs, Chang emerged from the shadows and looked up before moving ponderously and purposefully towards the door of the study.

8

DEATH IN VENICE?

The gondola moved smoothly across the Canale di San Marco, and Bond let his gaze drift to the Isola di San Giorgio and the imposing colonnade of its beautiful white Palladian church. On all sides was beauty and a quality of light that Bond only found in Venice. A water bus went by and the waves of its wake made the gondola pitch and toss through the broken reflections of the tall buildings. Bond's thoughts turned from beauty to duty.

A blow-up of the photograph taken of the blueprint in Drax's safe had revealed the words VENINI GLASS printed in one corner. It had taken little effort to discover that a company trading under that name owned a shop in St Mark's Square. Considerably more energy had been expended in trying to find out what the object depicted in the blueprint was, but without result. That it was some kind of small satellite was the considered opinion of Q's department, but the purpose for which it had been designed remained obscure. It was unlike anything currently being used in space for research or relay purposes.

The jetties of the Piazzetta loomed up and Bond's gondolier skilfully brought his craft in between the weed-encrusted piles. Bond stood up and stepped on to the planks. 'Wait for me here, Franco.'

Franco tipped his ribboned straw hat towards his eyes. '*Si, signore.*' He was a tall, well-built young man with black curly hair and long-lashed eyes, whose innocence was all above the surface. Beneath his smooth olive skin he was as hard as tungsten. He worked for Station G, whose sphere of influence covered northern Italy from Turin to Trieste.

The day was cold and the tourists thin on the ground. Bond walked past the Libreria Vecchia and towards the brick mass of the Campanile, the *paron de casa*. Around him the footsteps echoed hollowly and he began to hear the perpetual ghostly murmur that circulates through the colonnades like the accumulated whispers of history. He paused to admire the mosaics in the romanesque arches of the Basilica and moved on towards the Clock Tower. The hour began to strike and the two fused bronze figures on the roof swung back their hammers and struck the great bell in turn. The pigeons rose and then quickly dropped to the paving stones in search of food. They glanced at Bond hopefully with heads cocked on one side, but soon perceived that he was not a man who fed pigeons. Wings drooping and eyes alert to any crumb or grain, they hustled aside to let him pass.

Bond studied the shops near the Clock Tower. Very near the Merceria archway he saw what he was looking for. A canopy bearing the name Venini Glass. Tucked away in one corner with a discretion that was unusual was the Drax symbol. Bond looked about him as he had done when pausing outside the Basilica and felt reasonably certain that he was not being followed. He stepped forward under the arcade and entered the shop. Ranging on every side were shelves piled high with multi-coloured glasses, jugs, bowls, vases and ornaments, all fashioned in glass.

A very pretty girl was quick to step forward. 'Could I interest you in something?'

Bond found that his eye had unaccountably strayed to a glass model of a four-poster bed, and was quick to remove it. 'I'm tempted to say yes immediately, but maybe I'd better take a look round.'

The girl smiled and made a graceful sweep with her arm. 'Please, go anywhere you wish. You may visit the workshop if you like.' She pointed towards the back of the shop and left Bond in order to pursue another customer.

Bond made his way down the aisles and decided that on the whole he preferred antique glass to modern. There were a few showcases displaying antique pieces that appeared to a layman's eye to be worth a fortune. He passed them and paused in the doorway that led to the workshop. The light beyond was dim and the focus of attention inevitably became the furnaces and the glowing globules on the ends of the glass workers' rods. The sweat glistened on the chests of two men stripped to their under vests who were expertly fashioning a complicated multi-handled squat vase with the aid of pincers that manipulated the molten strands of glass as if they were spaghetti. What they were doing captured the interest of a small group of tourists, one of whom was fiddling with his camera at a speed scarcely inferior to that with which the glass makers were working.

Bond crossed to the tourists and then found his attention straying to another man who was working away from the others in a remote corner of the workshop. He was blowing what at first glance seemed like glass phials. Bond watched, admiring the skill with which the man picked up a blob of molten glass and inflated his cheeks until they seemed to be stuffed with a couple of tennis balls. The globule quivered and suddenly expanded like a balloon. A deft twist and a tap, and the glowing glass cylinder joined nine identical shapes in a tray. Bond looked at them and experienced an immediate sensation of *déjà vu*. An identical, four-inch glass phial with a swollen neck had been illustrated on the engineering drawing. There was no mistaking the convex protuberances. As Bond watched, the craftsman put down his rod and carried the full tray to an open service lift. He laid it carefully on a shelf and pushed a button. The globes disappeared from view. Bond saw the man glance at him suspiciously as he turned, and so he quickly swung round and followed a sign above another of the doors that led into the workshop which read 'Museum of Antique Glassware'.

Without looking back, Bond went through the door and along a dark brick and stone corridor that brought him into another showroom. Here there was none of the crush of the shop proper, and many of the exhibits were in glass cases. A girl in a beautiful but simple white cashmere suit was showing round a party of tourists. '. . . and this perfect bowl is the work of Bruno Venini, the founder of this establishment. Born in Padua in 1451, he came to Venice at the age of eighteen and, five years later, opened a small workshop on the island of Murano . . .'

Bond forgot about Bruno Venini as the party moved on to a second showcase and he saw who was detaching herself from the rear of the group. Holly Goodhead. Her hair hung loosely about her shoulders and she was wearing a thigh-length woollen jacket in red and blue stripes and wide navy blue trousers. She let the party draw ahead of her and then skirted some showcases to arrive at a door in the corner of the room. She glanced round quickly and Bond stepped back into the passageway. When he peered out she was opening the door and looking inside. Bond saw her head tilt. After a moment's pause, she closed the door and rejoined the party, who were being informed that a fastidiously ornate model of a sailing boat would fetch over a million dollars were it ever placed on the market. The party moved out of the room with a chorus of respectful 'oohs'.

Bond crossed swiftly and opened the door. He looked into a small courtyard with a flight of stairs going up to a heavily studded wooden door. There was a gateway with a wrought iron gate and beyond that a vista of green slimy wall with grey water beneath it. Bond closed the door thoughtfully and hurried in the direction that the party had taken.

Holly was walking across St Mark's Square as Bond came up beside her, making an exaggerated gesture of astonishment. 'Why – Dr Goodhead. What a surprise!'

Holly's lip curled slightly. 'I can only hope your presence here is a coincidence, Mr Bond. I dislike being spied on.'

'Don't we all,' said Bond agreeably. 'It makes me almost as piqued as having my brains scrambled on a sabotaged centrifuge.'

Holly's tone was almost prim. 'Really, Mr Bond, you appear to suffer from a persecution complex.'

'Events tend to encourage it,' said Bond drily. 'Can I ask what brings you to Venice?'

Holly waved a dismissive hand at a photographer who was angling for a shot. 'I'm addressing a seminar of the European Space Commission.'

Bond shook his head admiringly. 'Heady stuff. I keep forgetting that you're more than just a very beautiful woman.'

Holly stopped and faced him. 'Mr Bond, if you're trying to be ingratiating, don't bother. I have more important things on my mind.'

Bond's expression became serious. 'They're what I'd like to talk to you about. How about dinner this evening?'

Holly shook her head. 'This evening I'm giving my address.'

'Can you think of a reason why we can't have a drink afterwards?'

Holly smiled a thin smile. 'Not immediately – but I'm certain I shall.'

She started to walk away but Bond was quickly at her side. 'The least I can do is escort you back to your hotel. The Danieli, I imagine?'

Holly's eyes narrowed. 'You have been spying on me.'

'No, it's the direction in which you're walking. The

Y.W.C.A. is the other end of town.'

Holly suppressed a smile as they passed the Ducal Palace and crossed the long bridge to the Riva degli Schiavoni. 'I might ask you what you're doing here. The 747 came down in Alaska, didn't it?'

'I'm more interested in where the Moonraker came down,' said Bond. 'I didn't find anybody in California who was prepared to look farther than the other side of the Bering Strait.'

'Perhaps you didn't talk to the right people.'

There was a note of criticism in Holly's voice that Bond found puzzling. Apart from Drax and Holly, Trudi was the only person he had questioned in detail. 'How's Trudi Parker?' he asked casually. 'She seemed to be getting a bit bored with her job.'

'She's dead,' said Holly calmly.

'Dead?'

'Rather a horrible accident. Mr Drax was out shooting and the Dobermanns attacked her.'

'And nobody was able to control them?'

'She'd wandered off into the woods by herself, apparently. The dogs must have picked up her scent. Chang went after them but when he got there it was too late.' She shuddered convincingly. 'It's horrible, isn't it?'

Bond felt like throwing up. Just a few days before he had been making love to the girl. Now she was dead. Perhaps because of him. His bitterness was laced with strong measures of guilt which he funnelled instantly into a determination for revenge.

'Accidents appear to be proliferating,' he said grimly. 'You must fear for your own life sometimes.'

Holly looked at him levelly. 'I think we both have our fears, Mr Bond.' She held out a hand in a gesture of dismissal. 'Good luck with your inquiries.'

Bond shook the hand. 'And with your address. I'll see

you later.'

Holly's expression was sceptical but she said nothing. She turned on her heel to continue walking along the quay.

Bond's face was set in grim lines as he retraced his steps to find his gondola. Trudi must have been killed because somebody knew that she had been in the study with him. His own life had probably been spared because two 'accidents' in the space of a few hours would have aroused suspicion even in Drax's stronghold. But here, in Venice, he was vulnerable again. It was open season for James Bond. He lengthened his stride and found Franco fending off an American matron who was clearly more interested in his body than his gondola.

Bond adopted a mealy-mouthed English accent. 'I'm frightfully sorry but I'm afraid I engaged this chap for the day.'

The woman's eyes challenged him contemptuously and the word 'faggot' almost formed itself on her lips. She turned away, making no secret of her disappointment.

Bond stepped into the gondola. 'Have you seen anything unusual, Franco?'

'A man with binoculars has been watching the Piazzetta for a long time from the top of the Campanile. You see –' he nodded discreetly as he began to paddle '– they glint in the sunlight.'

Bond looked and nodded. It might be a tourist. It might be somebody reporting his movements. He must keep on the alert but not fall prey to exaggerated fears. 'Take me up to the Rialto,' he commanded.

'Si, signore.' Franco took the gondola away from the cluster round the jetties and headed towards the church of Santa Maria della Salute and the mouth of the Grand Canal. Bond sat back in comfort and looked at the façades of the noble buildings; the warm pink brick and the blackened stone. The water lapped noisily and there was a sad smell of age and decay. Bond thought of Trudi again and felt a fresh pang of bitterness and misery sweep over him. He was in a dirty business and kind, ordinary people with whom he came into contact ran the risk of dying. As he grew older it was something that worried him more. His increasing awareness of the limitations of his own mortality was making him more compassionate about the lives of others. It was something, he considered ruefully, that in due course could make him a liability to the service.

Franco turned into a narrow waterway at the Grande Hotel Europa e Britannia and the noise and bustle of the Grand Canal was replaced by the mournful *slap, slap* of muddy brown water against the slime-covered stones. Buildings rose on either side like the walls of a canyon and Bond turned his head to see a fat rat watching him from the mouth of a pipe. Far above there was an unnerving cackle of female laughter and the grinding noise of a window being forced shut. A low bridge loomed up and Franco almost knelt as they went beneath it. On all sides they were enclosed, and the atmosphere was claustrophobic. Bond slid his hand down to his waist to feel the comforting outline of his Walther PPK, keeping his eyes moving warily. There were balconies far above, and suddenly a flowerpot seemed to tremble. Bond flinched and then saw that the movement was caused by a cat picking its way along a balustrade.

No sooner had he relaxed than a funeral launch appeared, nosing its way into the canal ahead of them. The launch was black with an elaborate coffin mounted forward of a low cabin. Wreaths lined its sides. Before the coffin, the helmsman, dressed in black and wearing dark spectacles, controlled the launch. The sight was a depressing one at the best of times, and in this dark and narrow waterway was made doubly sinister by its surroundings. Bond found his attention caught by the Charon at the helm. The dark spectacles gave the man an appearance that was unaccountably evil. And the hat. It was odd that the helmsman of a funeral launch should wear a flat black cap. Bond looked at Franco, who had taken off his straw and was holding it respectfully across his chest. The launch was a dozen yards away. The helmsman crouched over the wheel. Bond could make out shadowy figures in the cabin.

Bang!

With a noise like the lid of a jack-in-the-box springing open, the top of the coffin burst into the air and a man sat up clasping a sub-machine gun. His first volley of shots ripped into Franco's chest and expelled him from the boat as at the tip of a lance. Bond threw himself flat and thrust out an arm. His finger collided with a button which he pushed as a second volley of sub-machine gun fire honeycombed the woodwork behind him. There was a grinding noise that struggled for survival against the metallic bray of the automatic, and the gondolier's platform slid back to reveal an inboard motor and a tiller. As Bond grasped the tiller, so the engine roared to life and the prow of the gondola leapt into the air.

The boat surged forward as another hornet swarm of hot lead lacerated the air above Bond's head. There were shouts of rage and defiance and loud scraping noises as the launch swung round to give chase. Bond found himself menaced by another gondola and steered a perilous passage between it and a wall before emerging in an open basin. There was no indication of which exit to take so he swung the tiller over and sped up the narrowest waterway he could find. Only a few yards' progress was necessary for him to realize that he had made a mistake. Ahead lay a high brick wall signalling that he had entered a cul de sac. Still lying at full length, he manipulated the tiller and passed under a narrow bridge. Behind him he could hear the manic screech of the launch's motor. It was closing the distance between them fast. There was a sound like somebody stamping on a matchbox, and Bond looked back to see that the coffin and the top of the cabin structure had been torn off as the launch roared under the low bridge. The helmsman did not give up easily. He knew that if he caught up with Bond he could run him down as a motorist with a couple of beers inside him might smear a rabbit just for the hell of it.

Now the brick wall was looming up fast. Bond cut the engine and turned to face the way he had come. The prow of the gondola thumped into the wall. Bond was shaken but pulled out the Walther PPK and held it before him in two hands. The muzzle wavered slightly between the two circles of dark glass that showed above a mouth parting in triumph. Bond knew that it had to be – now! A sharp crack and the helmsman's head jerked out of view.

Bond did not pause to congratulate himself on his marksmanship but leapt sideways for a metal railing running along the sidewalk. His hand closed on it and his feet braced against the wall. He jerked himself up and threw a leg over the rail as the launch smashed through the gondola and into the wall. There was a violent explosion and a wave of heat that singed the hair on the back of his head. Bond staggered against the wall and squatted down with his arm across his face. Behind him the launch burnt with a hungry crackling noise that soon extinguished the faint screams coming from the concertina-ed wreckage. Windows opened, people began to shout and cry out, a crowd converged. Bond found himself standing next to the American woman who had tried to obtain Franco's services. She looked at him, puzzled.

'Ghastly,' said Bond. 'Quite ghastly. I think there's been some kind of frightful accident.'

9

AN EAR FOR MUSIC

The night was black. The gondola could only be seen when light from a passing motor boat splashed into the inlet. It glided to the heavy wrought iron gate and stopped. High above where a narrow strip of sky showed between the tall buildings, the clocks of Venice began to strike ten. A pencil-thin column of light shone on the wrought iron and there was a clink of metal. Seconds passed, and with a click the gate swung ajar.

James Bond listened attentively and then slipped through the gate and quickly crossed the courtyard he had scouted in the morning. He came to the flight of steps and bounded up them silently on his rubber-soled shoes. In the distance, two cats started a brief skirmish. At the top of the steps was an archway and beyond it a dimly lit corridor. Bond paused until the only sound he could hear was his breathing, and entered the corridor. It was damp and cold and bisected at a distance of about forty feet by another corridor running at right angles. Bond advanced, coming to two heavy iron doors. Set into the wall beside them was a plaque like the surface of a pocket computer. The numerals glowed red in the semi-darkness. The bricks of the corridor were old but the doors were new. There was no handle, no lock. Bond was studying the smooth inscrutable face of the doors when he heard the sound of footsteps approaching. Another door behind him offered sanctuary. He lifted the latch and pressed. The heavy oak swung back and he stepped into darkness. The smell that assaulted his nostrils was more offensive than anything that damp or decay could muster. It was accompanied by a rustling sound that seemed to come from all around him. Bond had the impression of many shapes moving and of shelves stacked with sharp red eyes. The shelves held cages. Cages full of rats.

Not loath to turn his back, Bond swung round and applied his eye to the crack of the almost shut door. A man wearing a white coat and carrying a sheaf of papers loomed into view. He stopped before the metal doors. With a sigh of exasperation he raised a finger and tapped out five numbers on the illuminated panel. The colours of the numbers selected changed from red to yellow and the man pressed one of the doors. It opened and the numbers reverted to red as the man went through and the door closed behind him. Bond had little time to see what lay beyond; only that it seemed to be a store room. He waited for the man to emerge but minutes passed and nothing happened. What was he doing down here at this time of night? It seemed that there was going to be only one way of finding out.

Bond emerged from the livestock store and approached the panel. He hoped that an alarm signal would not be triggered off if he pressed the wrong combination. It had not been easy to see exactly which numbers the man had pressed. Bond concentrated and tapped. Five-one-one-three-five. For a fraction of a second nothing happened, then the numerals were flooded with yellow. Bond pushed open the door and quickly slipped inside.

He was now standing in a dimly lit outer office flanked by filing cabinets and stacks of variously shaped boxes. A second room could be seen through a glass window that one might have expected to find in the viewing chamber of a maternity hospital. It looked into a brightly lit laboratory. Bond advanced carefully, wondering what was going on. The reason for the rats was now obvious. They would be used in experiments. Looking across to the far wall, he could see two of them standing up with their paws against the bars of their cage. They were sniffing inquisitively as if asking themselves the same questions as Bond.

What was this laboratory doing in a glass factory in Venice? There was no indication that anything that was happening had a bearing on the manufacture of glass ornaments. It was just feasible that Drax might be developing some special strain of glass or plastic, but none of the equipment that Bond could see supported this conjecture. Besides the array of test tubes, beakers, balances and microscopes, the laboratory was dominated by a long and complicated distillation system that looked like a miniature oil refinery, a welter of glass pipes and coloured tubes connected to an array of bottles and retorts. The last part of the process took place within a sealed glass case and Bond could see that the distillate was being manoeuvred by a series of mechanical arms operated by two scientists who crouched outside the case. One of them was the man he had watched tapping out the combination. Drop by drop a quantity of the distillate found its way into a glass phial. The full phial was sealed and passed along a conveyor belt in a convoy of six to slide down a gentle slope, where it rested until a guillotine-like glass shield had descended behind it, sealing it off from the main distillation process. One of the scientists now operated another glass screen which permitted the phials to be withdrawn and placed in a giant refrigerator unit. The delicacy of the whole operation and the care taken to seal off the distillate suggested that it must be highly toxic.

Bond felt his pulse racing. Now he was on to something. He must get hold of a sample of the distillate. As he craned forward, he received a surprise. One of the scientists moved away from the refinery and returned, pushing two spheres like those that Bond had seen on the engineering drawing in Drax's safe. Each was mounted in a structure like a baby's high chair and Bond noted the curiously shaped hexagonal section around the middle of the globe.

One scientist pulled open the lid of the conning tower and the other carefully inserted a phial freshly filled with distillate. The lid snapped back into place and the process was repeated with the second sphere. The operation completed, the two scientists carefully manoeuvred one of the spheres to the end of the laboratory and steered it gently out through doors which opened automatically as the trolley approached.

Hardly had the doors closed than Bond had entered the laboratory and was moving swiftly to the distillation system. He pulled open the door of the refrigerator and selected one of the phials from the batch that had recently been introduced. Others were covered by a thick rime of frosting. He listened attentively for sounds of the scientists returning and then crossed to the remaining sphere. He must check that the contents of the phial in his hand were identical to those of the sphere. The lid of the conning tower was spring-loaded and it was necessary to lay the phial he had taken from the refrigerator on one of the wings so that he could grapple with it. He had just succeeded in opening the lid when he heard the sound of returning voices.

Telling himself to keep calm, Bond carefully inserted his thumb and forefinger in the opening and closed them about the lip of a phial. He started to withdraw it and felt the phial tremble as it worked free from his desperately pinching fingers. Cocking his little finger, he was able to support the lid and liberate his hand to grasp the phial just before it dropped. The automatic doors slid open as he ducked down and tucked the phial into the breast pocket of his pullover. Skirting the racks of instruments and the work benches, he returned to the outer office and gently pushed the door closed behind him before rising to his feet.

Experience told him that this was the moment to get out and not push his luck, yet he could not resist looking back into the laboratory. The two scientists had returned to the second globe and were preparing to manoeuvre it towards the automatic doors. Damn! Bond nearly spoke the word as he realized that he had left the phial taken from the refrigerator on the globe's centre section. The scientists could scarcely fail to see it. He was turning away when the trolley began to move and he heard a cry of alarm that penetrated even the thick glass of the observation panel. One of the scientists lunged forward desperately and the trolley lurched. Bond realized what must have happened. The first movement of the trolley had caused the phial to roll off the globe. What seemed like a puff of green smoke hung in the air and a bright red light in the ceiling of the laboratory started flashing at the same time as a piercing alarm bell began to ring. With a hissing noise, a green airtight seal appeared around the framework of the door by which Bond had entered the laboratory. As he watched, horrified, the scientists began to stumble towards the automatic doors. One collapsed against a rack of instruments and dragged them with him to the ground. The other reached the doors to find that they did not open. He beat at them with his fists and tried pathetically to prize them apart with his fingers. Within seconds he was clutching at his throat and then sliding down the doors to disappear from view. The air inside the laboratory was now tinged with green and a sinister coating of green appeared on the inner surface of the viewing panel like slime on the side of an aquarium. Only the rats seemed unaffected and still nosed inquisitively against the bars of their cages.

Bond took a wary breath and felt the outline of the phial against his chest. It would have been less dangerous had it contained nitro-glycerine. Eager to escape from the hellish scene before him, he pressed the switch that opened the door to the corridor and quickly retraced his steps to the flight of steps and the courtyard. Now the alarm bell was only a distant buzz and the wrought iron gate that led to safety was only a few paces away. Bond quickly crossed the courtyard and pulled open the gate. The gondola was not there. He looked towards the intersection that led to the main waterway and saw that it was drifting twenty yards from where he stood. He turned and found himself face to face with Chang. His hand moved for his gun, but it was still coming up to the firing position as the side of Chang's hand caught him in the neck like the edge of a spade. The Walther PPK clattered to the cobbles and Bond fell after it, feeling as if every nerve in his body had been paralysed. A flailing foot swept the pistol aside and another glanced off his rib cage. Had the blow landed on target it would have stoved in his ribs like the planks of a rotten barrel. Some inner voice of self-preservation brought him to his senses, and he rolled aside and scrambled to his knees. Chang came in again with foot raised, but Bond ducked beneath it and ran for the door that he knew led into the showroom. He felt something damp against his chest and offered a quick prayer that it was only water. If the phial broke . . .

With his neck throbbing as if an electric current was being passed through it, Bond threw his shoulder against the door and turned the handle. Behind him he could hear Chang grunting in pursuit. The man moved like a great ponderous crab. The door opened and Bond darted amongst the darkened shelves. Moonlight flooded in above the drawn blinds that faced out on St Mark's Square. Somewhere near by there was an orchestra playing. The acrid smell from the workshop permeated the room. Bond waited in the darkness, listening. He heard Chang panting and then the sound of his heavy breathing becoming fainter. A deadly game of hide and seek was about to begin. Bond considered the best course of action. The windows were too heavily stacked with merchandise to make diving through the sheet glass a healthy proposition. There was also the phial to think about. The main entrance would make the best point of escape, but that was probably where Chang was waiting.

Bond started to pick his way slowly between two rows of shelves groaning under the weight of the antique glass they had to bear. If he could just get to the – *CRASH!* Like a hurled bale of cloth, Chang launched himself through a shelf and on to Bond. Glassware shattered in all directions and Bond felt a piercing pain as he was borne backwards into another shelf and through that to the floor. The wind was crushed from his body. Chang's breath against his face stank of the lust to kill. Bond scrabbled desperately for any weapon that came to hand and his fingers closed around a sliver of broken glass. He drove upwards and there was a shrill bellow of pain as the fingers burrowing into Bond's windpipe loosened their grip. Bond struck again and wriggled sideways, feeling fragments of broken glass lacerating his shoulders. His right hand was slippery with blood. Chang struggled to hold him but Bond broke free and picked up a heavy glass vase shaped like an open-mouthed fish. He swung it with all his force and connected with Chang's temple as the Chinaman tried to rise. The vase shattered but Chang grunted and kept coming. There was a line of blood across his neck and upper shoulder where Bond had gashed him. Bond staggered backwards and found that the way to the front of the shop was cut off. Chang stood with the light behind him and his massive arms standing away from his body. If anything, his tortoise head seemed to be sunk deeper into his shoulders so that he looked like an unbreakable Humpty Dumpty. He came forward, his elbows brushing the shelves, and Bond shrank back towards the sullen heat of the workshops. Chang's eyes glinted with impersonal hatred, like the slits in a gun turret, but his small, obscene mouth had opened to reveal two rows of tiny teeth parted like those of a predatory fish.

Bond felt the opening to the passageway behind him and

quickly ducked inside. He was still numb from Chang's first blow, but with every movement the chains that shackled his reflexes were loosening. He drove his feet forward and moved into the darkness of the workshops. Darkness illuminated by the glowing crucibles that were never extinguished. At the far side of the workshop was the outline of a wooden staircase. Bond ran towards it and collided with something that resounded like a gong being struck. He staggered back, feeling fresh pain, skirted the object and prepared to move forward. *Click!* A light flicked on behind him and he turned to see Chang grinning at him triumphantly. One blunt hand reached out and Bond stiffened as apprehension gave way to terror. Chang was grasping one of the glassblower's rods that had been left at the mouth of a glowing crucible. It came away with its tip white-hot and Chang slashed at the air as if wielding a sword. He took a step forward and suddenly straightened his arm. Like a tracer bullet, the rod sped for Bond's head. Such was the unexpected speed of the delivery that Bond had no time to duck. There was the sound of ice cracking and Bond's vision fragmented. Before his sizzling eyelashes the white-hot tip of the poker turned to red and then a furious pink. Bond was standing behind a sheet of plate glass which had received the full impact of the rod. Its tip had been arrested inches from his face. Bond stepped back from the spider's web of glass and completed his journey to the staircase.

Now Chang let out a bellow of frustrated rage that was terrible to hear. Chang's foot was on the bottom tread of the staircase as Bond reached the first landing, and he could feel the structure shaking behind him as the Chinaman charged in pursuit. He dashed up the next flight and emerged in a small loft littered with packing cases. Some were open, and in them he glimpsed spheres like those he had seen being filled in the laboratory. There was a pulley system in the corner, suggesting that the loft was used as a store room.

Bond ducked down and listened to his heart pumping, registering the words stencilled on a packing case before him: C.&W. Rio de Janeiro. Interesting. But maybe a lead that had arrived too late. As Chang burst into the loft, Bond attempted to utilize his wrist gun. He jerked his wrist back and there was a sharp crack followed by an explosion of fragments and a cloud of brick dust from the far wall. Deadly but hardly accurate. Chang launched himself forward but checked as Bond sideslipped behind one of the packing cases. Chang's expression as he glanced down at the contents showed that he was well aware that whatever was in the packing cases needed to be treated with respect.

Bond ran for a small door in the corner and up a last flight of creaking cobweb-strewn steps. His head rose above floor level and he found himself in a room crowded with antique machinery and illuminated by a translucent circle of light picked out with roman numerals. In a flash it came to him that he had emerged in the works chamber of the Clock Tower. He was standing behind the clock face. The pulleys, cog-wheels and chains that surrounded him were all working parts of the clock. There was no way out of the chamber apart from the staircase by which he had entered. Here he must stand and fight. Pulling back a bunch of chains, he swung them in Chang's face as the Chinaman's head appeared above floor level. The effect was no more than that of a goad on an elephant. Chang roared his rage and blundered through the chains as if they were a bead curtain. A swinging blow broke through Bond's guard and seemed to lift his head a couple of inches from his shoulders. Again the numbing sensation set his teeth on edge and momentarily paralysed the right side of his body. He dropped his shoulder and lashed out with a left hook that struck Chang flush on the side of his recessed jaw. Chang smiled. It was not the involuntary smile that a boxer gives to prove that he is hurt. It was a smile that said, 'I have taken your best punch and found it less damaging than a pat on the cheek.' Bond retreated into the machinery and Chang followed, the grim smile still on his face. From around them there came a whirring sound and Bond heard one of the near-by clocks begin to strike the hour. He knew what the noise meant. The machinery was winding itself up to strike. At any moment the two Moors above their heads would start to hammer the bell as they had been doing for over four and a half centuries.

Chang's eye-slits glistened in the half-light. As the machinery ground into action, he spread his elbows, preparing to strike. One arm swung back, but as Bond flinched, anticipating the blow, there was a cry of surprise. The sleeve of Chang's robe had become entangled in the turning teeth of a cog. As he spun round to tear at it with his free hand, so a second cog-wheel moved into conjunction with the first and crushed his hand in its metal teeth. Chang fought to free himself as Bond snatched up a heavy weight on the end of a chain and swung it like a medieval battle weapon. The first blow crunched against the side of Chang's head and Bond lashed out again while the two Moors began to beat out their own macabre accompaniment to the screams and the mad grinding of the machinery.

With an agonized yelp of pain, Chang tore his arm free and turned to receive the full force of the metal weight against his jaw. His mangled hand pawed the air in front of Bond's face and Bond felt warm blood sting his cheek. Chang staggered forward, desperately trying to lay hands on Bond, who fell back almost to the clock face. As Chang made one desperate rush, Bond stepped aside, lashing out again. The weight of the blow struck Chang on the back of the head and he pitched forward, stretching out his arms to break his fall against the ghostly circle of light. There was a splintering sound and a sudden rush of night air into the room as Chang disappeared, leaving a jagged hole in the clock face.

From below, the sound of the orchestra playing in the square ended as abruptly as if a needle had been lifted from a record. It was replaced by a chorus of horrified screams. Bond let the weight drop from his numbed fingers and staggered forward to peer through the opening. Chang was lying face downwards on a table that had collapsed beneath his weight. A dark stain was quickly spreading over the spotless white tablecloth. Bond ducked back to avoid the startled faces that were tilted up to him and started to move fast for the stairs. It was time to be on his way.

10

THE QUICKNESS OF THE HAND

Holly Goodhead moved to the edge of her balcony and spread her arms wide. Nosing against the wide, lamp-lit quay was a huddle of small steamers and ferry boats. A few seamen and tourists were hurrying home to their beds and directly below a waiter was folding the royal blue sun umbrellas over the coffee tables. The cold winter sunshine had produced little passing trade. Now the Canale di San Marco was a pinpoint blaze of lights and in the distance the Lido showed up against the night like glistening beads of dew on a spider's web. Holly drank in one of the most beautiful views in the world and turned to enter her suite. Her address had been well received, but a combination of tension, exhilaration and relief made her welcome the thought of sleep. She was stretching out a hand for a standard lamp when a second hand closed over hers. She pressed the switch and the light clicked on to reveal Bond staring down at her, his eyes hard, his mouth a ruthless slit. His hair was dishevelled and there were bruises on his face that she would gladly have added to.

'What the hell are you doing here?'

Bond's expression did not relent. 'Convalescing. Your friend Chang just tried to kill me.'

Holly flared her nostrils and willed her heartbeat to return to normal. 'And you think I had something to do with it?'

Bond released her hand contemptuously and moved around the suite, turning on more lights. 'The thought had flashed across my mind.' He moved to a bureau and picked up a slim gold retractable ball-point pen. 'What's Drax up to in that laboratory?'

'Why don't you ask him yourself?'

'I intend to.' Bond started to doodle on a pad.

Holly placed one hand on her hip and ran the other through her hair. 'Are you leaving me your telephone number?'

Bond smiled grimly. 'I don't see the point.' He held up the pen before his eyes and pressed its base. A hypodermic needle darted out like a snake's tongue. Bond winced. 'Ah – now I do.' He pressed again and a fine jet of colourless liquid squirted into the air. 'Not what I want to get stuck with tonight.' He pressed a third time and the needle retracted. Bond pocketed the pen and continued to prowl.

Holly followed him uneasily. 'Why don't you fix yourself a drink, James?'

Bond flashed an icy smile. 'I see we've gravitated to first name terms at last.' His hand rummaged through the cosmetics on the recessed dressing table He picked up a small scent atomizer and sniffed it.

Holly smiled winsomely. 'You approve?'

Bond directed the atomizer at the mirror and pressed its top. A sheet of flame emerged as from a flame-thrower, and his image was obliterated. The blackened mirror cracked and rained glass on the dressing table. Bond wrinkled his nostrils and, holding the atomizer between finger and thumb, replaced it. 'It's a trifle overpowering, isn't it?'

Hardly pausing, he moved to Holly's handbag and emptied its contents on the embroidered counterpane of the large double bed. A small leather-bound pocket diary with a slim pencil tucked into its spine appeared in his hand. He directed the diary at an armchair and squeezed. The 'pencil' was fired like a dart to bury itself in the stuffing of the chair. 'No doubt tipped with cyanide,' said Bond as if making an inventory. He picked up a pair of thick-rimmed spectacles and examined the decoration by the hinges. A tiny tube was visible pointing in the direction in which the wearer would be looking. Bond put on the spectacles.

Holly shook her head. 'They do nothing for you.'

Bond held a blotter in front of his face and tapped the top of the spectacles as if ruminating on something. There was an almost inaudible hiss and a dart scarcely larger than a thorn was embedded in the blotter. 'They'd do less for me if you were wearing them,' said Bond. He pressed the side of a powder compact and a wicked-looking blade flicked out. 'You do have some rough toys.'

'A girl has to look after herself these days,' said Holly.

Bond smiled grimly. 'I know Third World armies that aren't this well equipped.' He pulled apart a lipstick holder to reveal what looked suspiciously like a miniature detonator and explosive charge. The cylinder of a Zippo lighter was divided so that not only could it light a cigarette but squirt Mace in the face of an attacker.

Bond shook his head. 'I bet you pulled the arms off all your dolls.'

'I never had any dolls,' said Holly. 'I always used to be out on the streets with a catcher's glove.'

'With a baseball bat, more likely,' said Bond. He pressed one of the clasps on the side of the handbag and a telescopic aerial began to glide silently into the air. There was a sub-dued crackle of static electricity and the second clasp glowed with the numbers of radio bands.

Bond tossed the handbag on to the bed beside its con-tents. 'I've seen this equipment before, Holly, and it wasn't in Macy's.' He paused for a moment before he crossed to a drinks trolley. 'It was being developed by the C.I.A. An old friend of mine, Felix Leiter, gave me a sneak preview.' Bond turned his back to throw some ice cubes into a glass and top it up with Chivas Regal. 'I think you probably know him.' There was no reply from Holly. 'Because it occurs to me that the C.I.A. placed you with Drax. Correct?'

He waved a hand towards the trolley in invitation. Holly shook her head. 'Correct.' Her face softened into a conciliatory smile. 'Could it be that this is the moment for us to pool our resources?'

Bond studied Holly over the top of his glass. It was the first time he could remember her smiling like that. So warm. So guileless. So insincere. He put down his glass. 'That might have its compensations.'

Holly took a step towards him so that she was close enough to be touched. Her long silk gown could have been tied tightly across her low-cut nightdress but it was not. Bond drew her to him and kissed the corner of her mouth gently. His eyes were still suspicious.

'You think I'm trying to hide something, don't you?' said Holly.

Bond raised his eyebrows and suppressed a smile. 'Yes and no,' he said drily.

Holly watched his eyes warily circling the room. 'Haven't you done enough detective work for one evening?' She broke away and started replacing the contents of her handbag.

Bond caught a glimpse of his battered face in a mirror and smiled ruefully. 'I am tempted to call it a day.'

Holly smoothed down the counterpane seductively and placed her bag on a bedside table. She crossed to Bond and winced as she saw his hand. 'You'd better let me take a look at that.' She unfolded his fingers one by one and examined the deep cut across his palm. 'I've got something in the bathroom.'

Bond smiled. 'As long as it's not in your handbag.' He rested his nose against her hair. 'I suppose you're right, Holly. We would be better off working together.' She tilted back her head to look at him and he closed his free hand over hers. 'Détente?'

Holly nodded. 'Agreed.'

'Understanding?'

Holly twisted her head quizzically. 'Possibly.'

'Co-operation?'

'Sometimes.'

'Trust?'

Her mouth came up to his fast. 'Why do you have to talk so much?'

Four hours later, Bond lay naked beneath a sheet, feeling Holly nuzzling into his shoulder. She let out a small contented sigh and draped an arm across his chest. Bond drove a tiger from his loins and stretched out a furtive right arm. His Rolex Oyster Perpetual, glowing in the darkness, told him that it was time to leave. He slid from the bed, gently replacing Holly's arm on the warm sheet. Holly made another contented noise and burrowed into the pillow. Bond suddenly thought how vulnerable she looked and pulled the sheet up about her shoulders. His clothes lay mingled with hers and a shaft of moonlight played on the label of the woollen jacket that had caught his eye in the glass shop: 'Victoria Bevan, Handmade Knitwear. Great Shelford, Cambridge, England'. Dr Holly Goodhead obviously cast her net wide in the pursuit of excellence. Bond felt a pang of nostalgia as he looked down at this link with a country that meant more to him than any other in the world. England in winter matched the bleak asperity of his spirit, yet an immediate return was out of the question. His only lead directed him to more tropical climes. He breathed in the cool night air and briskly pulled on his polo-neck pullover. There were five hours to daybreak and he had work to do.

Holly permitted herself another sigh as she shifted her position to take full advantage of the warm space left by Bond and listen to the sounds of him dressing. There was a nearly inaudible exhalation as he pulled on his shoes, and she heard a floorboard creak as he moved to the door. The handle turned. A pause, a click. The door was shut again. Holly lay still and listened for several seconds. 'James?' Her voice was bruised and plaintive. She raised herself on one elbow and looked around. There was no sign of Bond lurking. Quickly she sat up and brushed the hair from her face before picking up the telephone. She waited, irritably flicking at the tip of her nose. Nobody would have believed, looking at that serious, composed face, that an hour before she had been indulging in the most passionate love-making of her life.

The ever-hopeful voice of an Italian night porter sounded on the end of the line. '*Si, signora?*'

The voice was as cold as that of a mid-western Baptist schoolmistress making her first trip east of the Great Lakes. 'Send up somebody for my bags ... At once, please.'

A thin net of rain fell on St Mark's Square as Bond turned up the collar of his Aquascutum raincoat and waited respectfully on the less brisk pace of M and Frederick Gray. It was a few hours after he had left Holly's suite and the more than prompt arrival of both his secular bosses was decidedly an embarrassment of riches. He was reminded of Gray's immortal lines:

> How happy could I be with either,
> Were t'other dear charmer away!

'This had better be good, Bond,' snapped Gray. 'There was a late sitting last night and I hardly had time to clear my mind of that damned division bell before your message came through.'

M felt it necessary to intercede on behalf of his protégé. '007 doesn't usually press the panic button unless it's serious, Minister.'

Gray uttered a noncommittal grunt and looked round the square. Small groups of armed *carabinieri* lurked in the archways with as much self-effacing discretion as Italians are capable of mustering. 'I take it you've covered everything with our Italian friends?'

Bond nodded briskly. 'Yes, sir. It's all been taken care of.' There was a slight edge of disdain to his voice which suggested that he was not overfond of Frederick Gray.

Gray either did not notice or did not care. 'Poor devils. I expect they're doing this kind of thing in their sleep these days.' The tone was pious and complacent. It intimated that the Moro kidnapping could never have taken place in Britain. If pressed for an opinion, Bond would have been less optimistic.

The façade of the Venini Glass shop loomed up, with a few early morning sightseers peering in inquisitively. The police, wrapped in their heavy blue overcoats, nudged them back with their elbows. An inspector stepped forward and saluted. Bond addressed him in Italian and the three Englishmen moved into the shop, leaving the two plain clothes men who had flown in with Gray and M standing at the doorway. The beautiful shop assistant who had greeted Bond on his first visit thrust herself forward and unleashed a volley of excited Italian. Bond nodded to one of the policemen who drew her aside, still protesting.

Gray looked embarrassed. 'I hope you know what you're doing, Bond. I've played bridge with this fellow Drax.' M delivered a cold look which Gray rightly took as a reproach. 'He's a very influential figure in Anglo-American affairs. Sort of diplomat without portfolio. Chaps like him wield an awful lot of international influence.'

Bond said nothing but led the way through to the courtyard. The prow of a police launch was visible through the wrought iron gate. Two policemen stood at the top of the flight of steps. Nobody could fault the speed and thoroughness with which the Italians had moved. Bond swallowed. His throat was dry. A few yards away lay the remnants of something inexplicably evil. He was not looking forward to seeing inside the laboratory again.

At the top of the steps they were met by two *carabinieri* and a plain clothes man carrying a canvas bag. The plain clothes man shook hands solemnly and led the way down the corridor. He paused outside the steel doors and turned to Bond.

'This is it?' asked Gray.

'Yes, sir.' Bond took the canvas bag and withdrew three gas masks. They dangled from his fingers like squid.

Gray looked incredulous. 'Gas masks?' His voice was an imitation of Lady Bracknell's. 'Now look here –'

'I don't think it's wise to take any chances.' Bond's voice was firm but calm. M said nothing but stretched out his hand for a mask. Gray gave an exclamation of impatience and followed suit. The plain clothes man and the *carabinieri* retired down the corridor towards the courtyard.

'Haven't done this since the war.' M's voice almost savoured the nostalgia as he pulled on his gas mask. Gray followed suit as if being asked to put on a funny hat at a children's party. When satisfied that the two men were properly protected, Bond pulled on his own mask and approached the door control panel. His chest heaved as he raised a finger. Five-one-one-three-five. Nothing happened. He tapped the numbers again with the same lack of result. Beside him he could see Gray's eyes behind the mask straining to catch M's. Bond turned towards the door and experienced a shock. Where there had once been smooth metal there was now a handle. Bond felt uneasy. As Gray cleared his throat impatiently, Bond turned the handle gently and felt the door opening. He pushed it forward and stepped into the room to receive his second surprise of the morning.

What had once been the outer office had disappeared. Of the laboratory there was no sign. In their place was a long vaulted chamber hung with Aubusson tapestries and Renaissance paintings. Bookcases projected at regular intervals from the walls and the gold leaf on the hand-tooled leather covers gleamed in the thin morning light that entered from the high diamond-shaped windows. A huge brass candelabra hung from the ceiling, and the room was sprinkled with tasteful items of antique furniture. It was from one of these that a familiar figure rose. The pink satin upholstery of the chaise longue paid an insipid compliment to the red hair and the rufous complexion, but there was no mistaking Drax's awesome bulk in any surroundings. He surveyed his visitors with an amused smile tinged with mockery.

'Why, I do believe it's Frederick Gray. What a surprise!' He approached with arms outstretched as Gray tore off his gas mask. 'And in distinguished company, all wearing gas masks.' His smile embraced the trio. 'You must excuse me, gentlemen. Not being English, I sometimes find your sense of humour a trifle difficult to follow.'

Bond felt the words sting him like a whiplash. What a damnably clever fellow he was up against. To underestimate Hugo Drax for one second would be to risk paying a forfeit of one's life.

Frederick Gray's eyes blazed with anger and embarrassment. He removed them from Bond and accepted Drax's hand. 'Frightfully sorry about this intrusion – I think our lines of communication must have got crossed.' He foundered and turned to M for help.

'Good morning, Mr Drax,' said M calmly. 'Do you happen to have a laboratory on your premises?'

'A laboratory?' Drax sounded surprised. 'No. There are the workshops, of course, but nothing that you could call a laboratory. The art of glass manufacture as practised here

101

has changed little over the centuries.'

'And no more accidents?' said Bond coldly. 'Such as the incident that led to Miss Parker's death?'

For a second a tiny pinpoint of red glowed in the centre of Drax's ill-matched eyes. 'An incident certainly, but not an accident. Somebody broke into the glassworks last night. Chang, my personal assistant, appears to have surprised the intruder in the museum – it is where any thief would have gone. I cannot be sure of exactly what took place because Chang was murdered.'

Gray turned to look at Bond and then controlled himself. 'How terrible. You have all our sympathy.'

'Thank you,' said Drax. 'I take it that this is not the crime you are investigating?'

'Not directly,' said M. 'Although the events may be connected.'

'That is always possible,' said Drax. He looked at Bond without love. 'I hope you will keep me abreast of all developments.' He smiled. 'I believe that is the rather convoluted expression you English employ in these situations?'

'Sometimes,' said M noncommittally. Bond could tell that the old man had not warmed to Drax – though that was hardly going to help him in his present situation. 'I think we'd better leave you in peace.' M nodded gruffly to Drax and led the way towards the door, with Gray grovelling two steps behind.

Outside in the square the situation was different. No sooner clear of the puzzled onlookers and scarcely less confused *carabinieri* than Gray launched into the attack. He ignored Bond and addressed himself solely to M. 'That was the greatest humiliation of my life,' he hissed. 'I ask you to put your best man on this case and what do I get? A paranoid lunatic who has apparently committed a murder. Not only that, he drags us out of bed to become accessories!' The voice was approaching breaking point. 'I want him replaced immediately! The man needs a medical report. God knows what the outcome of this affair is going to be.'

M listened stoically until Gray had exhausted himself and stalked off across the square, detonating clouds of pigeons. He watched him go and then crossed to Bond's side. He felt in his pocket and withdrew his pipe. 'What the hell is going on, 007? Have they got at you with drugs again?'

Bond shook his head. 'No, sir. There was a laboratory there. Drax is a damned clever operator, that's all.'

M looked sceptical. 'He must be if he can remove all traces of the structure you described in a few hours.'

Bond felt inside his jacket. 'He couldn't remove this, sir.' He produced the phial and handed it to M. 'This is what they were distilling. I'd like Q to analyse it. But exercising extreme caution. It killed two men.'

'One more than you,' said M drily. He closed his hand around the phial and looked up at Bond. 'What am I going to do with you, James? You heard what Gray said. You've got to come off the assignment.'

Bond's eyes twinkled. 'Compassionate leave, sir?'

M looked from his beloved pipe to the phial and pocketed the former. 'Where did you have in mind?'

Bond's voice was level. 'I've always had a hankering to visit Rio de Janeiro, sir.'

M nodded. 'Oh, yes. I recall you mentioning it on the way from the airport.' His voice suddenly took on a harsh edge. 'Very well. But no slip-ups, 007. Otherwise we're both in trouble.'

From the first floor of the Venini Glass shop, Drax watched Bond and M walk away across the square. A thin but triumphant smile played around his ugly mouth. To see the proud English picking at a dish of humble pie was always a pleasing sight. Drax crossed to a telephone and punched out thirteen numbers authoritatively. There was a pause and then the ringing phone was answered. Drax quickly announced himself and dealt with the worried inquiries. 'Yes, yes. There is no further cause for alarm. I have taken care of everything. A minor crisis has been averted.' His tone became urgent. 'But, one important thing: as from now, all merchandise must be re-routed. It is possible that you may be receiving visitors. Nosey visitors. Have no qualms about disposing of them.' There was a spurt of acquiescence from the other end of the line. Drax waited for it to expend itself. 'There is also the matter of a replacement for Chang. What have you achieved?' Drax listened and showed his uneven teeth in a smile. 'Excellent. If you can get him, I will be well pleased.' More assurances flooded his ears. 'You've got him on the next flight? Splendid. Most gratifying. You have done well.' Drax replaced the receiver on the sound of thanks being expressed for gratitude and stretched back in his chair until the joints creaked. In a few hours he had retrieved the work of a lifetime. Now the future – his future – seemed assured.

The high-pitched electronic screech cut through the voice of the flight announcer and the security guard sprang forward. The giant figure was almost wedged in the electronic arch, the shoulders braced against the sides and the head stooped. A quick search revealed nothing that might have triggered off a reaction, and yet the ear-splitting racket continued. Another security guard hurried up and a crowd began to form. It was at this point that the man's mouth broke open and he showed his teeth in a terrifying glare.

Two rows of shiny, jagged steel teeth.

The alarm note rose to an even higher and more frantic pitch and the last call for the flight to Rio de Janeiro was completely blotted out.

11

STEEL TEETH IN RIO

Bond decided that the most beautiful views in Rio de Janeiro were looking out to sea; from the Copacabana beach to the Ponto de Leme and the Ilha de Contunduba with the uneven brown and green heights of Niterói in the background. All that and the beach itself, a magnificent sweep of sand like a great playing field speckled with football pitches and volley ball courts, where all colours of skin from honey to jet black twisted, turned, dived and leapt to steer balls over nets or between posts, and where to lie still beneath the tropical sun and listen to the Atlantic waves thump against the flattened strand was a confession of apathy tolerated only in tourists and exceptionally beautiful girls. Behind the beach and the broad divided highway the unremarkable hotels and apartment blocks stood shoulder to shoulder like white pickets in a fence. Held back behind them was the jungle. Two and a half thousand miles of it, stretching to the Pacific *cordillera*, and still within the boundaries of Brazil.

Bond pressed a button and the window of the Rolls-Royce purred down to bury itself in the coachwork. It seemed amazing that in only five and a half hours' flying time Concorde had borne him from Europe to half-way down the coast of South America. The mist-shrouded Charles de Gaulle Airport belonged not only to another continent but to another season. Here the air was warm, balmy with fragrance; the light, lucid and clear. In Paris the lights of cars had shone dully through an opaque screen; people walked in a cloud of their own breath.

The Rolls came to another halt in the slowly moving procession of traffic and Bond sniffed the smell of freshly roasted coffee and watched the ebb and flow of humanity scurrying about him. The soft drinks and hot dog vendors, the shoe-shine boys darting between the pavement cafés. The fat American tourists with their cameras wobbling on their bellies like an extra roll of fat. A gaggle of sweating workmen hoisting carnival decorations into the air. A small boy chasing an errant football amongst the slow-turning wheels.

The traffic began to move again and Bond glanced behind him with the wariness born of a hundred missions. A Ferrari Dino was threading through the pursuing automobiles at a speed that invited disaster. As he watched it nearly mounted the centre section and attracted a blare of horns before nipping into a space three automobiles behind.

Bond smelt danger. 'Take the next right!'

Bond saw the chauffeur's eyebrows rise as he glanced in the rear-view mirror. '*Sim, senhor.*'

The Rolls pulled out and with a discreet squeal of tyres cut across the oncoming traffic and accelerated into a defile between apartment blocks. A tumultuous volley of motor horns informed Bond that the Ferrari was on his heels. He glanced back and had an impression of a pretty dark-haired girl wearing a headscarf. Her expression was determined as she leant forward over the wheel. Bond's was grim as he leant forward to the driver. 'Lose her.' This time the reply was given by the limousine. Before Bond had time to brace himself, the wheel was flung over and the Rolls careered up a private driveway between two blocks of apartments, swerving past the entrance to an underground garage. The driver of a family saloon prepared to meet his maker as the Rolls bounded towards him – and opened his eyes to see it transformed into a Ferrari. There was a squeal of brakes and both automobiles screeched nose to tail into a narrow tree-lined street. Traffic was building up at an intersection and there was a further flurry of horns as the Rolls jumped the queue, narrowly avoiding the oncoming traffic and a lorry which was swinging in from the left. Coming down a steep incline to the right was a tram, the rear platform crowded with passengers, some clinging to its sides like refugees.

Bond watched the Ferrari streaking up behind him and called out fresh instructions to the driver. The Rolls bounded across the tram lines and then accelerated up the road which the tram had descended. The Ferrari skidded to a halt as the tram momentarily blocked its path, and then roared off in pursuit.

Hanging on to the side of the tram, the middle-aged unshaven man with the ragged trousers ending just below the knees watched the Ferrari disappear and wondered why the impeccably dressed foreigner wearing a light-weight tropical suit had leapt from a Rolls-Royce to take up a position beside him. Bond smiled sociably, but said nothing.

At first glance Number 1784 did not look any different to the other apartment blocks facing Copacabana Beach. It was slightly taller, perhaps, and the architecture more discreet than that of the newer hotels, but there was nothing to mark it out as one of the most valuable pieces of real estate in the world. Bond climbed the steps past the carefully tended pots of shrubs and inserted the thin platinum key he had been given into the signed slot at the entrance. The glass doors slid open obediently and he walked into the air-conditioned coolness of the hall. His eyes took a few seconds to get used to the restrained half-light, and it was in this brief period that a swarthy besuited figure materialized beside him.

'Mr Bond? We have been expecting you.' He looked beyond Bond to the glass doors. 'Your luggage?'

'Coming.' Bond smiled his agreeable smile. 'It was so

pleasant I thought I'd walk.'

'Of course.' It was clearly policy not to argue with clients. 'My name is Alvarez. Should there be anything you wish while you are staying with us – anything at all – it will be my pleasure to procure it for you.'

'Thank you' was almost too short a reply with which to greet such munificence, but Bond uttered it, whereupon he was conducted to an elevator the size of a miniature ballroom. No sooner had the door closed than it seemed to open again, and Senhor Alvarez announced that they were on the twenty-first and top floor of the building. He led the way across a mahogany floor polished to the sheen of turtle shell and respectfully withdrew Bond's key from his fingers.

'The locks have been reprogrammed to receive your personal key, Mr Bond.'

Bond nodded and watched as the sliver of platinum was inserted in one of a pair of doors that could have received a grand piano without the jambs coming within a couple of feet of scratching the varnish. With an impresario's panache, Alvarez flung open the door and extended a hand. The penthouse seemed to stop just short of the African coast.

'The President's suite!'

Bond looked about him. 'You must have a lot of presidents.'

The remark seemed to nonplus Alvarez, who hesitated uneasily.

Bond reclaimed his key and guided the startled manager back towards the door. 'Don't bother to show me round. If I get lost I'll call a cab.' He closed the door with a polite smile.

Bond's first estimate of the size of the suite had been exaggerated, but the living room was still the size of a hotel lounge. Furnished in the same way as well. Pillars, arches, scattered groups of low furniture and tall potted plants brushing against a roof that showed more glass than plaster.

It was an impersonal room. Opulent certainly, but not a place to curl up with a good book. The sheets of coloured glass that formed one long wall had been pulled back to give the effect of a Mondrian painting. Bond walked through to the terrace beyond. The view was impressive but not quite in the way that he had anticipated. Certainly the near-Olympic sized swimming pool was a revelation and the view of Rio from the Sugar Loaf to Ipanema a tourist brochure writer's dream. What was unexpected was that the pool had an occupant. She was swimming with a lazy crawl, her slim honey-brown body carving a shallow furrow through the crystal water. It was the stroke of someone who swam a lot, economical, unhurried, the feet drumming up a small wake of froth. The back was bare and there was no white line across the tan. A compressed triangle of faded blue half covered the neat buttocks. Bond watched the girl's shoulder muscles ripple as she pulled herself out of the water and turned to face him. She sat on the edge of the pool and shook out her wet hair, seemingly impervious to the fact that her breasts were uncovered. Taking her time, she stretched out a hand and hooked on a bikini top as Bond had seen men slip into a shoulder holster. She fastened the bikini under her breasts and stood up. Bond started to walk round the pool. The girl surveyed him haughtily. He might have been the postman arriving with a buff envelope.

'Do you come with the apartment?'

The girl finished patting her face with a large white towel and looked at Bond through deep brown eyes. 'It depends who's renting it.' She laid the towel on a reclining seat and moved to a drinks trolley that was positioned beneath a wide sun umbrella. The canvas flapped in the breeze. 'Vodka martini, isn't it?'

'With very little martini, thank you.' Bond watched his drink being made and approved of the eyelash thickness of lemon peel that scythed its way to the bottom of the chilled glass. 'You drive well.'

The girl's face suddenly lit up in a smile. 'Not usually as fast. My old instructor at Hendon would have burst a blood vessel. I'm sorry I missed you at the airport.' The girl handed him his drink. 'By the way, my name is Manuela. I work for Station VH. We've been asked to assist you.'

Bond smiled. 'M thinks of everything.' Apparently including girls who were taught to drive at the police driving school at Hendon.

Manuela nodded towards the penthouse. 'Do you think you're going to be comfortable?'

'I don't suffer from vertigo or agoraphobia, so I should be all right.' He sipped his drink. 'You mix a very good martini.'

'Thank you.' She looked about her. 'Don't you think that this must be some of the most palatial accommodation the service has to offer anywhere in the world?'

'I've slept in beds that were less comfortable than the carpet,' said Bond. 'How did we get our hands on it? I feel I ought to write to my M.P. about squandering public funds.'

'You've no need to bother. It used to belong to a German war criminal. He left it to us in his will just before he died.'

'Oh, yes,' said Bond, 'I think I remember reading something about it. He fell to his death, didn't he?'

'From this balcony actually,' said Manuela. She stretched out a hand. 'Can I refill your glass?'

Bond held up a restraining hand. 'No thanks. Something about this place preaches temperance. Tell me, Manuela, do the initials C and W mean anything to you?'

Manuela thought for a moment and nodded. 'If you're referring to Rio, most certainly. There is a firm here called Carlos and Wilmsberg. They are very big in the import-export business. They are a subsidiary of the Drax Corporation, I think.'

'Where are they based?'

'They have a big warehouse and offices in Carioca Avenue.'

Bond's eyes narrowed. 'Good. I want to pay them a discreet visit tonight.'

Manuela shook her head and smiled. 'I think you may find that a little difficult.'

Bond's jaw set in a determined line. 'Nevertheless, I want to do it.'

Manuela held his glance for a moment and then turned away to pick up an aerosol can of suntan lotion. 'Very well. We can try.' She squirted some cream against her calf and leant forward to start massaging it. Bond transferred his gaze to his watch with difficulty. It was just after three o'clock. His hand stretched out and started to massage just above Manuela's fingers. She raised her head to look into his eyes and her lower lip hung forward temptingly. The merest tremor ran through it as Bond's fingertips touched hers. Bond's mouth parted slowly. 'Tell me one thing, Manuela – how do you kill five hours in Rio if you don't samba?' Her lips had formed half a smile when Bond's hungry mouth obliterated it.

By eight o'clock the noise on Carioca Avenue could have been used to disguise the Salerno landings. Fireworks, samba bands, cheering crowds, celebrating groups, happy individuals. All the sounds of a Latin people enjoying carnival as if the other 364 days of the year were expendable inches on a slowly burning fuse wire. Bond looked up at the packed grandstands and the mile-long procession of floats and extravagantly dressed samba schools receding into the neon distance and marvelled at the irrepressible energy that was erupting all about him. The samba rhythm was like a never-ending line of breakers pounding at his

111

eardrums. The perfervid throbbing was an extension of his pulse. Nobody seemed to be capable of standing still. Everywhere was bobbing, weaving, lifting, jumping, bumping movement. With hardly a drop of liquor in his body, Bond could imagine that he was drunk on colour and sound. Carmen Miranda danced by with Charlie Chaplin, and a black girl, glistening naked beneath a wind of fisherman's netting, draped an inviting arm across his chest. Almost instantly she had disappeared behind a wall of waddling egg-shaped clowns who in turn gave way to coffee-coloured girls in silver lamé sheaths and tight-fitting bonnets whirling like dervishes.

Bond turned to make sure that Manuela had not been swept away by the crowd. Her own costume plunged almost to the waist at the front, and lower at the back. She had big puffed sleeves on her arms and a petticoat effect of overlapping polka-dotted skirts that sprang out from the clinging garment at knee level. Large circular ear rings dangled to her shoulders and her black hair curled back from a semicircle of beaten gold. Dressed in his black dinner jacket, Bond felt that he was hardly exhibiting the abandon that the occasion demanded. Manuela fought her way to his side. 'That's the warehouse on the next corner.'

Bond looked over the heads of the milling crowd and smiled ruefully. 'And not a soul about. Next time I'll pay more attention to what you say.'

Manuela looked up at him reproachfully. 'You're too impetuous, James. We could easily have waited until tomorrow.'

Bond appeared not to hear her. His face set quickly into a hard, determined mask as he dropped his shoulder into the mob of revellers and bore remorselessly forward. Manuela shrugged and followed him. She could no more understand this man than she could the reason she had so suddenly given herself to him. It was not the way she normally behaved. Still, as her still quivering body could easily bear witness, this was no ordinary man.

Twenty yards away in the main stream of the carnival procession, the movement of Bond and his companion attracted interested eyes. They rolled inquisitively from the holes in the face mask of a grotesque carnival figure towering several feet above the other revellers. Half clown, half giant robot, the figure seemed to suffer from a crisis of identity. Or at least from a lack of preparation in comparison with the other carnival figures, whose lustre reflected nearly a year's work. As Bond and Manuela entered a narrow alley, so the figure in its turn veered to the left and started to move clumsily against the tide, in pursuit.

In the alley Bond looked up at the gaunt structure that towered above him. The Carlos and Wilmsberg warehouse was not a modern building and would have been more at home amongst the dark satanic mills of the Yorkshire Ridings than in its present setting alongside a carnival route. The windows were barred and black with grime, and a high railing ran around the edge of a deep light well. An iron gate that led down to a basement door was padlocked. Bond let the dancing throng push past him and signalled to Manuela to join him at the gate. 'I'm going to have a look round,' he said. 'You wait here and don't dance with anybody else.' He leant forward to kiss her. Manuela's pleasure was dissipated when she saw that the gesture was no more than cover for an assault on the padlock.

'You're not very nice,' she said. 'I think I'll go off with the first man who comes along.'

'Make it the second,' said Bond. 'There's no point in restricting your choice.' There was a click and the padlock sprang open. Bond handed it to Manuela, slipping a thin strip of metal back into his pocket. 'I'd like you to keep this as a memento of our meeting. Hook it on again when I've

113

gone down the steps.' He pushed the gate open a few inches and had disappeared before she could say anything.

The basement door was more difficult because it was bolted on the inside. Bond had to operate a small glass cutter on two of the opaque glass panels before he could reach through and slide back the bolts. A bottle shattered farther along the alley and the foundations of the building seemed to be shaking in time with the samba rhythms. The noise was ear-shattering. If anyone was waiting for him on the other side of the door he would never hear them. The last rusty bolt slid back and Bond withdrew his arm and concentrated on the lock. Within seconds he was applying gentle pressure to the door with his shoulder. He let it open a few inches and then pushed forward hard and sprinted for the first cover that presented itself. He ducked down behind a concrete pillar and watched the door swing in the moonlight. Nothing moved around him, so he re-laxed his grip on the Walther PPK and straightened up. Even with the door closed he felt as if he was trapped in a tin box with somebody banging on the lid. Never for one instant did the noise of carnival relax its attempt to grind his eardrums into bone dust. A zig-zag staircase threaded its way up through the floors, and the coloured lanterns in the street blinked through the windows like a light show in a cheap nightclub. Bond put his finger to bed against the trigger of the Walther PPK and started to move forward.

Down in the alley Manuela held her position against the railings and fended off men who asked her if she wanted to dance or make love, or both. In the wall opposite was the entrance to a club, and like a spring tide pouring in and out of a cleft in a rock an unending flow of singing, dancing revellers ebbed and flowed through the garishly lit entrance. The view behind them was like an agitated Turner sunset. Unable to restrain her foot from tapping with the rhythm, Manuela stepped forward and craned to see what was happening.

At the entrance to the alley the figure in the grotesque carnival costume paused unsteadily and the dark, seemingly empty eye sockets levelled on the scene like gun barrels. A reveller attempted to serenade the clumsy giant with a cardboard guitar and was dashed to one side with a force that spun the toy into the basement. An attempt at remonstration faded away abruptly as the figure took a menacing step forward and revealed that no stilts or padding were needed to build up its size. The man in the costume was over seven feet tall.

Bond reached the third floor of the warehouse and pocketed his pencil torch. No extra light was necessary to see that the chamber was empty save for a few broken packing cases and twists of binding wire strewn around like modern sculptures. Patterns in the dust and fresh footprints showed that materials had been moved out recently. Bond climbed to the fourth floor and the fifth. The picture was the same. The warehouse was empty. Bond was disappointed but hardly surprised. After Venice it was logical that Drax would take steps to cover his tracks. Bond reached the top of the warehouse and looked through the skylight. A firework display was lighting up the sky like an aerial bombardment. Turning from the skylight, Bond saw something glinting on the floor. It was a label with a line drawing of an aeroplane taking off against the background of the Sugar Loaf. Along the bottom in silver lettering were the words DRAX AIR FREIGHT and the Drax symbol. Bond pocketed the label and hurried down the stairs.

In the alley, Manuela turned from the entrance to the club to watch the firework display. All heads were tilted towards the sky. All heads but one.

The giant carnival figure was watching Manuela. The heavy head sat square on the Frankenstein shoulders. The cold eyes took on a stone-like hardness. An enormous foot swung forward to close the distance to its prey. The stick of a spent rocket tumbled down into the basement with a shower of sparks and Manuela turned to see the figure nearly upon her. A huge hand rose to remove the headpiece and she was looking into a face more terrifying than any mask. It was as blunt and uncompromising as the blade of a shovel, with the features dragged down lugubriously to a bulging lantern jaw. The eyes stared down at her without expression and the wide mouth opened to reveal a nightmare. Two rows of jagged, stainless steel teeth parting like the jaws of a vice. Manuela started to scream, but what was one more scream in a night full of whoops, yelps, shrieks, hoots, cheers and unabating clamour? A hand spread round Manuela's neck like the steel of a pitchfork and thrust her back towards the railings. Fireworks exploded and a tidal wave of bodies surged from the club in a disjointed samba train. The alley was full of milling people. In their midst somebody was being murdered. Manuela gasped as her back was thrust against the railings with a force that drove the wind from her body. It seemed as though her attacker was trying to push her between them. His mouth opened wide and his head twisted to one side. With renewed horror, she realized what he was going to do. He was going to bite her with those obscene teeth. She kicked and clawed with all her might, but the expression in the man's eyes did not change. He might have been programmed like the robot his costume made him resemble. A weight of dancing, laughing bodies thrust against them and she screamed for help. At least her mind told her that she screamed. But any sound was drowned the instant it left her mouth. Only the din of carnival hurled mocking laughter in her ears. Her head was bent back and she prepared to die.

Bond saw the puffed sleeve pressed through the railings as he emerged from the basement door. For a second he thought Manuela was dead, but then the arm moved feebly. He charged up the steps and saw the great head begin to drop as if stooping to drink from a trough. Spreading his shoulders against the wall he kicked through the railings with all his force. The steel-capped heel of his shoe struck sparks as it collided with the fearsome teeth and there was a grunt of surprise and pain. The figure loomed up as if from the undergrowth of some primordial jungle and eyes that had looked before on Bond did so again with the blazing intensity of deadly hatred. For a second the glance was held and then a catherine wheel exploded amongst the crowd and a great weight of fleeing bodies bore the snarling giant away as if he was some pebble joggled across the hissing shingle by a receding wave. Bond unhooked the padlock and a fresh swirl of revellers from the club filled the vacuum, forming another barrier against the man with murder in his mouth.

Bond dropped to his knees and took Manuela in his arms. Her throat was red and her dress torn from her shoulder, but there were no traces of blood. Bond looked about him warily; he watched the girl open her eyes: 'Didn't I tell you about talking to strangers?'

'Oh, James –' Words failed her, and she clung to his arm and started to cry. Bond drew her to her feet and away from the claustrophobic menace of the alley. Manuela rubbed a hand across her face but her eyes were still wide with terror. 'Who was that – that man?'

'His name's Jaws,' said Bond. 'Don't worry, you're never going to see him again.' He hoped that his voice carried more conviction than he felt.

Manuela tried to smile. 'I was right. We should have stayed at home.'

Bond kissed her on the forehead. 'You're going to stay at home. I'll drop you off.'

'There's no need. I'm all right.' Manuela attempted to stand up by herself and started to waver. Bond caught her just before she fell.

'You're a marvel,' said Bond, 'but you're still going home.' Out of the corner of his eye he saw a battered taxi driven by a man wearing a skeleton costume; the driver seemed to have caught the atmosphere of the evening. He steered Manuela towards it. She put up no resistance.

'What did you find in there?'

'A lot of storage space. Everything has been moved out.'

'So you're no further forward?'

Bond signalled to the cab driver, who had just helped a couple of American tourists in petrol splash shirts to lose weight to the tune of twenty dollars. 'Maybe, maybe not. Where does Drax Air Freight operate from?'

'San Pietro Airport. Do you want me to take you there?'

'Just point it out if it's on the way home.' Bond took a careful look round and helped Manuela into the cab. The driver in his skeleton costume was lighting a cigarette. 'You want to give that up,' said Bond. 'They're bad for your health.'

12

SUGAR LOAF – ONE LUMP OR TWO?

Carnival was dying as Bond took the cable car to the top of the Sugar Loaf. Drunks were finding that gutters no longer fitted as comfortably as they had a few hours before, and were beginning to limp home. The fires on the beaches were dying down to blackened embers and there was more litter on the streets than dancers. Even the unquenchable samba was a hydra-headed sound weaving from many different quarters rather than the blunt all-conquering rhythm that had once bludgeoned the eardrums with a single beat.

The cable car reached the first sharp prong of rock and the doors crashed open. Bond was alone save for two middle-aged men who stepped out and walked purposefully towards the boarded-up fronts of souvenir stalls situated below the steps that led from the cable car station. That these men were going to open the stalls in the hope that a few tourists remained sober enough to visit them was beyond doubt. They had not looked out of the windows once since entering the cable car. They had seen one of the most breathtaking views in the world a million times, going up and going down. It was wallpaper to them, their face in the shaving mirror, the wife's head on the pillow. They did not see it any more.

Bond crossed to take the second cable car, looking up to the great slack weight of wire sagging above a thousand-foot drop. He was alone in the cable car and almost beyond the reach of the faint samba beat that eddied up from the streets and beaches and open places below. The doors closed and the wires began to hum. As the car jerked forward, so the twin car began its descent; a small red square that detached itself from the concrete mouth above like a bloody tooth. Bond looked down to the long grass and across to the skirt of foliage that clothed the side of the Sugar Loaf. Time and the elements had scored deep claw marks in its side and it looked easy enough to scale. To the right was the sea and to the left the peak of Corcovado, almost twice as high as the Sugar Loaf and with the statue of Christ at its summit, its arms spread wide, offering perpetual succour to the volatile city that sprawled beneath it. Bond decided he preferred Nelson's Column, but his preference might have been either patriotism overcoming aesthetics or a pragmatic faith in secular saviours. Below and to the left was Botafogo Harbour affording snug retreat to some of the most expensive yachts in the world, and in the distance a glimpse of the freeway that swept impressively across the Bay of Guanabara. The sun had hauled itself up in the sky and was flooding distant peaks with dazzling light. The inside of the cable car was warm. All was there to content the soul of man, but Bond was uneasy. The beauty around him was no deeper than the surface of a maggot-eaten apple. Somewhere in the big city Jaws would be looking for him. Jaws, whose steel teeth he had believed to be rusting on the ocean bed. Jaws, who had apparently miraculously escaped the great white shark and the sinking tomb of Stromberg's Atlantis. Was he now working for Drax? Time, Bond reflected ruefully, would probably find a way of answering that question.

The cable car docked and Bond walked out and down a flight of steps to a small tree-girt plateau. There was a café with outside tables and a scatter of gift shops, mostly shut. Bond resisted having his photograph taken to be superimposed on a plate and headed for a wide esplanade affording views of the boats at anchor in the harbour and the Copacabana and Flamengo beaches. Beyond the latter was a tongue of land jutting out into the sea which looked as if it had been manmade. On this were the familiar runway patterns of an airport. As Bond looked down, an aeroplane began to take off. It was taxiing slowly and Bond guessed that it was a cargo aircraft. Feeling in his pocket for a coin, he hurried forward and commandeered one of the telescopes at the edge of the esplanade. The coin dropped and a washed-out image of the airport swam before his eyes. Bond swung the telescope and picked up the aircraft just before it reached the end of the runway. It lifted into the air and began to fly on a course directly towards the Sugar Loaf. At the moment that he could make out two figures in the cockpit, it banked sharply and headed out to sea. Clearly visible on the fuselage as the aircraft came broadside to his position was the lettering DRAX AIR FREIGHT with the Drax symbol on either side of it. Bond let the telescope escape his grasp and rose thoughtfully. As he turned, it was to see that he was not alone on the esplanade. Standing twenty yards behind him and taking a pair of binoculars from her eyes was Holly Goodhead. Her expression, like his, was thoughtful. She was wearing a long white evening gown of becoming beauty and chasteness. The addition of the binoculars lent an incongruous note, as if she had chosen the wrong dress to go to a race meeting. Bond was unable to resist smiling as he approached her.

'Haven't we met before somewhere?' He placed a hand gently on hers.

Holly scowled up at him. 'The face is familiar –' she withdrew her hand '– as is the manner.'

Bond raised an eyebrow. 'You didn't seem to object too much in Venice.'

'That was before you walked out on me.'

'Nearly tripping over your suitcase.' Bond laughed scornfully. 'Come on, Holly. You weren't planning to stay around to see if I ate muffins for breakfast.'

121

Holly banished the fifth carbon of a smile. 'So?'

Bond placed an avuncular arm beneath Holly's elbow and began to lead her towards the cable car station. 'So don't let's waste any more time working against each other. I'm quite happy to share everything I've found with you.'

'Which presumably means you haven't found very much.'

Bond shook his head. 'Such cynicism is an unattractive trait in one so young and lovely. Let me supply evidence of my good intent. I've checked Drax's warehouse in town and it's empty. He's obviously moving everything out.'

Holly's eyes were cool. 'That comes as no surprise. Six of those planes have taken off since I've been here.'

'And do you know where they're going?' Bond watched Holly's expression carefully as she replied.

'Do you think I'd still be here if I did?' The answer made sense and her eyes did not flicker. Bond was inclined to believe her.

'Probably not. Right,' he nodded towards the open door of the cable car, 'we'd better find out.'

Holly paused warily. 'I'm not certain if I really trust you.'

Bond shrugged and stepped into the cable car. 'I'm not certain if I really trust you. It makes it more exciting, doesn't it?'

Holly hesitated and then stepped into the car. The door slammed shut behind her and the car jerked forward into space. She and Bond were the only people aboard. Bond looked up to the glass windows of the docking station but could see no one. There was something about their situation, isolated in space, that scared him. A sudden premonition of evil in the surrounding air.

'Where do you suggest we start?'

Bond had no time to reply to Holly's question before the car suddenly jerked to a halt. She fell against him and quickly transferred her weight to a rail. The car swung in the air disconcertingly. 'What's happened?'

Bond reached out a hand. 'Give me your binoculars.' Holly handed them to him and Bond turned them on the lower cable car station. As he focussed the glasses a door opened in the side of the engine room and a stooped figure emerged and unwound to its full awesome height. An icicle of terror buried itself in Bond's stomach. He reached up and pulled down the steel ladder that was attached to the roof of the cable car.

'What's wrong?' Holly's voice was tense.

Bond handed her the binoculars. 'We've got a problem. Take a look at him.'

Holly focussed the glasses. 'The giant? Do you know him?'

'Not socially. His name's Jaws. He kills people.'

Holly's voice mixed fear and disbelief. 'It's not possible. He's pulling down the cable!'

Bond was already scaling the ladder and forcing open the trapdoor in the roof. 'With Jaws, anything is possible. Come on!' He thrust his shoulder into space and turned to indicate a length of chain hooked across the door opposite to the one by which they had entered. 'And bring that chain.'

On the platform of the lower cable car station, Jaws saw Bond emerging from the top of the car and smiled to himself. The thick oil on the cable squeezed between his fingers and the tight plait of reinforced steel fibres descended under the impetus of his bulging arms until it was level with his bared teeth. Jaws opened his mouth wide and clamped the two rows of serrated steel around the cable. Exerting enough pressure to open a locked gate, he bit deep into the metal fibres, feeling the strands part as if they were decoration on a candy bar.

Bond had just scrambled on to the swaying roof and was reaching down for the length of chain when there was a

crack like an ice floe breaking up. The cable car tilted
sharply sideways and a hissing cobra of cable serpentined
backwards to snap at the air above his head and fall limply
into the valley. Bond slid down the roof and was just able
to grasp one of the cable guides. His feet dangled in space.
A wind had blown up from nowhere and whistled eerily
through the wires. Holly's worried face appeared through
the hatch. 'Hang on!'

Bond closed his eyes and felt his feet kicking against
empty air. He spoke through clenched teeth. 'The thought
had occurred to me.' He waited until the pendulum swing
of the unbalanced cable car had become less manic and
chose his moment to lunge upwards for the edge of the
opening, drawing his legs after him. After two tries he was
able to press against the top of the cable car as if balancing
precariously on the side of a steep roof. One glance at what
lay below was enough to make him feel physically sick. The
ground dissolved into a mist and the pattern of the wind
racing through the grass transferred itself to the inside of
his brain. He closed his eyes tight and clung like a bur
until the nausea had passed.

'James!' Holly's voice intimated further disasters. 'He's
getting into the other car.'

Bond twisted his head and looked down. He had expected that at any second the remaining cable would snap
and the car plunge into the gully. What he saw was scarcely
less alarming: Jaws hauling himself on to the roof of the
lower cable car. He must have swung out like a giant gib-
bon from the station. It could only mean that he had an
accomplice in the control room. As if to prove the surmise,
Jaws made a clumsy backwards gesture with his arm, and
the two cars began to jerk towards each other. Once again,
Bond was forced to cling on for his life. Suspended by only
one cable, the upper car was swinging like a lantern. Bond
pulled himself into the roof opening and eased out his

124

Walther PPK. 'I think we're going to have a visitor.'

Holly clung tight-lipped to one of the rails as the car swayed. 'How are you going to use that thing?'

It was a question Bond chose not to answer. Reeling from side to side at a crazy angle, there was no chance of getting off a well-aimed shot. He would have to wait until Jaws was on top of them. That was not going to take long. As a gust of wind made the car shudder, the lower car planed remorselessly towards them. Jaws knelt on the roof, his steel teeth glinting in the sunlight.

'Hang on to that chain,' said Bond. He drew himself up out of the sloping hatch and tried to aim at the approaching car. Suddenly there was a puff of smoke and one of the windows below him shattered. Jaws had fired first. Instantly he heard Holly choking and a thick pall of yellow smoke swirled up through the hatch. Bond's eyes began to pour water and he felt his fingers tensing. In a desperate effort to breathe and cling on, he let the pistol slip from his fingers. It slid down the roof and dropped into space. Now the lower car was abreast of them and the two red boxes jerked to a halt, swinging like heavy fruit. Across the space that separated them Jaws, grinning malevolently, towered scarcely less dramatically than the Corcovado behind him. As Bond struggled to clear his head, Jaws launched himself through the air and landed with a metallic thud on the roof of Bond's car. The cable screeched under the impact and the whole structure shuddered. Bond tried to rise, and a huge boot sailed past his head and dented the roof housing. Jaws crouched, riding out the motion of his arrival and preparing to deliver the *coup de grâce*. Bond edged sideways, with another glimpse at the terrifying drop beneath him, and then saw an arm appearing over the far side of the car. It was Holly who had scrambled out of the shattered window. Her lips were pressed together in concentration and fear, and there was something gripped in her left hand. Bond recognized the scent atomizer he had found in Venice. Jaws turned to meet almost scornfully the new challenge. Drawing himself up, he took a careful step forward like a spider closing in on a helpless prey. Holly raised her hand and – *whooosh!* a fine jet of flame hit Jaw's steel teeth. With a bellow of pain and rage he backed away, almost losing his balance. One huge foot pressed down and stumbled. The other met empty air as it disappeared through the open hatch. With a cry of alarm, Jaws toppled backwards and dropped inside the car. Bond threw himself forward and pressed down the hatch. He lay across it and within seconds felt himself being lifted into the air as if he was no more than a layer of dust. Holly directed a second tongue of flame into the opening and there was a scream of response. The pressure against the hatch disappeared.

'God bless America,' said Bond. He took the chain from Holly's shoulders and swung it round the cable. The sound of breaking glass below told him that Jaws was following Holly's route. 'Come on!' Bond insinuated himself into the linked halter and stretched out his arms to Holly. 'Cling on to me!' Holly looked past Bond to the fearful abyss and the distant cable car station. 'Come on! It's our only chance.' Still Holly hesitated. Behind her there was a roar and Jaws's raw red features appeared over the side of the car. Holly launched herself forward and threw her arms around Bond's neck. He pushed with his legs and suddenly they were dangling in space and the cable cars receding behind them. Bond heard Holly cry out in fear and she clung to him as if wishing to squeeze the life from his body. The wind plucked at their clothes and the speed of their descent built up with the wild screech of the chain against the cable. Bond felt the steel links cutting towards his bones and looked up through watery eyes to see a new source of terror. The cable car was descending after them. Whoever was in the control room had seen what was happening and was determined that they would not escape. If the cable car caught up with them they would be battered to death before Jaws got his revenge-crazed hands on them. And the car was catching up. There was a new throbbing through the wire as it closed the distance. Bond twisted his head and looked down towards the bottom station. It was now so near that he could see the silhouette of the man at the controls and people pointing skywards. Behind them Jaw's malevolent face was pressed against the glass, eager for the moment of impact. He loomed up like a tram driver staring down from his cab.

Bond saw a green hillside falling away in uneven steps and shouted in Holly's ear. 'You've got to jump!' Her grip did not slacken. 'Now!' The wires were screaming, the ground below a kaleidoscope. He broke Holly's grip and let her drop. The chain seemed to have bitten so deep into his flesh that he could not escape from it. Desperately he twisted as the wind tore at him Twenty feet before the concrete chasm, he wriggled free and let himself drop. He felt himself falling faster than ever until his legs hit the steep slope and his shoulder crashed against the side of the ravine. He rolled over half a dozen times and ended up embedded in a clump of cane with a small landslide of stones following the path his bruised and battered body had taken. Above him there was the sound of a violent impact and a continuing angry roar like a house falling down. A further avalanche of stones and fragments of brick and concrete chased each other down the hillside. Bond's mind cleared fast as he realized what must have happened. Operating on only one cable, the car with Jaws in it had failed to stop and had crashed into the station. Any normal man would have been killed immediately but Bond thought back to the sinking of Atlantis and was not sure that Jaws would have perished. If he could survive that, he could survive anything.

'James!' The voice coming from farther down the steep hillside was distraught. Bond expelled a sigh of relief at the cost of considerable pain to the right-hand side of his rib cage. Holly sounded plaintive but peripatetic.

'Over here.' Bond had pulled himself into an uncomfortable sitting position when Holly scrambled round the bamboo to his side. Her eyes quickly registered the hand pressed to the torn lapel of his dinner jacket.

'James! Have you broken something?'

Bond smiled ruefully. 'Only my tailor's heart.' He stretched out his arms in an attempt to rise and suddenly found that Holly was inside them. Her mouth came on to his, warm, moist and strong. Bond enjoyed it, then twisted his head aside. 'What was that for?'

Holly's eyes shone into his. 'For saving my life.'

'Remind me to do it more often.' They kissed again and the embrace was orchestrated by the sound of an approaching ambulance siren which stopped as they separated. 'They must have private medicine in Brazil,' said Bond. He leant forward to kiss Holly again and saw her mouth wrinkle in pain. 'What's the matter?'

Holly winced again. 'My ankle.'

'Let me take a look.' Bond squeezed her arm sympathetically and drew back. Holly braced herself stoically and looked heavenwards. After a few seconds her eyes returned to earth. 'That's not my ankle, James.'

Bond advanced up her body and took her in his arms. His lips brushed against hers. 'You're such a stickler for detail.' They kissed hungrily as a fresh fall of shale announced that someone was approaching down the hillside. Bond looked up to see two squat, dark-skinned men approaching, carrying a folding stretcher. They wore white tunics and trousers. Once again he marvelled at the speed and precision of the Brazilian health service. The larger of the two men stopped beside him and started to unroll his stretcher.

'I'm sorry,' said Bond, 'I don't think we need you. We're all right.'

The man beamed down at Bond with a smile that had been dipped in arsenic. 'No you're not.' The handle of the stretcher came away in his hand to become a cosh, and Bond moved too late. The blow struck him on the side of the temple and the light went out.

13

ORCHIDACEAE NEGRA

A fuzzy grey image before Bond's eyes deepened to black and then throbbed into a noncommittal brown. A face appeared, bobbing up and down with the motion of a vehicle moving over rough ground and Bond recognized the man dressed as a medical orderly who had struck him down on the hillside. Bond closed his eyes again and tried to move his hands. They were tied with cord and resting on his stomach. His legs seemed to be secured with a strap. Something pressed down on his forearms. He opened his eyes slightly and saw that a second strap around his chest was holding him down on a stretcher. He was in the back of an ambulance and beside him was Holly, similarly bound to another stretcher. Between them, with his back to the doors, was seated the complacent bulk of their guard, with eyes like bloodshot marbles. They bulged out of his face as if likely to slide down his cheeks with the next jolt of the ambulance. A small wet tongue washed the man's lips and Bond realized that he was looking into the face of a psychopath. He tried again to separate his hands but without success. Whoever had tied him up had been a professional.

As Bond watched, the guard ran his eyes over Holly from head to toe and rinsed his lips again. Bond knew what he was thinking. He turned his head slightly and saw that Holly knew as well. Her eyes were wide open with wary fear and she was concentrating on the man as if trying to hold him at arm's length.

Bond saw that there was no more point in feigning unconsciousness, so he opened his eyes. The throbbing behind his left temple was like an ice-pick hitting at his brain. A wave of pain like a meths drinker's hangover swirled through his head.

Like a child in a strange nursery, the guard felt in one of the pockets alongside the bunks and withdrew a slim leather case. He clicked it open and a glint of steel matched the crazed light that came into his eyes. The bitten fingers delved into the case and emerged with a long-bladed scalpel. Bond saw Holly flinch.

'Don't cut yourself.'

Bond's remark was intended to divert attention to himself but it did not succeed. The guard scowled at him and then glanced lovingly at the blade before returning his attention to Holly. Bond looked about him desperately. Just above his feet, in the corner by the door, was an upright fire extinguisher clipped to the wall. Bond wondered if he could reach it with his feet. Before him the guard bathed his shiny lips and leant forward to Holly with the scalpel in his outstretched hand. She twisted her head to one side and tensed her body in terror as the blade slipped beneath one of the straps of her evening gown and severed it with a swift movement.

Bond jerked his body forward and drove upwards with his feet. A toe collided with the base of the fire extinguisher and the plunger was depressed. With a noise like an egg being broken, a miniature volcano of foam erupted to splash off the ceiling and over the occupants of the ambulance. The guard swung round to see what had happened and then, too late, spun back again. He turned just in time to see Bond's feet driving for his face. The blow connected with the side of his jaw and he crashed backwards against the doors, dropping the scalpel on the floor. As it slithered towards Holly, she withdrew her bound hands from beneath the restraining strap and twisted with all her strength to pick it up. Her fingers closed about the handle and she held it out desperately towards Bond. He reached out his tied hands, and with two slashes from Holly his arms were free at the cost of a nicked wrist. As the stunned guard launched himself forward again, Bond stopped him with a vicious right jab and tore at the strap that held him to the stretcher. He freed himself and joined battle with the guard as Holly swung wildly but unavailingly with the scalpel. Bond's ankles were still bound but he struggled upright and pinned the guard against the swaying wall of the ambulance. As the man drove his knee up, Bond parried the blow and connected with a short left to the jaw that spun him round.

At that instant the ambulance jolted over a pothole and the guard plunged backwards on to the stretcher, with all Bond's weight on him. With a sharp crack the stretcher broke free from its moorings and crashed against the doors. As Holly screamed they burst open and the stretcher carrying both men plunged out into a cloud of dust. Bond felt the breath leave the guard's body as it absorbed the impact, and he rolled sideways to end up lying by the side of a dirt road. When he stood up the ambulance had disappeared and there was no sign of the stretcher. The dust began to clear and he took a few faltering steps down the road. A hillside became visible, falling away to the left, and half-way down it, facing a main road from which the track had branched off, was a large advertising hoarding. The back of the stretcher projected from a hole in the bottom of the hoarding. The poster showed a pretty stewardess and the words: 'British Airways. We'll take more care of you'.

On the wide expanse of pampas the three figures in gaucho costume riding abreast would have attracted attention from tourists. But tourists were a commodity that the region lacked. It was grazing land to the east of the Mato Grosso and behind the Serra do Roncador. Indifferent grazing land where men who scratched a living had to be as tough as the horses they rode and the cattle they branded. Brasilia to the south-east had the modern architecture and the embassies. They had the saddle sores and the mosquitoes. One of the riders gestured down a shallow valley and the three horsemen rode towards a long, low building with a red tiled roof and tidy squares of grazing land marked out by picket fences. A flock of white doves took off as they galloped into the courtyard, and peeling shutters creaked in the hot sun. The red dust settled as the men slid from their horses and flicked the reins round the bar of the hitching rail. Two of the men walked along the veranda. The third, and tallest, pushed open the swing doors and went into the building. The room he entered had bare whitewashed walls and was cool thanks to a high ceiling and a slowly turning fan. On one wall was a heavy wooden cross. A staccato clatter ended as the man came in, and Miss Moneypenny looked up from her typewriter.

'Why, if it isn't the Magnificent 007.'

Bond swept off his hat and beat some dust from his chaparejos.

'Mine not to reason why, Moneypenny. Is M expecting me?'

'He's champing at the bit.' She looked up at him with an expression of amused affection and nodded towards a door behind her.

Bond squared his shoulders and moved forward. 'One of these days, Moneypenny, I'm going to put you across my knee.'

'And one of these days I'm going to love it.' She blew him a kiss as he opened the door.

Bond found himself in a square courtyard. The first thing he smelt was cordite. Somebody had been firing weapons. Shattered fragments of human figures were strewn across the ground. Against a bullet-pocked wall a man sat with a poncho pulled around his shoulders and a sombrero tipped over his face so that it was invisible. He gave the impression that he was shutting out the sight of the firing squad that faced him with rifles raised. An order rang out and there was a burst of gunfire. But not from the firing squad. At the word of command, the sombrero tipped up and the poncho parted to reveal an automatically controlled machine gun which mowed down the clay figures of the firing squad and made a further contribution to the débris in the courtyard.

'Ah, there you are, 007.'

Q hove into view wearing his tropical working uniform of bush jacket and baggy shorts. He was followed by a harassed assistant clutching a clipboard who looked as if he had difficulty in keeping up with his master. In this respect he was not alone.

'Good day, Q.'

'Be with you in just a minute.' Q paused to watch a gaucho whirling a bolas above his head. The weapon was released to sail across the courtyard and wrap the balls around the neck of a much-decorated general with a smorgasbord of medal ribbons across his chest and one arm raised in a fascist salute. The balls exploded and the general's head disappeared. In its place was a jagged hole which revealed the neck opening of the plaster bust. Q turned to his assistant. 'Have that ready for Army Day.'

'This is all very fascinating, Q. But I think M –'

Q held up a restraining hand. 'Just a minute, 007. This really is interesting.' He nodded to his assistant who broke off from making hectic notes on his clipboard and signalled to a man dressed like a security guard who was holding a slim cylindrical torch. The torch was levelled at a second man and a brilliant strobe light flashed intermittently from its head. As Bond watched, horrified, the target melted away like a candle placed on a hot griddle. Bond knew that he was looking at a wax dummy, but the fearful destructive

134

potential of the strobe torch inspired awe and dread.

'Right,' said Q cheerfully. 'Rather splendid, isn't it?'

Bond said nothing but wondered if scientists were born with a scaled down range of human feelings in order to make room for extra quantities of grey matter. There was something unnerving about the whole of this backwoods camp for espionage, infiltration and sabotage. Q, in his silly ass English way, could have taught the C.I.A. a few lessons.

Behind the courtyard was a stone building with shuttered windows, and an armed guard outside the door. Q opened the door and ushered Bond inside. The room was in near darkness and set up with a slide projector and a screen as if for an illustrated talk. On one wall was a large map of Brazil that stretched from floor to ceiling. M switched off a desk light and rose hurriedly to his feet as Bond came in. 'Ah – morning, 007. I'm glad you could make it. We were beginning to get worried about you.'

Bond noted that all trace of this worry had disappeared from M's voice. 'Any news of Holly, sir?'

'Dr Goodhead?' The use of the official title was almost a reprimand for familiarity. 'I'm afraid not. The C.I.A. haven't picked up anything either. She must still be held somewhere.'

If she has not been murdered, thought Bond. 'And Drax?'

'He's gone to earth. He left Venice for a destination unknown. We don't even know how he went.'

'Suspicious,' said Bond.

'To us, yes. But not to anyone else. He could have gone to the country for a few days. There's still nothing official to connect him with the disappearance of the Moonraker. And why should he steal his own shuttle?'

Bond frowned uncomfortably. 'Damned if I know, sir. All I do know is that he's cooking up something pretty unpleasant. I feel it in my bones.'

'Regrettably, your bones can't be used as evidence in a court of law,' said M drily. He turned to Q. 'I think we'd better move on to what Q has to show us. That might throw some light on the matter.'

Q moved to the projector and indicated a couple of chairs beside him. 'We're talking about the analysis of the phial you picked up in Venice, 007. Your diagnosis was spot on. A highly toxic nerve gas capable of causing death in seconds. But – and this is very strange – none of the experiments we've conducted show it to have any effect on animals.'

Bond digested the information with a growing sense of unease. 'What about the formula?'

Q fiddled with a tray of slides and a formula was projected on to the screen. Bond studied it for several seconds. Most of the chemical symbols meant nothing to him, but there were two words that struck a particularly incongruous note. '*Orchidaceae negra?*' He looked towards Q for confirmation. 'Is that really some kind of orchid?'

Q nodded. 'A very rare one. It once grew in great numbers in the Yucatan Peninsula in Mexico but was believed to have become extinct until very recently. Then a missionary brought one back from the upper reaches of the Amazoco.'

'A long way from the Yucatan Peninsula,' mused Bond.

'Most decidedly,' said M. He approached the wall map and circled an area with a blue chinagraph pencil.

Bond studied the map and the tortuous passage of the river to the sea. 'So this is the only place in the world where this particular element of the nerve gas can be found?'

'As far as we know, yes.'

Bond considered. 'And we have no information about where those cargo planes were flying to from San Pietro Airport? Surely they must all have been logged.'

'Only two flights were logged. To Bahia and Recife. They were carrying maintenance teams to overhaul equipment on Drax installations. Nothing unusual.'

'Holly saw six planes taking off.'

'There's no record of that, 007. That's the important thing. Those planes, however many there were, could be anywhere. They don't have to land at civil airports. The jungle abounds with strips servicing logging camps and mining operations.'

Bond's eyes returned to the circle of blue on the map. 'So this is all we really have to go on. I'd better take a look.'

'We think so,' said M soberly. He turned to Q. 'Your department has, I believe, developed something that should assist 007 in his task.'

'Not for the first time,' said Q, almost petulantly. 'What would be new would be if Bond could avoid destroying it almost immediately after he'd signed for it!'

Hours later Bond thought of Q's words as he sat at the helm of the sleek vessel he had nicknamed the Q-craft. It had the lines of a motor launch, but with an exceptionally shallow draught, a powerful engine and a brightly coloured awning stretching above his head like the wings of a bird. The river up which he travelled was the colour of mud and tall, foliage-strangled trees crowded the banks, dangling snake-like lianas into the slowly moving water. The air was full of disembodied bird calls and the hum of mosquitoes. The trees pressed in so menacingly that Bond felt that he and his narrow craft were running a gauntlet; that at any moment the creepers would be wielded like knouts to scourge his back. With the sun locked out and the light fading into the palisade of trees, the river was not a cheerful place. Every foot travelled was one farther away from civilization, and the smell of rotting vegetation and the never-ending impression of being fed into a tunnel from which there might be no return pinched the spirit like lead shot.

Fighting off the insects, Bond steered a course against the detritus of the forest that came drifting downstream. Hours passed and the river became narrower, until the tops of tall trees on either bank almost met across the stream. Clumps of weed began to form untidy barriers and the Stygian gloom deepened swiftly into night. Bond moored some distance from the bank and debated between sleeping in the tiny, airless cabin and on deck. He decided on the latter and lay down beneath a hastily erected mosquito net to listen to the sounds of darkness. Splashes, rustles, buzzes, burs, the shrill shrieks of hunting owls, the terrified squawks of their prey. Nature feeding upon itself. Sharp teeth sinking into flesh and the senses tuned, always tuned, to the approach of larger, sharper teeth. Lulled by the sound of nature keeping its bloody balance, Bond eventually fell asleep beneath a starless sky.

When he woke up he was cold and there was mist upon the water. Somewhere beyond the trees dawn would soon be breaking; there was already a premonition of light. A string of stinging welts on his arms and face proved that the mosquito net had been too hastily erected. Bond washed down a handful of Paludrin with a swig of Old Hickory – brought to deal with real emergencies – and started the engine. There was a reciprocating clamour of startled noise from the banks as the Q-craft broke free of the choking weight of débris that had drifted against the prow during the night and started upstream.

Soon Bond had to make a decision. The river ahead was divided by an island of vegetation and disappeared into two sluggish channels overhung with trees and choked with weeds and lily leaves like circular green upturned tin lids. Neither seemed promising and he wondered if he had taken a wrong turning when night had been falling. He examined his hopelessly inadequate chart and took a compass bearing before following the fork that showed a dark line bisecting an open expanse of speckled surface weed. At least somebody had passed this way recently. He cut back the engine and moved gently through beds of thick reed punctuated by areas of open water often littered by flocks of fowl that took to the air with a thunderclap of wings at his approach. Although there were occasional clumps of vine-covered trees, the waterscape was taking on a far more swamp-like aspect. Not that this acted as a salve to the spirit. There was still a feeling of claustrophobia, of being hemmed in and closed off from the outside world. Not without pangs of alarm, Bond wondered how easy it was going to be to find his way back. He adopted the habit of stopping every few hundred yards to look back and see if there were any memorable landmarks. He soon realized that this was a waste of time. One patch of open water amongst the clumps of reeds looked exactly like another.

For half a day Bond continued without a change of scenery. Then he entered another narrow river winding through jungle. So serpentine were the bends in the stream here that he was able to look through a gap in the trees and see a second stretch of water running parallel to his. Half an hour later he had reached the stretch he had seen. Night fell without him being able to make a clear estimate of the distance he had travelled in a straight line. He prepared some rations which, if barely palatable, at least succeeded in destroying his appetite; and passed another fitful night during which refuge in the cabin was forced upon him by torrential rain that started to fall soon after it became dark, and dropped as if from some waterfall in heaven.

The next day brought his first contact with human beings. The rain had ceased and he had got under way upstream when a dugout canoe appeared round a bend in the river. In it were five tiny men wearing strips of cloth around their waists and carrying spears. They dropped the spears when they saw Bond and snatched up paddles. At a speed that was impressive, they dug their paddles into the water and headed in towards the bank, to disappear into a side tributary.

After that incident, Bond had the impression that he was being watched. Occasionally there were bird calls from the bank that evoked a strident response almost too spontaneous for anything found in nature. Creatures unseen rustled away through the undergrowth. Bond felt his nerves being stretched to breaking point. Oppressive surroundings and a growing sense of isolation wound the capstan. There was nothing to see but the thickening jungle and the winding river, yet he could never relax. A drifting log or a sub-merged rock causing an accident or a mechanical fault that could be simply repaired within sight of civilization could here be his undoing. And there was always the fear that an arrow or a spear would sail out from the river bank. That a war canoe would silently steal up on him when he was sleeping. It was a voyage that did not pity faint hearts.

By midday on the fourth day the river disappeared into a sponge of swamp and Bond's spirits took another dive. There was no discernible current that he could follow and the thick reeds were taller than the boat. It was like being lost in the bristles of a scrubbing brush. The reeds scraped the sides of the Q-craft and closed in behind. Once again Bond was tortured by the fear that he had taken a wrong channel and was ploughing into some limitless wilderness from which there would be no return. The fuel situation was becoming critical and he had only his compass to go on. He estimated that he was almost in the area marked by M, but he could not be sure. His last radio contact had been made when leaving the main river and he judged it unwise to open up the set again in case there *was* someone or something here to intercept the signal.

For an hour he brushed through reed beds that were so thick as to be almost impenetrable, and then the waterscape opened up and clumps of feather-topped cane became islands in a water garden of lilies and flowering tubers. These in turn gave way to stretches of open water bordered by reed and jungle and containing flocks of cranes and geese that rose into the air as he approached. To see some birdlife and be free of the stifling reed beds lifted Bond's spirits, and he opened the throttle slightly to let the Q-craft skim towards what looked like the beginnings of a large lake. The boat emerged from the last clumps of reed and was indeed riding across a wide expanse of water. The surface was smooth and clear and Bond saw rings that showed where fish were rising. But there were no birds. After the teeming backwaters that he had come through, Bond wondered why. What could there be here to frighten them away? The answer came in the form of a large spout of water that rose just forward of the bow. Bond thought momentarily of some giant fish or crocodile – before he heard the tell-tale screech. He had come under fire. A second shell exploded astern and he swung the rudder over to head for the shelter of the reed beds. Moving directly towards him with its bow out of the water and cannon blazing was a high-powered speedboat. Bond threw the wheel over again, only to see two more boats converging on him. The water round the Q-craft was boiling with shell fire. There remained one direction to take. Across the lake. Bond opened the throttle wide and headed for a gap in the trees on the far shore.

Behind him the three speedboats gave chase, one in advance of the others. Bond studied the control panel of the Q-craft and quickly ran through the instructions he had been given. Poor Q. He produced equipment for every contingency and yet was furious whenever one arose. Bond jabbed a button and there was a *clunk* from the stern which told him that two release chambers had opened. More pressure on the button and two cylindrical objects like depth-charges were tossed out to float on the surface twenty yards apart. As the first pursuing boat thudded across the water it steered between them, the helmsman imagining they were mines that would explode on impact. He was right – but not entirely. The mines were also magnetic. As the speedboat passed between them they leapt from the water like flying fish and slapped against the hull. After a moment's pause there was a violent explosion which sent a column of orange and yellow flame roaring heavenwards. Wreckage spattered the water and the blasted hull of the launch sank immediately.

Bond's tight-lipped expression eased momentarily. One down and two to go. As he tried to coax some more speed out of his craft, he saw a notch cut out of the jungle ahead where the lake must feed a river. He had an impression of white water. Cannon fire still hammered around his ears and another shell exploded dangerously close. Bond glanced at the controls again. The small lever on the left. That might be the answer. He pulled it down and turned his head to see a thin cigar-shaped torpedo drop into the wake behind the Q-craft. Almost instantly it broke free and veered towards one of the pursuing speedboats like a water snake, the nose just breaking the surface. The helmsman saw the danger and was swift to take evasive action. He steered towards his companion boat and the torpedo swept past the bow. A shout of triumph rose in the air and was quickly stifled. The torpedo made a one-hundred-and-eighty degree turn and homed in on its prey. Like a dog about to sit down the launch spun round on itself, but the torpedo was not thrown off. Remorselessly it closed the gap and the magnetic head smashed into the stern. A second column of flame, smoke and fragments burst into the air, and the stricken boat began to settle fast.

Now Bond was in the white water at the beginning of the river. Small angry waves thumped against the bottom of the boat and spray broke over the shuddering bows. Bond looked ahead and saw the water becoming more turbulent. He must be entering some rapids. In principle this should not be too serious. With its high-powered engine and shallow draught the Q-craft was built for this kind of work. Bond now saw and heard something that froze his heart. Round a bend in the river was a cloud of spray about a quarter of a mile wide and rising at its highest to at least sixty feet. There was also a deep, throbbing roar like nothing he had heard before. It could only be a waterfall. A waterfall of such dimensions as to dash to pieces anything that was swept over it. Bond swung the rudder and felt the boat in danger of broaching. A fresh hail of bullets creased the air above his head and shattered the cabin glass. There was no turning back, no steering for the bank. The river was now a boiling flood, the roar even louder. Spray began to drench the boat. Bond squared his jaw and steered straight for the point where it rose highest. Behind him the last pursuing boat was in difficulties. Horribly aware of what lay ahead, the helmsman had tried to turn back, and the boat had broached. Lying across the stream, it was drifting helplessly at the pace of the water and threatening to capsize at any moment. All attempts at wiping out Bond had been abandoned in the interests of self-preservation; a sentiment that had expressed itself too late. Bond glanced back to see the boat turn on its side and fill with water. It disappeared into the spray.

Bond's heart pumped like a steam hammer as he fought to stay in control of his senses and hold the Q-craft head-on to the racing water. The spray stung his face like hail and the roar of the falls threatened to burst his eardrums. Ahead the frothing white water was giving way to an apron of smooth cream as the river stretched itself over the lip of the precipice. What lay below was swathed in a heavy pall of mist. Bond's numb fingers reached up and grasped the metal rod that ran beneath the awning of the Q-craft. To the left and right were two levers, sculpted close to the shape of the rod. Bond waited and felt the hull of the boat rasp against rock. He was now inside a cloud of spray, and below him was a sudden unnerving glimpse of what lay beyond the falls. It seemed like a great hole in the middle of the earth down which water from every side was disappearing. A hole so deep as to have no bottom. Bond pulled down the levers and immediately felt the awning come free and the wind attempt to tear it from his grasp. He clung tightly to the rod and as the Q-craft tilted over the edge of the falls what was now apparent as the wing-like structure of a hang glider swept him up over the terrifying drop.

14

THE HIDDEN CITY

Blinded by spray, Bond felt that he was as good as dead. The enormous flow of water going over the falls set up air currents which acted like an undertow on a swimmer. His frozen hands clung to the bar and he dangled, terrified lest any attempt to throw his feet backwards should destroy his already precarious balance. An up-draught carried him away from the lowering cloud of spray and he saw that what had seemed like a bottomless pit was in fact a deep gorge which sucked in water from three of its sides. Ahead of him, beneath a suspension bridge of misty rainbow, the re-formed river escaped as a cataract between towering cliffs. Bond's heart fell fractionally faster than the hang glider. A down-draught was carrying him below the lip of the falls. He struggled to find a current of air, but knew that it was hopeless. He could never reach the surrounding jungle. He would have to follow the river down the gorge and hope that some landing space would appear before he ran out of supporting air. One look at the raging torrent, and his chances of survival seemed remote. The sides of the gorge were sheer save for occasional patches of vegetation, and the river raced through a shattered honeycomb of snag-toothed rocks. As the distance to them narrowed, he saw the battered shell of one of the launches breaking apart like a bundle of kindling. That was the fate that awaited him. It was like a nightmare in which with a jolt one is suddenly suspended in mid-air, drifting down, down, down towards a hostile landscape, twisting and turning but unable to arrest the descent. Bond felt a coldness which did not only come from fear. Beneath the level of the cliffs the atmosphere was glacial. The rocks glistened with spray and a bird rose upwards sharply, as if terrified by this strange intruder in its turbulent kingdom.

Now the bottom of the gorge was fifty feet away and all the air seemed to belong to the rushing water. There was nothing Bond could do to stay up. Only prolong the agony for as long as possible. A sheer rock face loomed up before him and he veered away at the last moment, dropping a heart-stopping ten feet with the suddenness of the turn. Angry spurts of water snapped at his heels and the gorge closed in above his head. The torrent jinked to the left and another wall of rock threw itself in his path. Bond forced his right arm up and pulled with his left. As the water rose high to whip against the cliff, he saw a scatter of jagged rocks and stones on the other side of the stream. An untidy mane of creepers strained against the current. Bond veered left away from the full force of the water and braced himself for impact. He came in close enough for the tip of the wing to scrape against the cliff and fell clumsily into a frothing mill-race of water.

The first impact drove his knees against his chest and the freezing water cut him to the bone. The battered framework of the glider was torn from his grasp and bounced away like a broken rainbow. Bond narrowly avoided being disembowelled on a submerged rock, and snatched at a cluster of creepers. His hands started to slip down the slimy tendrils, stopping at a joint to which he clung with desperation born of the threat of imminent death. The current swung him to the side so that he was within reach of a narrow beach of water-washed shale. Feeling the current relax its hold, he kicked sideways with his feet and threw out an arm to grab at a twist of root which projected from the rock face. His fingers brushed against it and then gripped. A last muscle-wrenching effort, and with both hands clinging to the root, he pulled himself from the maelstrom of pounding water. He lay on the wet stones and sucked in mouthfuls of air, thankful and surprised to be alive.

The roar of the water around Bond was still terrifying. Tucked on a ledge of shingle, he seemed almost to be beneath it. As he looked back upstream, the full might of the falls was hidden by the bend in the river, but a thick cloud of spray and mist hung in the air, grey and foreboding against the black mass of rock. The water only needed to rise a few inches to sweep him away again. As if prompted by the terror behind the thought, it began to rain. Bond knew what this could mean. A sudden storm upstream and the mighty weight of water being swept over the falls would rise by feet in seconds. He began to look around him desperately. The rock swelled out above his head and before him was an untidy jumble of glistening stones, the residue of a cliff fall. As Bond's eyes reached up, they narrowed incredulously. It was scarcely possible to believe what he could see through the fine net of spray and the falling rain. Revealed through a fading rainbow was a beautiful girl standing on a promontory of rock. She wore a long green robe split to the waist and a head-dress like a cap with streamers before and behind the ears. She looked not at Bond but upstream towards the falls. Bond turned away as the water surged against his foot alarmingly and when he looked back the girl had gone. Had she really been there? Had the journey and this terrible gorge begun to play tricks with his imagination? The roar of the water dinned into his ears and the cold pinched his limbs. If he could not find his way to higher ground within seconds he would be dead. The rain was now falling heavily, driving in under the rock. Bond edged along the thin shelf of glistening stones with the cliff face scraping his back. He could not see what lay directly above him, but his view of the opposite side of the gorge was depressing. A sheer cliff face loomed out like the bow of a ship, pitted only by horizontal contours of erosion. To climb it in his present condition would have been impossible.

Bond reached the end of the shale and launched himself clumsily at the lowest of the boulders. The shifting stones made an indifferent springboard and he was hard-pressed to get a handhold and haul himself up. A glance behind showed him that he had acted only just in time. The small beach had disappeared and the trailing tentacles of creeper that had saved his life were invisible beneath an angry white froth of wild water. Bond continued to climb, wondering how far the swollen stream could pursue him. Every surface was wet and covered with a green slime that felt like the skin of an eel. The cliffs towered above him like the walls of a deep tomb. He hauled himself up to the spot where he had seen the girl and rested, shivering uncontrollably.

At first he thought that he must have been dreaming. He stood precariously on an uneven surface of slippery, rain-lashed rock with a mass of glistening creeper trailing down the cliff. Then he saw that there was a dark shadow behind the creeper. He tugged the foliage aside and found that he was looking into the mouth of a cave. He pulled out his pencil torch and moved forward. The cave was small but the torch showed an opening and a flight of rough-hewn steps leading upwards. Bond's heartbeat quickened in excitement. He forgot about the cold and moved swiftly and silently up the steps. He climbed for a long time, his breath visible in the faint light of the torch, until he eventually emerged in a wide tunnel which sloped gently upwards. He followed it stealthily, and rounded a bend to see a glow of light far ahead. Silhouetted in its centre was the outline of the girl. As Bond extinguished his torch and shrank against the wall, she disappeared again.

Bond quickened his stride and began to feel the numbing

cold losing its grip. The circle of light grew larger and glowed green with sunlight. It was like approaching another world after the watery tomb of the gorge. A few more paces and he was actually able to stand at the mouth of a cave and feel the hot sun playing on his limbs. Above him was an escarpment and before him the jungle crowding in again with a profusion of giant cedars weighed down with flowering creepers. Of the girl there was no sign.

Bond stirred himself and pressed forward down a narrow, overgrown path that was obviously rarely used. Where did the girl in the strange costume come from? Bond racked his brains to remember where he had seen something like that costume before. The track opened into a narrow clearing and Bond found himself face to face with a mass of creeper-covered stones that had clearly once been a building. He looked about him and saw other piles of stones almost obliterated by the jungle. He had arrived at the ruins of an ancient city. There was a long wall that might have belonged to a public building; there a well choked by fallen masonry; a row of truncated pillars snapped off like broken teeth. And everything covered by a trelliswork of creepers that lay across it like a camouflage net. Bond picked his way between the buildings with difficulty, looking about him for the girl. There was no indication that the place was inhabited. He came out in another overgrown clearing and looked up to the tree line. Poking above the tangle of creepers were the uppermost stones of a building. Bond moved forward warily, brushing through some predatory thorn bushes. to find himself before a squat stone pyramid that soared a hundred feet into the air and was topped by a small temple. A flight of steps led up the face of the pyramid, and poised in the middle of them was the girl. She did not look at Bond but there was something about the way she stood, half turned towards him, that suggested she was waiting for him.

Hardly had he appeared than she moved forward and disappeared between two enormous stones. Bond felt uneasy but at the same time fascinated. He looked about him again, but there was no sign of human life. Birds called from the tops of trees and there was the swift liquid jabber of a monkey. He waited a few seconds and then crossed to the foot of the pyramid.

Q had spoken of the Mayan civilization in the Yucatan. This was what the pyramid reminded him of. And the clothing worn by the girl. Was it possible that some offshoot of the Mayas had been forced to emigrate south because of famine or internal strife? Surely he was not following the survivor of a supposedly extinct race which had somehow managed to propagate itself in the unexplored wastes of the South American rain forests? He started to climb the giant steps and marvelled that stones of this size could have been quarried by hand-held implements. Some of the blocks were upwards of five feet in height and twelve feet long. Bond reached the spot where the girl had disappeared and found himself at the mouth of a narrow passageway leading down into the heart of the pyramid. On the two stones at the entrance were superimposed paintings of warriors with spears. Bond looked behind him to see the jungle stretching away in all directions and then stepped down into the interior. Below him was a glow of light and half-way down the staircase the beautiful girl. This time she turned to face him, and her face split in a welcoming smile. As if confident that no other invitation was necessary, she turned and continued down the steps. Bond followed. To left and right, the walls were adorned with faded frescoes showing lines of marching men in short tunics and caps like the one worn by the girl whom Bond now considered his guide. The girl did not look round but continued down the steps towards the source of light. Bond was keyed up in the knowledge that a great secret was about to be revealed to him. The heart of the enigma must reside in the centre of the pyramid. With quickening pace he came to the end of the tunnel and looked about him in amazement.

His first impression was that he was in a cathedral. Great walls of coloured glass rose into the air and formed the back of the pyramid. Against them pressed the jungle, and the effect of integration was increased by the plants and creepers that climbed to meet the glass from the inside. Crystal rocks glowed as if illuminated internally and there was a serpentine pool traversed by a silver bridge. Nature had been harnessed as if in a Japanese garden, but here everything was on a giant scale and less formalized. Beside the arched bridge the girl waited for Bond like a refugee from a willow-pattern plate, and he had the strange feeling that he was in a world of make-believe. For a chilling moment he wondered if he had perished in the falls and been wafted straight into a purgatory that obliterated memory. He advanced to the girl and suddenly realized that he had seen her before. At the Venini Glass shop. Now the feeling of being in a dream took on nightmare proportions. The girl started to cross the bridge, then paused to see if he was following. Something about her look further agitated Bond's disturbed mind. The girl was looking, not to see if he was following, but to make sure that he was following. Bond started to skirt the pool. The water was clear, the surface merely disturbed by the gentle trickle of a waterfall at its far end. Only an alarmist would have been suspicious. But Bond was an alarmist when it came to the question of life expectancy. He traced the pattern of the paving stones around the pool and spun round as two more figures materialized through the foliage – girls dressed like the first. Again he recognized them. Astronaut trainees from California. They looked at him with smiling, expectant faces as if waiting for him to do something. He turned to the first girl. She was still on the bridge. She too was smiling. Waiting.

Bond put his foot down and immediately realized that something was wrong. The stone beneath his feet was not anchored but balanced over a void. Before he could move forward, it sprang into the air and hurled him into the pool. Bond hit the water and straight away struck out for the side. Subsequently it seemed to him that he had started swimming while still in mid-air. Whoever wanted him in that pool was not thinking of his cholesterol level.

His hands had just thudded against rock when a force like a steel whiplash wound itself round his chest. Bond was plucked backwards and received a terrifying glimpse of what had happened to him. Rearing before his eyes was the hideous open mouth of a giant anaconda. Its coils tightened round his chest and he started to shout before being dashed beneath the surface. The pressure on his chest might have been exerted by an enormous pair of nutcrackers. It seemed that at any moment his rib cage must break and crush his lungs in a jagged fist of broken bone.

Bond struggled and tore with his hands but the strength of the snake was too great for him. The breath was being systematically choked from his body. Bond took in half a mouthful of water and began to panic. His fingers clawed at the bottom of the pool and closed about a rock. He snatched it up and lashed at the swaying shape before his face. A blow connected solidly with the anaconda's head and its grip relaxed. Given new hope, Bond began to fight his way free of the coils. His fingers brushed against the side of the pool. Then the coils snatched tight again like a contracting spring. The huge weight of the snake bore him down. Beyond the knot of its coils Bond glimpsed ten feet of tail lashing the water like a hose. Twisting desperately, he pushed his fingers into the breast pocket of his tunic. Like a subliminal image he saw a picture of the retractable pen he had taken from Holly's room in Venice. His fingers closed about the tip and he drew it out folding it in his hand. As his tortured ribs seemed to meet beneath the pressure, he forced the point of the pen against the straining flesh of the snake and pressed the tip. Seconds passed and nothing happened. The grip did not weaken and the snake was still trying to force his mouth open so that he would drown. Then suddenly the coiled body was a weight that had no strength. Bond wriggled free and felt his rib cage expand. The snake hung in the water as if in suspension. It gave three convulsive twists and then lay still.

Bond swam to the side of the pool and hung on, breathing painfully. Then he hauled himself out and closed his eyes as he cleared his lungs. When he opened them it was to see a small mountain of wet leather against his face. The leather which gleamed dully belonged to the toecap of a shoe. Above the shoe was a tree trunk of sodden material that formed a trouser leg. Above the trouser leg was Jaws. His mouth was open and his teeth parted in a grin that shone down like a naughty deed in a naughty world. Bond rested his head on his hands and regularized his breathing. Something told him that he was going to need every ounce of breath that he could find.

'Mr Bond –' the voice echoed down from above, and conveyed a note of genuine regret '– you defy all my attempts to plan an amusing death for you.'

Jaws's hand reached down and picked up Bond as if he was a floating toy being retrieved from a bath. With disdainful ease he dumped him down before the owner of the voice.

Drax appeared down a flight of steps from what had presumably been a vantage point on a high rock. 'Why did you break off the encounter so summarily?'

'I discovered he had a crush on me,' said Bond.

Drax brushed the front of his black silk tunic as if picking off Bond's remark like a speck of dust. 'Always jokes, Mr Bond. A concomitant of the stiff upper lip, I suppose. The Englishman always laughs in the face of adversity. Well, I can promise you plenty to laugh at. It will be interesting to see if your sense of humour can keep pace with it.' He nodded to Jaws and turned on his heel. Jaws thrust out a hand and Bond staggered forward. The familiar faces of two more girls had appeared and he noticed that they shared a common expression with the first three: disappointment.

'I'm sorry about your pet,' said Bond.

The girls looked at him coldly and followed on like bridesmaids at a wedding.

Drax led the way towards heavy metal doors that slid open at his approach and revealed a scene totally in contrast to the conservatory calm of the glass chamber. Tiers of technicians sat before ascending screens of overprinted monitors and the sounds of disembodied voices calling out technical information rang out like those of brokers in a stock market. Bond quickly saw that all the monitor screens had one thing in common. They revealed different stages of rockets being prepared for take-off. Rockets that were clearly intended to propel something into space. Bond watched giant claws swing slowly back from the winged spacecraft and saw the familiar lettering on the hull: MOON-RAKER. Fresh words and symbols continuously flooded on to the flickering screens and Bond realized that he was watching the pre-launch procedure not for one but for several space shuttles. He turned to Drax, who was looking about him like a bishop in a newly consecrated cathedral.

'What the hell are you up to here, Drax?'

Drax did not deign to look at him. One of his brutish hands rose and plucked reflectively at the red fur on his face. 'It is a convention of the fiction beloved by parlour maids that the villain explains all before disposing of his victims. I do not intend to follow that precedent.'

'Not even the briefest elucidation, Drax?'

Drax turned away from the hustle and bustle of the control chamber and looked towards a domed glass case resting in an alcove. In Victorian days it would have contained an arrangement of small, brightly coloured stuffed birds. Now it held a beautiful black orchid, its flowers tipped with scarlet as if they had been dipped in blood. Bond recognized the slide he had been shown in Q's workshop: *Orchidaceae negra*.

Under Jaw's watchful eye, Bond moved to Drax's side. 'What about that orchid?'

Drax spoke as if to himself. 'The curse of a civilization. It was neither pestilence nor war that wiped out the race who built the great city lying around us. It was their reverence for this lovely flower.'

Bond looked again at the bland face of the orchid. Behind its sheen of surface beauty there was an impression of evil conveyed more subtly than through its colour. The very shape of the flower suggested that of a praying mantis. 'Come too near me and I will devour you' it seemed to say. Even within the heart of the flower there was a tiny foetal face crushed so tight that it seemed to be crying out in pain and despair, as if bemoaning a life it could never have.

'The flower is poisonous,' said Bond.

'In the long term, yes,' said Drax. 'Exposure to its pollen causes sterility. The unfortunate Mayas never realized that. Through every crisis of their dwindling civilization they turned to worship the flower that was responsible for its destruction. Poignant, is it not?'

'But you've improved on sterility haven't you, Drax?'

Drax smiled. 'If you choose to employ such quaint phraseology. Yes, I have. As you probably observed in Venice, those same seeds now yield death.'

'Except to animals.'

'And plant life as well.' Drax spread his hands. 'One must

preserve the balance of nature. Let no one say that at heart I am not an ecologist.' His smile was like a crack on a gravestone.

'Moonraker launch programme now commencing.' The voice coming over the public address system temporarily drowned the babble of voices flooding the chamber.

Drax raised his eyes to one of the screens and Bond followed them. 'You have arrived at a propitious moment, Mr Bond.' The voice was a contented purr. Bond saw a wide expanse of Arctic ice-cap. There was no sign of a human presence.

Another voice cut in. 'Moonraker One. Lift off!' Immediately the ice-cap shattered and the screen flooded with light. Through the light appeared the nose-cone of a rocket and attached to it a Moonraker shuttle. The assembly rose slowly into the air and then roared skywards, leaving a dense trail of smoke and flames. The picture changed instantly to a barren stretch of desert.

'Moonraker Two. Lift off!' A chatter of technicians' voices orchestrated the appearance of a second rocket and shuttle. The final stages of the countdown flashed up on the screen, and monitors around the chamber fed back changing temperatures and pressures. Bond glanced towards Jaws. He was watching the scene, round-eyed and open-mouthed, like a child looking up at an illuminated Christmas tree.

'Moonraker Three. Lift off!' Now the picture changed to a range of mountains and a third rocket and Moonraker soared into the air.

Bond's awe was nearly the equal of Jaws's, and coupled with it was a growing sense of alarm. Why were these shuttles being put into orbit? What was Drax planning to do? All the time, at the back of Bond's mind was the image of what he had seen at the glassworks. The two scientists sliding to the floor, their hands clutching at their throats.

156

The rats squeaking in their cages . . .

Bond glanced about him and saw that both Jaws and Drax were absorbed by what was happening on the screens. He started to edge sideways and felt something hard press into his ribs. A guard with a sub-machine gun prodded him back banefully. Drax addressed Bond without turning his head. 'I can understand your desire to leave us, Mr Bond. In fact, I endorse it. However, you will go when I wish it. My genius demands the respect of a little attention.'

Bond read the message on Jaws's gleaming teeth and turned back to the screens. He was now looking at a Pacific atoll. Palm trees shuddered and then disappeared from view as a dazzling effulgence blazed across the monitors. Bond was reminded uneasily of another Pacific atoll. 'We have lifted off,' said a satisfied voice over the public address system, and the blazing tail of the rocket disappeared out of the top of the picture. A dense cloud of smoke began to clear and the agitated palms stopped having hysterics. The screen suddenly went blank.

'Four shuttles in space?' queried Bond.

'Six,' said Drax shortly. He turned towards a technician sitting before a cathode-ray tube on which circles of light were converging towards a glowing centre which throbbed at one-second intervals. The technician spoke into a chest microphone. 'Moonraker Five on pre-set launch programme. Minus ten.'

The countdown began to be projected on to the console in electronic script as another technician spoke into his microphone.

'Moonraker Six on pre-set launch programme. Minus two zero.'

Bond turned to Drax. 'Tell me one thing. The Moonraker that was on its way to London and disappeared over Alaska. You hijacked that, didn't you?'

Drax's eyes roamed the monitors. 'You use the language

of the tabloids, Mr Bond. Let us say I repossessed my own property. It was a regrettable necessity. One of the Moonrakers I was intending to use in this programme developed a technical fault. I was not prepared to put the timing of the operation back.' He looked at Bond and a quick dart of red flashed in his eyes. 'As you know, I am not renowned for my patience.'

'And what is the operation?'

Drax held Bond's glance for a couple of seconds and then shook his head brusquely and dismissively. 'No, Mr Bond. You have distracted me enough.' He turned to Jaws. 'Mr Bond must be cold after his swim. Place him where he can be assured of warmth.'

Jaws showed half an inch of grinning metal as if sharing a private joke and propelled Bond towards a ramp leading deeper into the pyramid. Bond turned to face his captor. 'I'll see you later, Drax.'

The voice was a razor wrapped in velvet. 'Fleetingly perhaps, Mr Bond.'

At the end of the ramp was a network of dimly lit corridors, and Bond felt Jaws's hand grasp his arm and force him towards a heavy wooden door fortified by horizontal pieces of metal. The pressure of the grip told him that there was no point in trying to escape. Two bolts were slid back and the door opened just wide enough to receive Bond's body. With a thrust of Jaws's arm Bond was making acquaintance with the opposite wall while the door slammed behind him.

'James!'

Bond turned to find Holly launching herself towards him. He caught her by the shoulders and looked into her eyes. 'Thank God you're all right. You are all right?'

'Apart from a few bruises. And you?'

'The same.' He looked around the high, vaulted chamber furnished with a large circular table, surrounded by chairs.

158

It looked like an executive boardroom, but without windows. 'Where the hell are we?'

'I don't know. I haven't moved since they brought me here.'

Bond looked up at the ceiling far above their heads. It was almost as if they were at the bottom of a well. 'Drax is launching half a dozen Moonrakers. Four have gone already.'

'Do you know why?'

'I was going to ask you.'

Holly shook her head. 'Where are the other two shuttles?'

Bond started to prowl round the room. 'I think they must be near here somewhere. We've got to get out and locate them.'

'Let me spare you the trouble, Mr Bond.' The voice belonged to Drax and echoed down eerily from above. At the same instant, the ceiling above their heads split open and began to slide back. Bond sucked in his breath. He was looking into the menacing barrels of seven mighty rocket engines. A Moonraker space shuttle with its propellent tank and booster rockets was positioned vertically above their steep-walled prison supported by giant metal arms. Bond understood Drax's remark to Jaws about putting him where he could be assured of warmth. Holly and he were inside the exhaust chamber for launch rockets. Enormous panels, in the roof of the pyramid, slid back to reveal the sky far above; distant as the hope of escape.

'Even in death my munificence is boundless.' Drax's blunt silhouette loomed over the edge of the pit. His hands lathered air smugly. 'When this rocket lifts off I shall be leaving you in your own private crematorium.' He raised an arm and an elevator began to descend from the opening in the cabin of the Moonraker. 'Dr Goodhead, Mr Bond, I bid you farewell.' He delivered a mocking salute and climbed into the elevator. With a remote, whining whir it began to lift into the air. Bond looked at the rocket barrels of death, thinking of the billowing clouds of flame he had seen emerging from big rocket engines. When Moonraker Five lifted off with Drax in it they would be reduced to ashes within seconds.

'Moonraker Five. Four minutes to lift-off.' The technician's voice rang out like that of a mortuary assistant.

Bond avoided Holly's desperate eyes and reverted to looking round the walls of the chamber. The atmosphere was not stuffy despite the apparent lack of ventilation. He started to push a steel cabinet along the wall.

'What is it?' Holly looked at him keenly. 'Do you think we can climb out?'

'Not up that wall. I'm looking for an air shaft.' He dropped to his knees as he found a square opening in the wall a foot from the floor. He squinted through a criss-cross of metal bars and saw that there was in fact a narrow shaft, perhaps thirty feet in length. Beyond it jungle foliage showed temptingly. Bond seized the bars and gritted his teeth. He strained until the sweat ran down his cheeks but the bars did not budge. Holly knelt beside him with hope dying in her eyes.

'Three minutes to lift-off.' Maybe it was Bond's imagination, but there seemed to be an edge of mockery in the technician's announcement over the public address system. The metal arms were drawing back one by one from the rocket and the elevator and its movable shaft had retreated out of view of the pit. Most sinister of all, thin wisps of gas were emerging from some of the rocket engines as if from the bowl of a pipe. The whole structure of the rockets began to hum with activity.

'You can't move it?'

Bond did not reply but pressed Holly back against the wall. His fingers fumbled with his watch and Holly saw what looked like the winding device being detached from its side. Behind it was drawn a thin thread as if a spider was descending from its web. Bond knelt and swiftly pressed the small circle of metal against the point at which one of the bars emerged from the wall. There was an almost imperceptible *click*. The metal roundel adhered. Bond waved Holly farther along the wall and moved to take up a position beside her. The watch was still playing out thread.

'Two minutes to lift-off.' The technician's voice could now barely be heard above a low whining noise that was emanating from the rocket and increasing in intensity with every second. The stench of turbine exhaust fumes scraped at their throats.

Bond pressed his back against the wall and his hand moved to his watch.

Holly looked first at him with an ironic questioning in her eye, and then down to the thread. 'Are we supposed to pull?'

'Push.' Bond's finger jabbed against the watch and a pinpoint of red light flashed up the thread. There was a violent explosion and a cloud of smoke billowed from the mouth of the shaft. Bond started forward as the severed fuse retracted into his watch. The grille had been blasted aside. Only a few stubs of metal remained.

Bond gestured towards the opening. 'Get in!' His eyes were watering and he started to choke. Fumes swirled around him. The whole structure of the rocket was beginning to throb. The metal arms had swung back out of sight. The disembodied voices of the public address system intoned the critical stages of the countdown.

'One minute to lift-off.'

The knell of doom rang in Bond's ears as he scrambled into the shaft and started to crawl after Holly. In less than sixty seconds a merciless tongue of flame would be pursuing them, roasting them alive as if they were threaded on a spit. A stub of metal took a chunk out of his knee but he hardly noticed it. Behind him he could hear the noise building up towards ignition. The eldritch shriek developed into a giant roar. He blundered against Holly's heels and shouted at her to go faster. His knuckles were bleeding. Holly's body shut out air and light. He could see nothing before him. With a fresh pang of horror he realized that the shaft was narrowing. His shoulders brushed against rock on either side. There must be still another fifteen feet to go. At that moment he was convinced that they were never going to make it.

'Ten ... nine ... eight ...' Somewhere behind them the referee was calling the count over a fallen fighter. Bond imagined the blowtorch of flame rushing up between his legs and wanted to cry out in horror. 'Six ... five ...' Ahead of him. Holly suddenly disappeared. He saw a square of green light and another shaft joining at right angles the one they were in. 'Three ... two ... one ... ignition ... Lift off!' Bond forced himself forward following Holly into the side tunnel. Barely had he pressed into the opening than a rush of orange flame roared past, making him scream with pain. He heard the noise of his hair singeing and smelt the scorched fabric of his clothing. The pain was agonizing and for several seconds he thought that he was going to die. Then the flame disappeared as suddenly as it had come and there was only a wisp of acrid smoke. Somewhere in the distance a great roar swelled and then died away. Bond touched his burnt flesh and winced. Pieces of charred material were sticking to him and he had no idea how badly he had been injured.

'James!'

Bond urged Holly forward. 'Keep going. I'm all right.' He gritted his teeth against the pain and tried to find comfort in the fact that at the side of the shaft, somewhere near them, was a source of light and air. It was revealed as a grille giving on to a ledge of rock; the light was artificial and came from a lamp attached to the rock beside the grille. Bond heard the sound of a motor vehicle going past, and then another. The public address system was barely audible in the distance. Bond surmised that they must be in some tunnel leading off the control chamber. Holly waited at the grille while Bond attacked it with his bleeding fingers. This one was a wire mesh construction that could be easily forced open. He crawled out on to the rock and lay still, feeling the unbelievable balm of cool air against his cheeks. Slowly, some semblance of life returned to his cramped limbs, and with it the responsibility of action. So far nothing had been achieved save the salvation of their own lives. But Bond had seen enough to know that many other lives were at stake.

'Moonraker Six pre-set launch programme completed. Pilots proceed from base to launch area.' The announcer's voice was faint but distinct. Hardly had it finished speaking than an open vehicle came into view beneath Bond's perch. In it, sitting back to back along the length of the vehicle, were twelve of the astronauts that Bond had seen being trained in California. Six men and six women. They were wearing white tunics and for an instant their faces showed grim and purposeful in the lamplight. The vehicle rolled on its way.

'Come on.' Bond forgot about the pain of his burns and scrambled down the side of the rock to the broad passage-way. He held up a hand for Holly, but she was already beside him. From the direction from which the astronauts had come there was the sound of another vehicle approaching. Bond nudged Holly. 'Stand by. We may be hitching a lift.'

A jeep appeared down the track and the sight of the two passengers sitting behind the driver made Bond's heart skip a couple of beats. They were wearing the operational suits of astronaut pilots carrying helmets and vizors. Bond leapt in front of the vehicle and flung his arms wide. The amazed driver stood on the brake and the jeep skidded to a halt.

'What the hell do you think you're doing?'

The driver's spontaneous reaction came split seconds before he realized that there was something wrong with Bond's appearance. By that time Bond had walked calmly round to the side of the jeep and hit him on the point of the jaw. As he slumped backwards, Holly snatched up the sub-machine gun that lay beside him. The two pilots, handicapped by their cumbersome uniforms, hardly had time to get over their surprise before they were knocked senseless by a karate chop from Bond and an expertly aimed blow with the butt of the gun from Holly. Bond dragged the driver from the wheel and Holly jumped into his place to drive the vehicle into a dark alcove. She cut the engine and Bond looked at her admiringly. 'Right,' he said, 'I estimate we have about five minutes.'

Four minutes later the jeep pulled out of the alcove with two figures in astronaut pilot uniform in the front seat. It trundled down the broad passageway and within the space of a few minutes, after a tiny hesitation at an intersection, emerged from the dark tunnel into a brightly lit chamber that throbbed with activity. At one end, rearing majestically, was Moonraker Six, with its attached fuel tank and rockets to take it into space. Resting against the structure like protective fingers were curved steel girders. They opened in unison as the jeep appeared from the tunnel. The huge rockets were trembling and beginning to make the high-pitched whining noise that had characterized the pre-lift-off build-up of Moonraker Five. The mobile elevator, against the cabin entrance to the space shuttle, was beginning to make its descent. A door over the passenger hold slid closed and the vehicle that had been transporting the twelve astronauts reversed beneath the gantry.

Two armed guards stepped forward and one of them raised his arm as the jeep approached the descending elevator. He held out his hand and for a few seconds neither the driver nor his companion did anything. Then the driver raised his hand to the breast pocket of his uniform and produced an identity card with photograph attached. His companion followed suit. The guard glanced at the cards. 'You guys cutting it fine, aren't you? Did ya stop for a leak?'

The driver nodded and stretched out his hand for his card. The guard hesitated for a moment and then returned the cards. He stepped back and the jeep continued to the waiting elevator. Above it the combined structure of the spacecraft and its boosters towered into the air, almost scraping the ceiling of the chamber. There was a grinding noise and the roof opened to reveal a diamond-shaped patch of blue sky. The two pilots stepped from the jeep and entered the elevator. With a hiss of compressed air it left the ground. Two pairs of eyes looked about them warily. Behind the glass of the control room, monitors, screens and consoles flashed up pictures, figures and print-out messages. The unceasing interplay of voices droned across the open space, to be heard even above the whining of the rocket turbine pumps which set the teeth on edge.

'Four minutes to lift-off.' This time the tone was calm and measured.

The elevator quivered to a halt before the open hatchway of the Moonraker control cabin and the two figures in pilot uniform raised an arm towards the control room like footballers acknowledging their supporters before the start of a game and ducked down to enter the shuttle.

'Three minutes to lift-off.'

The first pilot climbed into a padded seat, strapped himself in and depressed a button that tilted the seat so that he was facing in the direction in which the Moonraker would be travelling, his back horizontal to Earth.

'Two minutes to lift-off.'

The door hatch slid shut and there was a hissing noise as it sealed hermetically. Bond turned towards Holly who was strapping herself in beside him. Holly quickly flashed out an arm to flick off a switch.

'Don't say anything. We're on closed circuit until after lift-off.' Bond nodded and Holly's voice relaxed. 'We won't have to do anything. We're on a pre-programmed flight pattern.' She quickly flicked up a switch and Bond could hear again the interrupted sound of the countdown.

'– teen . . . thirteen . . . twelve . . . eleven . . .'

Bond folded his hands across his chest and gazed at the banks of dials and flickering needles. Everywhere there was vibration, movement and noise, and above all the terrifying roar of the fuel pumps getting ready to prime the engines for ignition.

'Eight . . . seven . . . six . . . five . . .'

Bond suddenly felt frightened. A fear that was physically painful. He was about to be shot into space with no idea of his destination or what would happen to him when he arrived – if he arrived.

'Three . . . two . . . one . . . ignition . . . Lift-off!'

Bond's shoulders bent to the curvature of his seat. He sensed the rocket detach from its mooring and begin to lift slowly into the air. Through the cabin windows he could see fumes and dust billowing up. The control room was obscured. Within seconds he would be exposed to the mind-scrambling stress of the G force that had nearly taken his life on the centrifuge trainer. The needles on the control panels danced madly. The speed started to build up. His stomach felt as if it was being pushed down his body at the end of a hot metal rod. James Bond closed his eyes.

15

RENDEZVOUS IN SPACE

After an unspecifiable length of time, Bond opened his eyes. Only a slight trembling of the fuselage suggested movement. Beside him Holly reached forward and pressed a row of buttons. Immediately screens situated near the roof showed pictures of the other Moonrakers. 'That's the rest of the fleet.'

Bond looked incredulously at the banks of instruments. 'And we don't have to do anything?'

'We can't do anything. We're locked into a pre-set flight programme. To break it and go over to manual we'd have to call control.'

'Not a good idea,' said Bond. 'Have you any thoughts about where we might be going?'

Holly flicked some more switches and a monitor showed a number of superimposed dotted lines. 'No, but we're all headed for the same rendezvous in space. We'll just have to wait and see.'

Bond glanced out of the window beside him and sucked in his breath. Above them, through wispy cloud, he could see what looked like the page of an atlas. Clearly recognizable was the isthmus of Central America. The sense of isolation provoked by this sight was profound. They were flying upside down. The unknown stretched ahead. He wondered whether they would ever be able to find their way back.

A light on the control panel started to flash and Holly spoke with warning in her voice. 'Don't be alarmed. All that's happening now is we're going to jettison our fuel tank and roll over.'

There was a noise like an undercarriage retracting and the fuselage gave a convulsive shudder, as if shaking free an encumbrance. The Earth seemed to rotate until it appeared below them.

Bond smiled at Holly. 'When I think of all the girls I know who would have been useless on this trip.'

Holly spoke with mock severity. 'Don't tell me about them.' She leant forward and flicked another switch. A monitor directly in front of their seats threw up a picture of the twelve astronauts facing each other in two rows of six. Now the men and women had split up into pairs. 'The personnel hold. They're behind us.'

Bond's eyes narrowed. 'And the animals went in two by two.'

Holly looked at him quizzically. 'What do you mean?'

'Something about this operation reminds me of Noah's Ark.' Bond leant forward and pointed to something on the screen. Spied on by the angle of the watching camera, a man and a woman were revealed as surreptitiously holding hands.

'Love is in the air,' said Holly.

'Maybe you're right.' Bond pondered. 'Perhaps space has the same effect on the libido as an ocean cruise.'

'It hasn't shown up in any of the logs I've read.' Holly's eyes continued to flicker over the control console and monitors. Bond settled back in his seat. There was nothing to do but wait, and even the pain of his burns could not overcome his desire for a cat-nap. He closed his eyes.

When he awoke it was to find Holly studying the bank of screens. The images of the Moonrakers were closing together.

'We're converging,' said Holly.

Bond looked at the screens. The blips on the monitors were moving in dramatically towards the centre. 'Are we meeting up in space?'

Before Holly could answer, Bond was thrown forward in his seat. The speed of the Moonraker had changed as though it had been pushed by a giant's hand. Almost immediately there was a sensation of movement, lasting a short time.

'That was the forward control rockets,' said Holly calmly. 'We're entering an orbit.'

Bond felt relieved and looked ahead, beyond the nose of the shuttle. A pinpoint of brilliant light showed up in the eerie darkness.

'What's that?'

Holly studied the radar scanner and Bond could see the curved line of the Earth's surface. Again a feeling of terrifying isolation gripped him. Holly's face was puzzled. 'There's nothing showing up.'

Bond strained his eyes to penetrate the darkness of space. Slowly a shape became discernible; a luminous globe from which projected six tubular arms carrying at their ends satellite globes. With every second the detail became more defined as a huge mass like a giant's mobile emerged from the Earth's shadow. Tubular corridors connected several satellites with each other and led to the central globe. A saucer-shaped antenna was mounted beneath the globe.

'A space station,' breathed Holly.

'It looks more like a city.' Bond glanced again at the scanner. Its surface revealed nothing. 'Why aren't we getting anything? Is the radarscope out of order?'

Holly quickly ran through a checking drill. 'No, it's functioning. Drax must have a radar jamming system.'

Bond's voice was thoughtful. 'So nobody knows the space station is there?'

'No.' Holly looked at him. 'What are you thinking?'

'Too many things,' said Bond. 'I'm almost frightened to think.'

Before them light touched the many surfaces of the space station and it shone like a bejewelled crown floating serenely in space. Bond glanced sideways and saw another Moonraker closing the distance between them. The dotted lines on the monitors were interlacing like the poles of a wig-wam.

'All Moonrakers prepare to initiate docking sequence.' The disembodied voice coming from above made Bond tense with anticipation. Now another Moonraker had appeared beyond the space station. The shuttles were surrounding the structure like wary minnows grouped around a bait. Holly began to busy herself with the battery of controls.

Bond smiled. 'You're a real little homebody, aren't you?'

'Do me a favour, Mr Bond.' Holly spoke out of the corner of her mouth and conteptuously brushed aside a wisp of hair.

'Moonraker Six – you are now in manual. Prepare to dock.' The voice spoke again and the airways crackled. Holly manoeuvred a control column and Bond felt the Moonraker moving forward towards one of the satellites. Above a series of concentric roundels there was painted a numeral 6.

'Six – initiate docking sequence.'

Holly took the shuttle forward and a docking tube below the 6 extended to receive the shuttle. Holly steered alongside it. Through the window beside him Bond could see a second shuttle dock with the satellite. Through the hatch a helmeted astronaut, floating weightless in the zero-gravity, entered the largest satellite. Bond watched in amazement as the man drifted across the satellite and disappeared into a tunnel that connected it to the main globe.

'Where's he going?'

Holly unclipped the strap across her chest. 'He's activating the artificial gravity control system. At the moment we

170

don't have any gravity. We'd all be floating around like balloons if we went outside. Once the rotation thrusters are fired, the station will start to rotate and we'll have artificial gravity. Then we can move about more or less normally.'

Bond looked grim. 'More or less normally until Drax catches up with us.' He unclipped himself and encountered the weird sensation of weightlessness as he tried to rise to his feet.

'What do you suggest we do?' asked Holly.

'Find that radar jamming system and sabotage it. Once we're visible from Earth they'll send somebody to investigate. I don't believe Drax is planning to run this place as a convalescent home.'

'Gravity conditions normal. Life support system nominal.' The voice came clearly over the intercom. A second voice cut in after it with an authoritative announcement. 'Moonraker Six – off-load at will.'

Bond looked at Holly questioningly. She flicked the switch that brought the personnel hold up on the screen. The astronauts were filing out into the satellite. Two lingered behind. Those who had been holding hands. They waited a discreet moment and then embraced passionately before moving to the door.

'Do you see yourself as a Peeping Tom in your old age?' asked Holly.

'At the moment I'd just like to see myself with an old age,' said Bond. He reached forward and flicked up the switch. 'Right. Let's mingle – and steer clear of Drax.'

From the satellite they moved into a long corridor with reinforced glass windows looking out into space. The main globe towered before them like the dome of a cathedral. Other astronauts were filing out of the hold of the companion craft. Bond kept his head down as he moved along.

'All personnel to Command Satellite. All personnel to

Command Satellite.' The announcement came over the public address system. Bond moved closer to Holly. 'Any idea what this is about?'

Holly shook her head. 'None.'

Bond looked at the purposeful group about him. 'We'd better tag along. If it's a "welcome aboard" address, we may learn what Drax is up to. Stay with me and keep your eyes open.'

'I always keep my eyes open,' said Holly firmly. She glanced out of a window and nudged Bond. 'Like right now. Look.'

At a point higher on the left Bond was able to see into another corridor tube leading from a satellite in which shuttles had docked. Clearly visible, with his bowed head still nearly scraping the ceiling, was Jaws. Striding along before him was Drax. Bond's eyes wandered from the deadly couple to a tube that was protruding from the side of the globe. In it, as if lined up for release, were three spheres like those he had seen in the laboratory at the Venini glassworks. Holly followed his eyes inquiringly.

'Did you see those in Venice?' asked Bond. 'I saw them being filled with nerve gas. Two people died.'

Holly looked alarmed. 'So what's he planning to do?'

Bond's expression hardened. 'I don't know what he plans to do, but I know what he *can* do.'

They stepped through a door and entered the command satellite of the space station. It was constructed on three levels, with an elevator shaft running like a spindle from it to the central globe. There were a number of apron stages. On one of these was a giant instrument resembling a telescope protruding from the roof of the chamber, and next to it a console incorporating three monitor screens and a bank of switches and buttons. Around the edge of the sphere was a circular walkway with more consoles and screens built into the outer walls. These were manned by

172

technicians in light green tunics. Long windows positioned at intervals looked out into space and towards the attendant satellites. From these the newly arrived astronauts were entering the chamber by means of the corridor tunnels, which criss-crossed at all levels, and fanning out around the walls.

While Bond was looking about him in silent wonder, the elevator came to a halt behind the giant telescope and Drax stepped out. As he appeared, so the lights dimmed, and beyond the windows could be seen a million tiny pin-points of distant stars. The feeling of being at the very hub of the universe was brilliantly conveyed. Bond was awed.

'First there was a dream ... Now there is reality.' Drax's voice echoed eerily, seeming to come not from his body but from the throbbing walls that surrounded his listeners. Lights began to play on the faces of the assembled astronauts to reveal that they were standing in couples. Their carefully selected beauty had a cold, impersonal quality which added to the feeling of unreality. Bond began to get an unpleasant pricking sensation down his backbone. The whole scene was like a meticulously orchestrated stage performance.

Drax slowly extended his arms to embrace the gathering. A penumbra of light played about his head and softened the brutish hardness of his twisted features. 'Here, in the untainted cradle of the heavens, will be created a new super-race. A race of perfect physical specimens. You have been selected as its progenitors. Like gods, your offspring will return to Earth and shape it in their image.' Bond looked towards Holly. Her face echoed his incredulity. The lights continued to shine and behind Drax, in the shadows, they glinted on the cruel, vulpine faces of armed men. With a start of horror, Bond realized what the scene reminded him of: one of the Nazi rallies of the 1930s. Excitement, pageantry, showmanship, distortion, lies, genocide. The last word flared up in his mind in blazing letters. Drax's voice continued. 'But you will not be ordinary gods. You have all served in humble capacities in my terrestrial empire. You have learned that humility which is the sovereign bond of kingship.' Bond looked again at the faces. The words were getting through to them. Chins were lifting, jaws setting with a new edge of purpose. They waited eagerly for what was to come. Drax extended his arms before him, his fists clenched. His voice rose slowly and demoniacally. Nobody could fault the delivery or the fervour. Only the words emerged as if dipped in some ghastly putrescence of the soul that made Bond feel physically sick. 'Your seed, like yourselves, will pay deference to the ultimate dynasty which I alone shall have created. From their first day on Earth your descendants will be able to look up and know that there *is* rule and order in the heavens.'

There was a silence and then everything was plunged into darkness. Only the ghostly luminescence of space and its myriads of stars were visible like shining dust through the long windows. Seconds passed and a globe appeared to glow with light and slowly start revolving as if it had arrived from space. The familiar shape of Earth could be recognized, the continents black against the glowing white of the oceans. Almost imperceptibly at first, the dark shape of the continents began to melt into the sea. The surface of the globe became smooth as if a slate had been wiped clean. Then in a blaze of light the land masses appeared, dazzling with an ethereal brilliance, whilst the oceans became dark. The impression of rebirth was dynamically conveyed. There was a gasp of awe which spoke its effectiveness.

Bond drew Holly to him and whispered in her ear. 'It's more vital than ever that we get to that radar jamming system and kill it. The idea of Drax as God terrifies me.'

Holly squeezed his hand. 'Me too. I guess it must be on

174

another floor or in one of the satellites. We'd better take the elevator.'

The lights came on and the globe stopped spinning. Drax had disappeared. As if leaving an auditorium after a moving performance, the astronauts began to disperse slowly, their faces drawn and preoccupied. Bond saw one girl wiping away tears. Poor fools. They had been brain-washed for victory like a college football team buoyed up for the big game. But Hugo Drax was much more sinister than any football coach. The side he was planning to destroy had over four thousand million people in it.

Mingling with astronauts and technicians, Bond and Holly followed one of the corridor tunnels to the elevator shaft. With a hiss the door slid open and Bond quickly turned to face Holly. Filling the elevator as if packed in it was Jaws. Bond pretended to be preoccupied by some detail on Holly's uniform and waited until her wary eyes returned to his. 'He's gone.'

Bond saw the broad back retreating down the corridor and led the way into the lift. There were five buttons and he pressed the middle one. The elevator moved slowly along its shaft and came to a stop. 'You must be careful –' began Holly.

'I know that,' said Bond. Sometimes he wished with Messrs Lerner and Loewe that women could be a little more like men. One did not always need to be reminded to take care. The door hissed open and Bond moved forward. He immediately found himself falling on his face.

Holly grabbed him. 'When I said you must be careful, I was referring to the fact that we have now arrived in a zero-gravity area.' Her tone was gracious.

'I'll listen next time,' said Bond apologetically.

'Do that.' Holly looked left and right along the gallery. 'Move slowly and press your feet well down. There's Velcro on your soles and on the floor.'

'So we're right in the centre of the space station?'

'Correct. Hence the zero-gravity. The nearer you get to the –'

Holly broke off her lecture as two guards appeared, moving purposefully around the gallery. At the waist of their dark green combat uniforms hung silver cylinders a foot in length and three inches in diameter. The heads of the tubes swelled priapically. Bond guessed that they must be laser torches. The guards appeared to be fully absorbed by what was happening inside the viewing panels of the globe-like structure that the gallery enclosed. They hardly glanced at Bond and Holly.

Bond waited until the guards had moved on and then looked inside the sphere himself. At first he thought he was looking beneath the surface of a swimming pool. Half a dozen young men and women appeared to be gliding through water. Then he realized that they were drifting weightlessly in zero-gravity; that the sphere was being used as a kind of space gymnasium. Before him a beautiful girl in a leotard hung suspended as if frozen in the middle of a swallow dive. Her arms were flung wide, her back curved, her unsupported breasts melding gracefully into the forward sweep of her body. The girl turned her head and her eyes met Bond's. She smiled. For a few seconds Bond forgot that he was a man who smoked and drank too much and lived on borrowed time.

Then Holly's hand drew him away like a child from a sweet shop window. 'Look at this.' She led him to another porthole. Bond looked inside and saw a smaller sphere containing two familiar figures: the astronauts he had seen embracing in the personnel hold of Moonraker Six. Now they were naked and drifting in zero-gravity as if performing a sensuous mating ballet. A soft pink light throbbed at the speed of a heartbeat and fingers stretched out to touch, stroke and caress. Slowly, the light dimmed and the two bodies began to join into one.

Bond turned away from the window. 'Somebody's taking Drax's advice to heart.'

'It's incredible.' Holly took a deep breath and shook her head. 'I just can't adjust to what's going on up here. It's like some kind of dream.'

'Or nightmare,' said Bond grimly. He started to move forward and nearly fell again. The image of the nightmare returned forcibly. To find one's limbs locked in perpetual slow motion whilst evil ran with the speed of a greyhound – that was a recurring horror of bad dreams.

'James, look!' Holly pointed to a sign above one of the tubular corridors that connected with the gallery: 'Satellite Two. Electronic Camouflage Unit'. 'This must be it.'

Bond glanced down the corridor and then back along the gallery. What he saw made him take Holly's arm firmly and steer her as fast as he could along the perimeter of the globe. Moving towards them awkwardly was Jaws. Fortunately he was staring at his feet like a débutant skier or he would certainly have recognized Bond. One glance at Bond's face told Holly that something was wrong, but she said nothing until they came to another corridor marked 'Galley'.

'Down here.' She nudged him with her shoulder and Bond found himself approaching a brightly lit room laid out with parallel refectory tables that abutted one of the walls. The room was half full of astronauts and technicians. Holly led the way to the table that was farthest from the door and occupied by only one other man. Bond rubbed an eyebrow ruminatively so that he would not be recognized. They sat down with their backs to the assembly and Bond glanced over his shoulder. Jaws had come in and was sitting by the entrance. It would be foolish to try and leave before he did. He cursed himself for not having continued round the gallery. Now more time was going to be lost before they could get near the radar jamming system.

Bond looked around again and turned to Holly. 'Where do we have to go for food?'

'We don't.' She indicated a list of dishes printed beside each place setting. Next to each choice was a recessed button. 'Choose what you want and press the appropriate button.' She pointed towards one of the walls. 'That's today's special.'

Bond looked through a glass panel and saw a large joint of roast beef revolving on a spit. A row of plates was positioned on a narrow conveyor belt beneath it. As Bond watched, a thin beam of light moved vertically down the beef and a slice dropped on the plate. The process was repeated and Bond realized that the joint was being carved with an automatically controlled laser beam. He thought of the laser torches being carried by the guards and winced. 'I think I can resist the beef,' he said. He made a quick choice of dishes and pressed the relevant buttons, adding as an afterthought one marked 'Red wine'. Two minutes passed, in which he kept a wary eye on Jaws's reflection in the outside glass, and then a hatch slid open at the end of the table. Two trays emerged and glided slowly down a shallow trough in the middle of the table. When they arrived in front of Bond and Holly they stopped. There was a click and the two trays were nudged off the feed line to arrive before the diners. Bond nodded approvingly at Holly. 'Impressive.' He picked up a small bottle of wine and examined the label. 'Kubrick 2001. Excellent year.'

Holly shook her head. 'You're incorrigible, James.'

'Worried, too. I don't like the look of those spheres we saw poking out of the side of the big globe. As soon as we've done something about the radar jamming system, we'll take a look.'

Holly put down her coffee cup and looked at Bond coolly. 'Is that an order, Commander Bond? If it is, I'm bound to disobey it. My rank is equivalent to that of colonel. I outrank you, James.'

'You chose an excellent moment to remind me,' said Bond. 'All right. Will you accept a respectful submission that we should take steps to check whether those spheres are full of nerve gas and ready to be launched?'

'I will,' said Holly graciously. She glanced round. 'And now I think we can be on our way. Jaws doesn't appear to be a heavy eater.'

'It depends who the heavy is,' said Bond. He pressed a button marked 'disposal' and a flap in the centre gully opened as the tray and its contents tilted to slide into it. The table was now ready to receive more diners.

Bond rose and followed Holly to the door. With the movement towards the centre of the station the sensation of weightlessness became more marked. They turned down the gallery and were approaching the corridor to Satellite Two when Jaws appeared again. He was leaning forward and gazing moodily into the zero-gravity sphere that had contained the gymnasts. The expression on his face was almost wistful. He was positioned opposite the 'Electronic Camouflage Unit' sign.

Bond cursed to himself and led the way up a steel spiral staircase which gave on to another circular corridor with doorless rooms leading off it. He looked inside one and saw that it was a dormitory with beds arranged in twos, separated by curved partitions like the petals of a flower. A couple of astronauts were sleeping in one of the cubicles, their hands stretching out towards each other across the intersection, fingertips touching as they rested on the floor.

Bond looked round warily. 'We might as well hang on here until the coast is clear.' He entered the room and lay down on one of the beds. Holly followed more gingerly. 'It brings back memories, doesn't it?' said Bond. Holly smiled. She turned her back and drew up her knees in a

179

foetal position. There were no bedclothes, only a firm pillow. Bond rested his head on it and concentrated on staying awake. With his burns causing pain, this was not difficult.

Hardly had he stretched out when another couple came into the dormitory and entered the cubicle opposite with predatory eagerness. They kissed passionately and broke apart to scramble on to their individual beds. At once, the man stretched out his arm and lifted up the small table between the beds. As this hinged back against the wall the two beds moved together and the sides of the partition curved up from the floor to meet and form a screen that hid from prying eyes what was happening on the double bed. Bond could only see two forms interlocking behind the opaque material.

He was turning towards Holly for a reaction when Jaws appeared in the doorway. Bond quickly lifted his table and a startled Holly suddenly found his hand over her mouth as the partition panels closed above them. 'Jaws!' Bond whispered the word and Holly's sharp nails withdrew from the flesh on the back of his hand. She lay still, looking with Bond towards the end of the beds. A huge dark outline showed that Jaws was standing in the middle of the dormitory. For seconds he did not move and then, as there was a gasp of pleasure from the beds opposite, the shadow withdrew. Bond waited a few more moments and then kissed Holly tenderly behind the ear before lowering the table. Noiselessly, the partitions slid back to their original position. There was no sign of Jaws. Bond swung his feet off the bed and made for the corridor. It was empty. Holly appeared beside him and they made their way back down the spiral staircase and along the gallery. There were few people about at this level, and they entered the tunnel leading to Satellite Two without passing anyone. Bond approached the door marked 'Electric Camouflage Unit' and peered through a glass panel. In the centre of a circular room was a bank of electrical circuits looking like a telephone exchange. Two technicians in white tunics were visible, seated before consoles at the far side of the room. They were watching monitors on which horizontal zig-zag lines chased each other from left to right. Bond turned to Holly and tapped his clenched fist against his palm. She nodded.

The tap on the door was so light that the first technician did not hear it above the noise of the equipment. His companion nudged him and jerked a thumb over his shoulder. Again, there was a discreet tap. The first technician sighed and stood up. Then he sighed again. Why should he always be the one to answer doors? He looked at his colleague and wondered whether to make an issue of it. Still, he was standing up now and it was hardly worth the trouble. Next time, Wilson could answer the door. He crossed the room and looked through the porthole. A handsome girl in a pilot's uniform was standing outside. Her face looked vaguely familiar. The technician pressed the unlocking device and a buzzer sounded. Immediately the door swung open fast and the girl rushed past and headed for the consoles. The first technician turned to follow her. At that instant he heard another sound. He turned back, but too late. Bond's fist caught him flush on the side of the jaw and he staggered backwards, his knees buckling. Another blow found the same target and he crashed against the centre stack, unconscious before he hit the ground.

The second technician turned as Holly burst into the room. He started to rise to his feet and reached beside him for his laser torch. Holly swung her arm and a vicious karate chop sank into his stretched neck muscles. Crying out in pain and surprise, he swung a right hook. Holly swayed outside it and struck again with the side of her hand. This time there was no sound save that of the man

181

collapsing at her feet.

Bond looked down at the inert form with admiration. 'Where did you learn to fight like that? NASA?'

'No. Vassar.' Holly moved swiftly to the centre stack and began pulling out banks of wires. Bond dropped to his knees and started trussing up the technicians. Holly took the laser torch and directed it at the circuit system. The thin ray of murderous green light played on the metal and smoke quickly rose into the air. The radar jamming system was melting into a foul-smelling glutinous mass. 'Switched off?' said Bond.

'You could put it like that. Let's say: non-operational.'

'So now we can be seen from Earth?'

Holly nodded. 'That's right. Let's hope that somebody is watching.'

16

CAN YOU SEE ME MOTHER EARTH?

Above Gregor Sverdlov's head there was six feet of air, twelve feet of reinforced concrete and thirty feet of snow. At the Soviet army listening post in the Severnyy Anyuyskiy Khrebet the winters were long. Longer, it was said, than the intervals between the arrival of the samovars of lukewarm tea sweetened with the new state sweetener that left a taste of bitterness on the tongue akin to poison. It was rumoured that the aftertaste was due to a special ingredient added to eradicate anti-revolutionary sentiments, especially those that might be induced by contemplation of the vital parts of women. Gregor Sverdlov rubbed his hands together and looked round hopefully for sight of the creature, believed to be female, who brought the samovar. It was the tea that he was interested in, not the woman. To look upon her unwholesome appearance was merely to duplicate what the state was trying to achieve with its bromide. The woman not only discouraged amorous thoughts, she drove them before her like Gadarene swine eager to find any cliff to leap over.

It was cold in the bunker. Not as cold as outside, where the radio masts lifted above the pines and the snowy wastes reached to the frozen waters of the Chaunskaya Guba, but cold enough to pinch a man's bones as if an undertaker with icy fingers was counting them. Gregor Sverdlov stood up, swung his arms across his body and strolled down the room. Another hour before he was off duty, free to trudge through the banked snow to the log cabin he shared with eleven other radar operatives. The stove would be nearly out and the airless fug only marginally preferable to asphyxiation, but it would be warm. It was something to look forward to. Something more immediate than the day eighteen months hence when he was due to be released from the army.

Gregor Sverdlov turned as he reached the end of the long console and cast a bored eye along the row of monitors. Immediately he started forward. Something was wrong. He pushed buttons and twisted knobs. Something was still wrong. The satellite Kalinin was not due over for another twenty minutes. Why was he getting this signal? Surely he had not fallen asleep? The very thought of having committed a crime so heinous made him shiver with a fear that took over his body from the cold. But if he had not fallen asleep, how could he have avoided seeing this object enter his area? It could not suddenly appear in space. He operated the space tracker and the advance position spotter and waited nervously and impatiently whilst the machine churned and groaned over the information he had fed into it. Eventually there was the sound of mechanical spewing and a small print card entered his hand, covered in crisp perforations.

Almost running, he crossed the chamber and pressed it down on the reception plate of the space image recorder. He pushed it home and waited as a pale translucence illuminated the screen of the large monitor. Ten seconds later an image appeared. An image so startling and unexpected that Gregor Sverdlov's hand was still shaking as he pressed the button that would put him in immediate telephone contact with his regional controller.

The bare foot attempted to hook the slipper from beneath the bed, and then abandoned the project. The red light had started flashing on top of the telephone, which meant that the President was waiting to speak. General Scott, U.S.M.C. withdrew the one arm that he had managed to thrust into his dressing gown when the telephone first rang and nodded his head aggressively in time with the speaker on the other line. Eventually his moment came to break in.

'Listen, General Gogol. How many times do I have to tell you? We didn't put it there. We are as perplexed and disturbed as you are.'

A wave of static broke over his words and he leant forward to pull back the curtain beside the bed. A siren was screaming and a lorry load of U.S. Space Marines converging on a shuttle and rocket positioned in the middle of a launching pad. The area was lit by searchlights like the start of a Twentieth Century-Fox film.

'General Scott?' The rasping Russian voice re-materialized out of the ether.

'Yes, General Gogol. I'm still here.'

'In the circumstances I am certain that you will have no objection if we make our own investigation. The satellite Kalinin is on a similar orbit collecting meteorological information –'

'We know about the satellite,' said Scott, allowing a hint of sarcasm to enter his voice. 'I had no idea it was collecting meteorological information.'

'The details are perhaps immaterial at this time,' said Gogol coldly. 'I propose that we divert Kalinin to investigate this intruder.'

'Reports suggest that you have already done so,' said Scott.

There was a mounting roar from outside the window which told that the U.S. shuttle had achieved lift-off. 'In the circumstances, I think that we will send up a vehicle ourselves to examine the situation. You will of course have no objections?'

There was a slight pause and then Gogol's voice came back colder than ever. 'No. We will be in constant touch to review the situation. Goodnight, General Scott.'

'Goodnight, General Gogol.' Scott put down the telephone and promptly picked it up again. The President was on the line. 'Yes, sir ... A shuttle is on the way ... Yes, the Russians will get there first ... No, sir, I don't think they had anything to do with it. I think they're as much in the dark as we are ... Yes, sir. If there is any doubt we'll take the initiative ... destroy it.'

Gogol leant back against the pillow and his brows wrinkled in concentration. Were the Americans telling the truth or were they trying to provoke the first confrontation in space between the two great powers? The implications of such a course of action could be far-reaching and terrifying. Fortunately the satellite Kalinin was well able to defend herself. She must be prepared to bring her defensive capability to bear in an L.P.A. role. In Soviet army terminology L.P.A. stood for Liquidation of Potential Attacker.

The two Drax guards moved slowly along the corridor and glanced hopefully through the porthole into one of the zero-gravity spheres. All was darkness. Frustrated in their voyeuristic impulses, they advanced towards the Electronic Camouflage Unit. When they had gone, Bond and Holly emerged from a side corridor and moved to a window that looked out on space. Below them and protruding from the side of the central globe was the cylinder that had contained three nerve-gas spheres. With a sinking heart, Bond saw that it now contained only two. 'Now,' he said, 'we have a problem.'

'Yes.' Holly was not looking at Bond but over his shoulder. Her eyes were wide with fear. Bond spun round and saw Jaws looming above him like an angry bear. His arms were spread wide and his teeth bared like two rows of organ pipes. The huge hands clenched and Bond ducked and dived to one side. As Holly raised the laser torch that she had taken from one of the technicians, Jaws grabbed it and squeezed. The metal extruded from his fist like toothpaste. Jaws struck again and a metal guide rail was snapped off to fly across the floor. Bond threw himself on it and rose to lash out with a blow that struck Jaws on the side of the jaw. There was a loud *dong* and the metal buckled. Jaws smiled. He came forward again and Bond jabbed with cruel force for his crutch. Again there was a *dong*. Jaws's face registered distaste, like a vicar being told a crude joke. He still came forward. Bond spun round desperately. Before his nose was the threatening bulb of a laser gun; behind that a Drax guard with a determined expression on his face. Two other guards were covering him, each with a laser gun. Bond raised his hands in submission. 'All right,' he said. 'Take me to your leader.'

Drax moved away from the giant telescope and dusted his fingers together. It was a gesture he indulged in when savouring moments of satisfaction. To see a master plan approaching its execution produced a series of such moments.

'Sir –'

Drax turned to the technician who was speaking from one of the consoles. 'What is it?'

'The Russian satellite, sir. It appears to have changed course.'

'So?'

'If my calculations are correct, it is now on course to intercept us.'

The red of Drax's scar tissue flushed to crimson. 'That is not possible.' He corrected this complacency with his next order. 'Check the state of the radar jamming system.'

A second technician manipulated the switches of his console and then spoke in a puzzled voice. 'Jamming power supply and back-up are out, sir. We can be observed.'

Drax gritted his uneven teeth. 'Make a personal investigation of the situation immediately and report back to me. And bring the operatives.' The last four words were spoken in a voice of fire and brimstone. The technician left with two guards, and a monitor voice spoke from the roof of the chamber. 'We are on schedule for secondary launch position in T minus thirty seconds.'

Drax nodded vigorously as if anxious to convince himself that all was still well. 'Launch second nerve-gas globe as scheduled.'

He moved to the window and looked out at the tubular spout like the thorax of a giant insect. After a few seconds a globe detached itself and drifted away like an egg laid in space. The last of the three spheres moved forward into the launch position. Drax turned away. 'Prime next batch of nerve-gas spheres and load re-entry tube.'

The elevator hissed open and Bond and Holly emerged, dwarfed by the figure of Jaws. Drax looked upon them coldly. His lip curled.

'James Bond. You appear with the tedious inevitability of an unloved season.'

Bond's glance was no less unloving. 'I didn't think there were any seasons in space.'

Drax smiled a thin, cruel smile. 'As far as you are concerned, only winter.' He turned to Holly. 'And the treacherous Dr Goodhead. The word "welcome" freezes on my lips. How happy I am that despite all your plodding efforts my finely wrought dream approaches its fulfilment.'

'I very much doubt it,' said Bond. 'Your dream, whatever kind of twisted nightmare it is, doesn't have a chance of becoming a reality. You're not invisible any more. You're soon going to have a lot of very inquisitive visitors.'

'I will show you how we deal with uninvited guests, Mr Bond.' Drax bit off the words and turned to the technician who had given warning that the Kalinin was changing course. 'What news of the Russian satellite?'

'On course to intercept us. Range two hundred miles. Three minutes to interception.'

Drax's face set like a death mask. 'Activate laser and destroy it.'

'It's not going to make any difference,' said Bond. 'You can't hold out for ever.'

'On the contrary,' said Drax without emotion. 'Time is on my side. Soon there will be no one left on Earth to defy me.'

A disembodied voice came from the monitor. 'Target co-ordinates matched. Ready to fire.'

'Fire!' Drax did not hesitate.

The moment he spoke, a ruled line of green light became visible streaking from a position corresponding with a turret on top of the centre globe of the space station. At an indefinable distance in space a brilliant splash of flame burst across the star field before disappearing as suddenly as it had appeared.

Drax turned to Bond with a smile of understated triumph. 'You see, Mr Bond, we are well able to take care of ourselves. Something which only a liar or a deranged optimist could say about you in your present situation.'

Again the monitored voice spoke from the roof. 'On schedule for tertiary launch position in T minus thirty seconds.'

'Proceed with launch.' Drax spoke calmly and moved to Bond's side. 'Perhaps you would like to watch, Mr Bond. Not every man has the opportunity to be present at the creation of a new world.'

'It's a refrain I've heard before,' said Bond.

'But never played on such a finely tuned instrument.' Drax waved his arms about him. 'Come, Mr Bond. Do not grudge me your admiration. Surely, even with English understatement, you would describe me as a genius?'

'With English understatement I would describe you as a blackguard,' said Bond. He advanced to the long window and looked down upon the spout of the launch tube loaded with the final sphere of the first batch of nerve-gas. As he watched, it was discharged into space and quickly drifted away, to disappear against a glowing pin cushion of stars.

Drax's voice purred out of the shadows. 'No doubt you have already divined the splendour of my conception. First, a necklace of death around Earth. Each of those spheres is capable of killing one hundred million people. I am releasing fifty of them at pre-programmed intervals. The human race, as we have had the misfortune to know it, will cease to exist. Then will come a renaissance, a rebirth, a new world.'

'Why?' asked Bond. 'Forgive me asking, but the question does spring to mind.'

Drax's brow contracted into an unforgiving frown. 'The reason is one that any man of normal intelligence and powers of observation should be able to grasp in seconds. It concerns population, Mr Bond. You are no doubt aware that the population of the world has increased from a figure beneath 2,300 millions in 1940 to over 4,000 millions at the present time. Have you any idea what the demographers prognosticate for the year 2070? A world population of 25,000 million! Does that figure not horrify you? A world crawling like a barrel of maggots and its population dying like flies. Pestilence, starvation, war. How can we hope to feed all those people, Mr Bond? By that time we shall have irrevocably poisoned our last remaining unexploited source of food, the oceans. There will be nothing left. Only one tried method exists for man to control his numbers: war. And what happens when there is war? Destruction. Not only of human life but of the one thing that still makes man's existence worthwhile: art. Books, paintings, buildings, the finest legacies of countless civilizations, all that can enrich the human spirit, will be lost as man's capacity for self-destruction exceeds his ability to control it. I revere this artistic heritage too much to allow it to be destroyed. I could turn my back and form my own civilization in space, but I believe that this would be to renege upon my responsibilities. I will not abandon Earth, I will save it! Our current civilization, if I can use such an implicitly laudatory term for it, will surely destroy itself. By accelerating the process I can protect those priceless monuments of history that it would demolish at the same time. I can give the Earth time to replenish its plundered resources, the sea will become pure, the air breathable again. I do not exaggerate, Mr Bond. Our own scientists have told us that within twenty years the trashy waste materials with which we pollute the atmosphere will have depleted the ozone layer around Earth dangerously. Skin cancer will increase alarmingly and the weather become more unpredictable. Droughts, floods, typhoons, holocausts. The precursors of the inevitable end. The slow, maimed, painful, purposeless end. Can you not see the irrefutable wisdom of what I am in the process of doing, Mr Bond? Without any racial discrimination I have selected the finest specimens, combining both mental and physical excellence. It is they and their offspring who will colonize the new Earth when the nerve gas has done its work and time has been left for nature to take her course. A new civilization can be built upon the framework of all that was best in several million years of human existence.'

'And the knowledge that it was born from the greatest act of mass murder in history.' Bond's tone was cold and contemptuous.

Drax shook his head sadly. 'It is always a mistake to bandy words with fools. I will not repeat it.'

He was turning towards Jaws when the observer spoke

urgently from his console. 'Unidentified craft closing distance fast. Recognition signals indicate U.S. space shuttle.'

'Laser it!' Drax spat out the words and turned back to Bond and Holly. His face was blotchy and glistening. A maverick tick invaded his misshapen eye. 'It occurs to me that your view of the demise of our last visitor was limited. I think you should be nearer to the next spectacle.' He smiled obscenely. 'Much nearer.'

Now the pinpoints of red in the mad eyes were growing larger. Bond followed Drax's gaze to the circular door set in the outer wall of the globe. With a new surge of fear he realized what was in Drax's mad, bad mind.

'Jaws . . . the airlock chamber.' Drax turned back to Bond and Holly. 'Observe, Mr Bond, your route from this world to the next. At least you will not be travelling alone. It appears that you will have some American companions. Doubly pleasing for you, Dr Goodhead. Your compatriots will be able to see you achieve your ambition to be America's first woman in space.'

Jaws moved forward with grim relish and depressed the metal lever on the door. It opened with a hiss to reveal a small compartment in which two men might stand crouched. What was clearly the outer hatch to space had a transparent window which was a twin of that in the first door.

Drax addressed his guards. 'Take them!'

Two men stepped forward, their laser torches trained on Bond and Holly. Bond shrugged and started to move across the platform. Within a few paces of the airlock chamber was an unmanned console. Prominent across its top were the words 'Rotation Thrusters – Artificial Gravity'. Bond's pulse quickened as he remembered Holly's words when they had been docking: 'We'd all be floating around like balloons if we went outside. Once the rotation thrusters are turned on, the station will start to rotate and we'll have artificial gravity.' And if counter-rotation thrusters were turned *off*? Bond glanced again and saw a handle recessed behind a transparent cover. On the cover were printed the words 'Emergency Stop. Do not use unless station secured'. If he could just get to that handle there might still be a chance. Even as he thought, the hard knob of the laser torch jabbed him forward.

'Enemy craft in range. Am matching co-ordinates.' The cold, impassive voice of the laser gunner echoed down from the empty air. It was all happening at once. Bond's destruction was as imminent as that of the investigating American shuttle. At any second the next batch of nerve gas spheres would start rolling out into space. Already three hundred million victims waited unknowingly for the death that would be their fate when the spheres entered the Earth's atmosphere and dispensed their deadly poison. Bond knew that he must do something – but what? The laser torch was still thrust into his back. He would die instantly if he made a dive for the rotation thrusters. Jaws showed his teeth in an uninviting grin. Behind him stood one of the astronauts Bond could remember being trained in California. Slim, handsome, an expression of detached superiority on his face. He looked like a monitor in an English public school watching a fourth former being led out for a thrashing. Bond looked back to Jaws. The lumpen features, the misshapen body, the totality that was so obviously an accident of nature. He turned and fixed Drax with his eye. 'Are Dr Goodhead and myself the only people being ejected into space?'

Drax's eyes narrowed. 'Of course, Mr Bond. Why do you ask such a facile question?'

'I was trying to come to terms with the rules of eligibility for this flying stud farm. You wouldn't disagree that only those who conform to your own physical and mental standards will survive?' Bond stared pointedly at Jaws.

Drax saw the look and hesitated before replying. 'You are attempting to raise emotive questions which are irrelevant. Jaws – expel them.'

Jaws's hand left the handle of the door to the airlock chamber. He took a step towards Bond. The guards closed in.

'Co-ordinates matched. Count-down to fire T minus sixty seconds.' The laser gunner's voice spurred the words from Bond's throat. He looked deep into Jaws's eyes. 'The questions aren't irrelevant to you are they, Jaws? How long do you think you're going to be allowed to survive us? Have you looked about you, Jaws? You don't conform, and that's fatal in this society.' Jaws hesitated and looked towards Drax. His face wore the expression that it had when he looked into the zero-gravity globe.

'Expel them!' Drax shouted the words and there was an edge of panic in his voice. It revealed itself in the sudden emergence of the Prussian accent. Bond gestured towards the open maw of the vacuum chamber. 'Come on, Jaws. There's room for all of us if we squeeze.'

'Expel them!' Drax took a step forward as the guards closed in. The laser gunner started his final count-down. Bond braced himself as Jaws's hands slowly rose. Then they clamped down on the two guards and crashed their heads together. Bond snatched up a laser torch and dived for the rotation thrusters. To a background of screams and shouts he tore open the transparent cover and hauled at the handle marked 'Emergency Stop'.

17

TAKE THE WEIGHT OFF YOUR FEET

Immediately Bond felt as if he was in a vehicle that had crashed into a brick wall. The handle tore itself from his grasp and he smashed against an unidentifiable object with a force that threatened to break both shoulder and collar bone. He slid across the floor and arrived against the wall of the globe. Around him was every article of furniture that had not been anchored to the floor, and most of the people in the chamber. The lights flickered madly and the air was full of the screams of men crying out in pain and terror. Bond tried to struggle to his feet and felt himself at the mercy of total weightlessness. Something bumped into him and he pushed it away to feel a sticky substance on his hand. It was blood. Blood from one of the Drax guards that Jaws had dealt with. The side of his head was smashed in like an empty eggshell. Bond shook free of the dead embrace and looked out of a window into space.

Keeping pace with the space station, a hundred feet from it, was a U.S. shuttle, the white star plainly visible on the fuselage. From an open hatch a stream of space marines poured out as if making an inverted parachute drop. Bond's heart exalted as he saw the white space suits, helmets and back-packs with built-in oxygen supplies and hand-operated propulsion units. Like a skein of geese the marines converged on the space station.

Bond turned away from the window as a streak of bright laser light passed above his shoulder. There was no sight of Drax, and Holly had also disappeared. The main action concentrated around Jaws who was manoeuvring an unanchored console like a battering ram. As Bond watched, he took advantage of the zero-gravity to force three Draxites back against the outer wall and press the life out of them as if they were the last half inch of a tube of toothpaste. Bond clawed his way with difficulty to a position near the lift column and aimed his laser torch at a Draxite who was drawing a bead on Jaws. The light snaked across the room and a thin spurt of flame sprouted from the man's neck. His arms spread out and he hung in space as if taking part in a levitation experiment. Bond twisted his head and looked out of the nearest observation slot.

Like fierce rain against a window pane, the rays of confronting laser guns criss-crossed the void. A stream of Draxites had emerged to give battle in space, and as Bond watched a space marine was hit in the chest. His suit momentarily swelled and then, as if fired from a catapult, he shot backwards, accelerating into infinity. Bond shuddered. What a death. For those who were disabled and drifted away the end was even more horrible. They would travel through space until their oxygen ran out and they slowly died. Without enough oxygen a man would suffocate and his space suit would become a tomb perpetually orbiting Earth. Burial in the sky. How many tin cans were there in space rattling with skeletons?

A bright light flared momentarily and Bond saw that one of the moored Moonrakers had been attacked and was aligned at the side of its satellite. Some of the Draxites were operating one-man globular space carts with laser guns mounted in the nose gun. They seemed to possess a defensive shield that made them less vulnerable to attack. Despite the opposition, the space marines were pressing in against the side of the space station like swarming bees. Bond knew that he had to help them get in; also to stop any more spheres of nerve gas being released. Picking his way through the floating débris he made for the exit tunnel which he estimated would lead him to the interior of the globe-launching tube. The other side of the chamber Jaws was still fighting for survival. And still winning. A Draxite who had strayed within reach of his great hands sailed across the chamber to fold against the elevator shaft like a rag doll that had lost most of its stuffing.

Bond pulled himself along a lopsided corridor, using the guard rail, and came face to face with a door marked 'Nerve Gas Launch Assembly'. The door was of steel, and Bond hesitated. Supposing some of the nerve gas phials had been thrown across the room and had smashed when he pulled the Emergency Stop handle? To open the door would be to step into certain death. So was he going to turn his back and crawl away? Bond took what he knew might be his last deep breath and turned the handle of the door. He pressed and waited, his nerves jangling. No deadly gas rushed to his lungs. Neither did the door open easily. The reason was soon apparent. A body was wedged against the other side, beneath a collapsed row of metal shelves. Bond squeezed inside the door and found that he was alone with a corpse and two badly wounded men in light green tunics. They had obviously been hurled against the side of the space station when it went into zero-gravity. Three nerve gas spheres were lined up in a metal cradle that led out to the launch tube. The launch tube was empty. This must be the second batch of spheres ready for launching. It was not conceivable that another batch had been released after the handle had been pulled.

Wielding his laser torch with extreme care, Bond directed the beam on the machinery that operated the launch mechanism. Within seconds it was knotting into molten worm casts. If Drax wanted to launch any more spheres he would have to manhandle them to the nearest airlock chamber. Bond finished destroying the launching apparatus and looked round the wrecked room. A conveyor belt of globes ran round the walls and disappeared through a hole to what was presumably another chamber where they were stored. Bond hesitated and then decided against tampering with the globes. The risk of accidentally releasing the gas was too great. The moment to sacrifice his own life might not be too far off, but it had not yet arrived with certainty.

Outside in space the battle still raged and the Draxites were fighting desperately to beat off the marines gathered against the side of the central globe. A space cart moved in on them and was caught in the crossfire of two laser beams. Its own fire was extinguished and it began to melt like a moth trapped in a lamp.

Bond looked up to the top of the globe. What he saw made him draw in his breath sharply. The scene of carnage that prevailed in the Nerve Gas Launch Assembly room was not duplicated in the turret that housed the laser gun. There he could see figures moving and the long barrel of the gun being brought to bear on the U.S. space shuttle, which was still keeping pace with the station's drift through space. Would the pilot of the shuttle be aware of what had happened to the Russian satellite? Almost certainly the position of the satellite would have been plotted and its sudden disappearance commented upon. No doubt this was the reason why the Americans had come straight in to the attack. They had treated the disappearance of the Russian craft as evidence of a hostile presence in space and not risked pausing to make a challenge.

Bond could almost hear the seconds ticking away. At any moment the laser gun turret might open fire and obliterate the shuttle. He must do something. But to reach the turret would be a labour of Hercules. The largest contingents of Drax's men would be gathered near the dormitories, which were directly below the turret. With the space station lopsided and in a state of zero-gravity he would have to fight his way, weightless, through a confused warren of passages dominated by those of Drax's men who were still in a condition to give battle. For support he could rely only on Jaws and Holly – if they were alive and if he could join up with them. He peered out of the window and another possibility entered his mind. All his plans were based on the premise that he should attack the turret from inside the station. But if he were to approach it via space ...

Bond prized open the door and clawed his way back down the corridor. He recalled passing an airlock chamber. Through the transparent viewing panel he had glimpsed that it contained two space suits. If they were equipped with propulsion units he might be able to let himself out of the airlock and manoeuvre his way to the turret. He pulled himself along the corridor again, knowing that he was battling against time. Ahead, three Draxites moved clumsily across an intersection. They looked towards him but took no action. They were concentrating on the threat from outside. Bond found the airlock chamber and pulled down the lever. The inner door swung open and he seized one of the space suits and started to pull it on. It was a cumbersome thing to wield at the best of times but in a weightless situation and with time running out, the effort frayed nerves and fingers. Eventually it was on and he secured the helmet and turned on the oxygen supply. Now he could breathe in space; but could he move through it? Bond contracted his gauntleted hands and felt his power supply convert to forward thrust. In principle this should propel him through space like a human jet aeroplane. In principle. Bond had never tried it in practice. Already he was sweating, and not only because of the space suit. He twisted uncomfortably and looked up towards the laser turret. The gun was traversing. He turned and looked for the shuttle. There was no sign of it. For a moment his heart stopped. Then he realized what must have happened. Either by accident or design, the shuttle had dropped back to a position behind one of the satellites that projected from the main globe. The laser gunner dared not fire for fear that he would destroy his own space station.

Feeling no other sensation beyond numbing fear, Bond closed the inner door behind him and was now entombed in the claustrophobic cubby hole that was the vacuum chamber. No Edgar Allan Poe story he had read as a child had adequately conveyed the sense of mouth-drying terror that now engulfed him. Instant death would almost have seemed a better choice than the one he was making. He forced movement into his paralysed right hand and felt the lever that secured the outer door begin to descend. With a speed that took him by surprise, it slid down and he toppled into space. A quick start of alarm was followed by surprise. There was no sensation of falling, of wind battering against the body, no slipstream to be drawn into. All that was happening was that the space station was drifting away like a ship silently gliding away from a man who has fallen overboard. Bond again had the sensation that he was in a dream; that no matter what he did, no matter how far he opened his mouth to scream, nothing was going to happen. But in a dream there was always that faint link with reality. Something at the back of your mind told you that this *was* a dream, that you *were* going to wake up. But here that link was missing. There was no thread to bind him to the globular insect drifting away like the dried-out husk of a great spider.

Bond came to his senses as panic engulfed him. He must use his propulsion unit! If he did nothing he would be left in an orbit of his own. Bond squeezed his hands and immediately felt a pressure behind him as if someone had given him a shove in the small of the back. The distance to the space station began to close. Relief was quickly counterbalanced by a new fear as a laser ray passed dangerously close. An American space marine had fired at him, thinking that he was a Draxite. Bond pulled out his laser torch and accelerated until he was against the outside wall of the corridor from which he had emerged. He turned anxiously and saw that his attacker was engaging a globular space cart that had appeared from behind one of the satellites. As battle was joined, Bond located the gun turret and started to move along the corridor towards the central globe. To take a short cut was to become involved in the main area of the space battle, and he did not want to risk a confrontation with an American space marine. Neither did he want the laser gunner to see him approaching. There was also a powerful fear of losing tactile contact with the space station. Bond had not forgotten his first terrifying impression of what it must be like to be marooned in space. He hovered close to the corridor and pressed on towards the central globe.

Suddenly he found that he was drifting away into space. He changed direction by pressing with his left hand, but the tubular arm of the corridor seemed to move even farther away. Bond fought mounting panic. What was happening? Had something gone wrong with his power control unit? Then realization dawned on him. Somebody had switched on the rotation thrusters. The space station was starting to revolve. The revelation electrocuted Bond as if he had touched a high tension cable. He turned his head and saw a second satellite corridor swinging towards him like a mace. He hesitated, then powered himself away from its path. It swept beneath him and he glimpsed men running down a corridor.

Now he was almost at the central globe, and he accelerated forward and tried to find something to cling to. The moving surface brushed him aside and he spun backwards to collide with the curved surface of a corridor arm as it built up speed. The force of impact glued him to its side and he was borne forward as if flattened against the spoke of a revolving wheel. Stretching out an arm, he found a perforated metal seam that followed the line of the corridor, and clung to it. Thank God he was near the centre of the station. Facing him across the void, he saw an American space marine trying to cling to a corridor arm from a position nearer to a satellite. Helpless against the build-up of centrifugal force, the unhappy man started to slide down towards the satellite and was then tossed into space like a screw of paper dropped on the edge of a spinning disc. Bond watched the man disappear into space and felt sick. Sick with pain, pity and – above all – fear.

18

A DREAM DIES SCREAMING

Bond blinked against the sweat that was soaking down through his eyebrows and twisted his head to look up at the laser turret just visible above the curve of the globe. The U.S. shuttle was now at its mercy. Bond looked along the metal seam he was clinging to and saw that it joined the central globe. Another protruding lip rose towards the turret.

Stretching out an arm, Bond gritted his teeth and performed the first painful movement towards achieving his goal. In what seemed an agonizingly long period of time, he had pulled himself to the central globe and made the perilous transfer to the vertical seam. Now he felt as if there was a pile of sandbags on his back pressing him against the surface. Each foot of progress had to be fought for at the cost of his fading strength. With ten feet to go to the turret, he saw the gun barrel being brought to bear again. He felt that he could almost reach out and touch it. The turret lunged out of the dome and he could see the portholes and the rectangular outline of a hatch in its side. Bond hauled himself along the seam and prayed that he would get there in time and that the small red square at the bottom right-hand corner of the hatch was what he thought it was. Five feet, four feet, three feet ... A face pressed against one of the portholes would have seen him clearly. He craned forward and saw the steel handle in its recessed cavity. Above it were the words 'DANGER! External Hatch Opening. Only to be used when station secured in N.P. situation'.

Tightening his grip with his left hand, Bond snaked out his arm and forced his fingers into the recess. They closed about the handle and he braced himself and pulled. Nothing happened. The handle merely flinched. Bond's heart sank. He had nearly exhausted his physical resources. At any moment the laser gun might open up. Hanging on in space, he was only going to make himself weaker. He ground his teeth together and strained again until his sinews shrieked. The handle lifted a quarter of an inch but no more. Exhausted, Bond clung to the surface of the globe and felt his laser torch pressing into his chest. Maybe that was the answer; if not the answer, the only hope. He withdrew the torch and directed it into the aperture, avoiding the handle. Two quick flashes and the metal glowed a dull red. Bond fumbled for the handle and in his hurry let slip the torch. He snatched at it clumsily and it brushed against his fingertips before drifting away, gathering speed fast. Bond knew that he was now irrevocably alone. If the hatch did not open he had no chance. He inserted his hand again and felt the sweat clinging to his body. His heart was wedged at the bottom of his throat. Summoning up his last reserves of energy he tore at the handle. Slowly it began to respond. 'Come on! Come on, damn you –' There was a loud *pop* like a champagne cork being withdrawn clumsily, and the hatch slid sideways with Bond still clinging to it.

As if they had been leaning against the hatch, three men were sucked through the door with a chaos of equipment that represented everything not battened to the floor of the gun turret. The men hung before Bond's eyes for a moment as if making a free-fall parachute drop and then were snatched from sight, disappearing fast into space. Bond swallowed, and clawed his way back round the hatch to the opening. He hauled himself up on the floor and slowly rose to a kneeling position. His breath was coming almost faster than the oxygen unit could cope with, and he paused before stealing out an arm and pulling the hatch shut. Now for the first time he really believed that he had succeeded.

The gun crew had been expelled into space; the immediate danger to the U.S. shuttle was over. He rested on his knees for a few moments and then drew himself up to stumble past the laser gunner's console and down the short flight of steps that led to a steel door. Bracing himself, he activated the opening mechanism and found himself emerging in a circular gallery which he guessed must be situated on the far side of the station from the dormitories. He closed the door behind him and immediately responded to the conditions of re-entry into artificial gravity. Now he could move normally, if clumsily. He tore off his helmet and moved towards the sounds of battle that were coming from below. From what he could hear, it seemed that the U.S. space marines had broken into the station. If they could wipe out the Draxites quickly there might still be a chance of catching up with the three nerve gas globes before they entered the Earth's atmosphere. There were so many events falling one on top of the other that it was difficult to select an order of priorities. Where were Holly and Jaws? Were they still alive?

Bond descended a spiral staircase and emerged into a long corridor that led to one of the satellites. There was a smell of burning and the lights flickered madly. Bond guessed that the space station was out of control. It only needed a severe breach in the outside wall and they would all suffer the fate of the gun turret crew. Space would suck them out like bone marrow.

Bond moved towards one of the satellites. Seen from this vantage point, he could get a clearer picture of what was happening to the central globe. He had taken ten paces when a figure emerged furtively from an intersection. It was large and it belonged to Drax. He turned and saw Bond. For a moment the two men faced each other, and then Drax read the look in Bond's eyes and took a step backwards. Bond said nothing but followed. Drax's hands stood away from his body, but there was nothing in them. His face was drawn. Hatred had been replaced by fear. Bond was looking at a different man from the one who had wanted to be God. The lights flickered again and there was a distant roar like thunder. The fabric of the corridor creaked ominously. It was almost as if some earthly storm was penetrating space. Intimations of the rewards for hubris. Drax took another step back. Behind him was an air-lock chamber and beside the entrance a Draxite and two U.S. space marines who had also died in the fighting. Bond stiffened as he saw what lay at the dead Draxite's fingertips. A laser torch. He paused and, as if alerted by the gesture, Drax glanced behind him. With a speed that belied his size he bent down and scooped up the laser torch. Now his expression changed. A blotchy red suffused his plastic cheeks. His distorted eyes leered triumphantly. 'At least I will have the pleasure of putting you out of my misery.' He began to raise the laser torch and his words were charged with cruel mockery.

'Desolated, Mr Bond.'

Bond began to raise his hands as if in a gesture of abject submission. Then with a sharp crack a vent appeared in his gauntlet. Drax clutched at the left-hand side of his chest. A dart protruded from between his fingers.

'Heartbroken, Mr Drax.' Bond's words were no less of a jibe. He stepped forward and depressed the lever of the inner door of the air-lock chamber as Drax's faltering fingers brushed against it. The laser gun had already dropped to the floor. 'Allow me.' Bond threw the door open with old-world courtesy and Drax staggered back to rest against the door that led into space. He looked from Bond to his chest as if unable to believe what had happened. 'Cyanide,' said Bond shortly. 'A new world starts in thirty seconds.' He started to close the inner door as Drax's hand rose to stave off the inevitable. Bond slammed the door ruthlessly and moved his hand to the lever marked 'Space

Door Release'. Without pausing, he depressed it. Glimpsed through the porthole, Drax's mouth was open wide, but he uttered no sound. His cheeks hollowed and his skin suddenly shrank on his body as if the core had been taken out of him. His eyes vanished and he hung in the air like a great, hulking scarecrow snatched up by the wind. Then he was drawn away by invisible strings, becoming smaller and smaller until he was no larger than the distant stars he had set out to emulate. Bond turned quickly as running footsteps brought Holly to his side. She clung to his arm. 'Thank God! What's happening? Where's Drax?'

Bond showed his back to the porthole. 'He had to fly.' There was another eerie sound of metal under strain. 'Come on. So have we.' He started to move back towards the central globe when a U.S. space marine appeared in the doorway. He saw Bond and raised his laser gun.

'No!' Holly threw herself forward.

'Dr Goodhead!' The man hesitated as a sergeant appeared behind him.

'Jesus Christ!' He looked at Holly and craned forward in disbelief. 'You're from NASA.'

Bond lunged forward to address the sergeant. 'I'm with her. What's the situation in the Command Centre?'

'We're in control but the station is breaking up. We're dropping into atmosphere.'

Bond staggered back as a violent explosion shook the corridor. Looking across to the next corridor arm he saw the metal begin to twist and the whole structure start to break away from the central globe. Like something in a slow motion film the satellite began to swing round towards them. The corridor ruptured and there was an ear-splitting scraping noise as metal ground against the top of the buckling corridor they were standing in. The huge mass of the severed satellite shut out their view of space and then scraped clear and spun clumsily into the darkness.

'Get the hell out of here! Back to the shuttle!'

An officer lurched past, shouting at the top of his voice. The sergeant looked as if he had no desire to hang around. 'Are you coming? We're docked on one of the satellites – if it's still there.'

Bond looked around him desperately and turned to Holly. 'There's still those three nerve gas globes. We can't just leave them.'

'What can we do?' Her voice was a shout. The corridor was beginning to bend. The sergeant had disappeared.

'There must be some way we can destroy them before they get into the Earth's atmosphere.'

'James! Look!' Holly grabbed his arm and pointed out of the window towards the command satellite. Moored against it was a Moonraker with a figure 5 on its side.

'Drax's shuttle.'

'It's armed with a laser gun. He showed it off to me after I was captured.'

'You think we could use it against those nerve gas globes?'

'What other choice do we have?'

As if to provide an answer, the corridor arm groaned under stress and all the lights went out. Bond started to run towards the satellite. There was a cracking noise and for a second he thought that the whole station was breaking up. Out in space a shape loomed from behind the central globe, and he saw that it was the U.S. shuttle. At least somebody was going to be saved. Bond threw his shoulder against the door leading into the satellite and prayed that the closure round the air-lock chamber of the Moonraker had not broached. After two steps into the chamber he could still stand on his feet and breathe air. The thin barrel of the laser gun emerged from the nose of the shuttle. Bond pulled back the hatch to the control chamber and dived across the seats. Holly scrambled in beside him and reached for a safety strap. There was a violent upheaval and Bond's head hit the cabin roof. The satellite lurched as if it had struck something. Bond knew that at any second the whole corridor arm was going to break off. If they did not get away immediately they would join it spiralling crazily into space. Holly jabbed at a switch and then jabbed again. Lines of tension cut deep into her face.

'What's the matter?'

'It's the docking system. I can't disengage it. It must be jammed.'

Bond swore and activated the exit hatch on his side of the cabin. As it slid back he jumped out and moved to the access hatch of the Moonraker. The whole binding rod assembly had been jerked sideways and was now buckled in its setting so that the thick metal pincers would not open. They stuttered feebly like the mouth of a dying fish. Bond dropped to his knees and tried to pull them apart. A second's effort told him that he was wasting his time. Behind him there was a sharp crack like an ice floe beginning to break up. Bond's forehead was lathered with sweat. Fear ran through him like a fast-moving current. He turned to see if there was anything he could use as a lever. Almost opposite the nose of the Moonraker was a turn-table launching ramp bearing one of the globular space carts. Bond turned again and found himself face to face with Jaws. There was a trickle of blood running down from the corner of his mouth and his clothes were torn. His eyes were those of a wild animal caught in a car's headlights.

Bond waited for the man to act. Was it going to be life or death? Jaws looked at Bond and then down to the binding rods. Without a gesture, he lumbered forward and sank to his knees. His huge hands closed on the metal bars and he pulled until the veins stood out on his forehead like pencils. One two-inch bar rose from its setting and Jaws dropped his head and closed his blood-stained teeth about it. There was a harsh grating noise and Bond saw the steel teeth slowly bite through the metal. It snapped, and at that instant the satellite dropped ten feet. Bond was thrown backwards. He rose to find that although one of the binding rods was free, the fall had caused the air-lock securing assembly to wedge deeper into its housing. Jaws tore at it with his hands but could not separate the Gordian knot of twisted metal. Bond joined him but their combined efforts quickly proved that the task was beyond human strength. Jaws rose, breathing heavily, and pressed his hands against the structure of the Moonraker. He pushed and looked to see what was happening to the metal housing. There was a faint upward movement. Jaws looked round the satellite. The cracking sound was now continuous, as if a crevasse was opening up. Jaws pointed to himself and gestured towards the space cart. Then he pushed Bond towards the door of the Moonraker. Bond hesitated but Jaws was already pulling open the hatch of the space cart. Bond pulled himself into the Moonraker beside Holly. She turned to him anxiously.

'What's happening?'

'I don't really know. I think he's going to try and push us out.'

Holly gave the disengage switch one more abortive flick and sat back in her seat. 'Jesus!'

Bond said nothing. Jaws was now inside the space cart, looking like a goldfish that had outgrown its bowl. As the craft started to tremble, another figure appeared in the satellite. A pretty girl in astronaut's uniform. She ran forward and beat on the side of the space cart. Jaws slid open the hatch and she scrambled in. Now there was a noise like a ship beginning to founder and Bond could feel the tail of the Moonraker tilting upwards. The satellite was beginning to break away; but the nose of the shuttle still held securely. It would be dragged down to inevitable destruction. Holly was manipulating the controls like an organ console. The space cart started down the ramp as if fired from a gun, and there was a crash that jarred Bond sideways and then back in his seat. He glimpsed Jaws's face pressed against the screen of the space cart and then felt the whole structure of the Moonraker jerk sideways. Suddenly the satellite dropped away and he was looking across the infinity of space towards a million stars. Beside him Holly whooped her delight.

'We're clear! We're clear!'

Bond looked to his right and saw the central globe of the space station folding in on itself like a deflated football. Somewhere in its heart flames erupted and were rapidly snuffed. The remaining satellites were breaking away, carrying their buckled corridors with them. As they fell through space to enter the Earth's atmosphere they began to glow red. One disintegrated in a meteor shower. Bond twisted his head and searched for the satellite they had just left. Had it carried Jaws and the girl to their deaths?

Holly manoeuvred the control lever and tapped Bond on the shoulder. 'Over there.'

Bond turned and saw that Holly had brought them round on a course almost parallel to that of a space cart with a large dent in its nose and its laser gun twisted up against the cabin window like a windscreen wiper. Behind the window was Jaws, an expression of dogged concentration on his face as he grappled with the controls. The pretty girl looked over his shoulder.

Holly shook her head ruefully. 'I don't know if that craft is capable of re-entry.'

Bond smiled. 'Jaws is capable of re-entering anything. How far is it to Earth?'

'About a hundred miles.'

'He'll be home before we are.' His face suddenly became grim. 'If there's anything to come home to.'

Holly said nothing but flicked on the radarscope. She knew what Bond was talking about. Out in space there were still three nerve gas spheres. Unless they were found and destroyed before they re-entered the Earth's atmosphere, three hundred million people would die, which could spark off an atomic war that would destroy the rest of humanity. Her desperate eyes searched the screen. It was blank.

19

DESTROY TO LIVE

Bond looked anxiously at the concentric circles on the radarscope. They moved as innocently and treacherously as the ripples left by a drowning man.

'How do we know they haven't already re-entered?'

'We don't.' Holly pummelled the controls and the Moonraker hurled itself through space.

'Look!'

'That's them.' Holly glanced knowingly at the three pinpoints on the screen. The one nearest the centre of the circles pulsed the most dynamically. 'We should make visual contact in a few seconds.'

'You mean, I should be able to see something,' said Bond. 'Why the hell don't you speak English?' He looked down at the ranging screen of the laser gun. 'And how do you fire this thing?'

'Very accurately if you want to save our lives.' Holly took her eyes off the controls to glance out of the forward window. 'Have you ever been to a fairground? Two red images will appear on that screen. They represent us and the individual nerve gas globes. Manipulate the two knobs until the circles overlap. They will then turn into one green circle. That means you are on target. Then press the fire button. I'll switch you on to automatic and programme through the positions of the spheres.' She spoke urgently but without any edge of panic. Bond, who loved order and calm in a woman, loved her at that moment. He looked ahead and saw something glinting in space.

'Here you are.'

Bond looked down at the ranging screen and saw that

two red circles had indeed appeared. Their movement was reassuringly slow. A quick correction of the right-hand knob and one circle drifted into the path of the other. Red turned to green and Bond pressed the buttons embedded in the centre of each control knob. A flash of blinding white light knifed out from the nose of the Moonraker and the green circle disappeared. The screen was empty. Bond looked ahead. Whatever had been glinting was not there any more.

'A sitting bird,' said Bond.

Holly did not turn her head to bestow congratulations. 'They'll begin to flap their wings in a minute.' As if to prove her words, the Moonraker began to shake violently. 'We're skipping on the Earth's atmosphere.'

Bond knew what that meant. Very much lower and they would start to burn up like the space station. Their angle of descent was totally wrong for re-entry. He glanced at the ranging screen. Two more red circles had appeared. They were dancing like ping pong balls on the surface of a saucepan of boiling water. He began to aim urgently. The red circles crossed momentarily and then swam away again. The green image had held for a fraction of a second. Bond wiped the sweat from his eyes and concentrated again. Around him the atmosphere was becoming unbearably hot.

Holly was staring out of the forward window, her lips pressed tight. 'We're in range.'

'I know that, dammit!' Bond's fingers tensed against the two range finders. Another violent shudder ran through the Moonraker. Suddenly the shaking eased. He twisted the knobs violently. Sweat dropped on the screen. 'Come on, my beauties!' It was like some game found in a Christmas stocking. Only on its result depended the lives of one hundred million people. Two red arcs crossed each other and the area of intersection widened towards the formation of one complete circle. Bond held his breath. If his heart was beating, he could not feel it. Red on red became green and his fingers thrust against the steel nipples. The snake's tongue of light scythed through the air. The screen went blank.

'How am I doing?'

'You're winning.' Holly's voice was tense. She looked at the control panel and bit her lip. Her face was glistening with sweat. Bond touched the side of the cabin wall and cried out. They were being roasted as if in an oven. He moved his feet to rest them on his heels. The ranging screen was empty.

'Pass me the next one.'

'I have.'

The ranging screen was still empty. On the radarscope only the faintest pinpoint could be seen. The Moonraker was bouncing like a ball rolling down a corrugated iron roof. A frightening brown tint was spreading through the perspex of the forward window. He could smell something burning. Soon it would be him.

'Where the hell is it?' Bond followed Holly's eyes to the control panel. On the upper right-hand side three separate needles were showing against the 'Danger' mark. Red lights were flashing all over the console. Everything was showing red except the ranging screen.

Holly spoke grimly. 'We've got another 50,000 feet. If we don't catch up with it by then, we'll burn out.'

Bond looked at the altimeter: 250,000 feet, 240,000 feet. They were dropping at an angle that was suicidal for re-entry. But they had no alternative. It was either that or leave a hundred million people to die.

'There it is!' Two red circles started to dance crazily on the screen. Holly was looking ahead to a tiny red sun bobbing in the distance. Bond knew why it was red. It was beginning to re-enter the Earth's atmosphere. Just like them. The red circles lurched towards each other and there was a flash of green. Bond pressed. The circles stayed on the screen. Red. Holly cried out in pain as she jabbed at the controls.

'I can't hold this course much longer. We'll break up.'

Bond said nothing. 220,000 feet. His eyes were almost falling out of his head. The heat was agonizing. The two circles overlapped momentarily and there was another stab of green. He pressed instantly. Again too late. The two circles rolled around the screen like socketless eyes mocking his ineptitude. A shrill, high-pitched buzz rang out from somewhere on the control panel. A whole section of lights began to blink in unison. 200,000 feet. Death, here is thy sting.

'I'm losing the controls. The wings are starting to burn.'

Bond concentrated on the circles. They might be the last thing he ever concentrated on. The Moonraker was being shaken up and down as if by a giant hand. The noise from the control panel was ear-splitting. Distracting red lights flashed at the extremities of his vision. Smoke was billowing under his nose. His heels were on fire. Holly was crying out in pain. Bond strove to stay in control of his senses. The two circles performed kangaroo jumps and then moved into the same orbit. Come on, come on, damn you! It was like watching a putt hover on the lip of the hole. A putt with a hundred million lives riding on it. The circles trembled and then mounted each other to give birth to green. Bond pressed hot metal and looked out of the forward window. An arrow of white light streaked towards a white circle tinged with red. The circle disappeared. A violent explosion seemed to throw the Moonraker upwards and Bond saw Holly haul on the control column. Then he passed out.

20

COMING DOWN TO EARTH

Frederick Gray moved down the long corridor feeling pleased with himself. How fortunate that he, a key member of Her Majesty's Government, should have found himself within reach of Houston at this time. He tried not to look too obviously at the camera crew who were filming as they retreated down the corridor before him. His picture appearing all over the world. What a well-deserved boost to his career. With the P.M.'s health in question and no successor immediately recognizable in a divided Cabinet, the opportunities for self-advancement were obvious. Frederick Gray, the man on the spot. All glory attached to Britain's unexpected space coup would adhere to him. With M and his myrmidons safely ensconced in London, he would be seen as the trenchant mastermind behind Britain's involvement. Which, of course, was just. He had pressed for the best man to be put on the job, and this fellow Bond seemed to have delivered the goods.

'Hold it just there, gentlemen.' The cameraman held up his hand and the phalanx stopped obediently. Cameras whirred. Frederick Gray saw the microphone boom above his head. He began to speak with the slow, pompous delivery that had bored millions of television viewers: '... A great day for Anglo-American co-operation and a great day for the world.'

The general whose name he had not caught looked at him in surprise. 'Yeah.' He moved from behind the shoulder that Gray had thrust in front of him and addressed the camera crew. 'We're going in to Mission Control now. I would appreciate it if you were to keep behind the prescribed limits and not crowd us. Thank you.'

An armed guard in white helmet and gaiters swung open the door and Gray stepped forward smartly. At first glance he appeared to have walked into a theatre, but there were rows of consoles instead of seats. Where the stage would be was an enormous map of the world with lines of illuminated dots showing the paths of orbiting satellites. Gray thought of the famous space shots that had been shepherded from this hallowed room and wished that he could remember the names of some of them. He should have got his private secretary to bone up on the necessary background information. A few well-chosen words might have impressed viewers with his alertness and knowledge of everything that was going on in the world. He saw that the microphone boom was out of range and felt better. 'Very impressive,' he said, just in case anybody was listening. The general turned and looked at him with scarcely concealed dislike. He hated all politicians, but British politicians acting as though they still had an empire gave him a special pain that was worse than his ulcer.

An authoritative man bearing the words 'Mission Control Director' on the breast pocket of his short-sleeved shirt stepped forward and nodded to the assembled company. 'Gentlemen, welcome to Mission Control, Houston. We have received a position report and should have visual contact at any moment. If you observe the wall map you can see the trail of green lights approaching the Indian Ocean. The red light that you see flashing represents our tracking ship. Once Commander Bond and Dr Goodhead come within range we should have audio-visual from the remote on-board T.V. monitors.'

Gray began to relate to the excitement that was building up in the room, but for different reasons. He had heard his name mentioned twice by the man who was talking into the hand-held microphone to the television crew. They were transmitting live, and would be received at every corner of the globe. Not since the landing of Armstrong and Aldrin had there been an event like it.

The Mission Control Director began to speak again. His eyes sought out Gray. 'We're particularly glad to have you with us, Mr Gray. Because of the historical significance of this mission, I'm having this patched directly to the White House and Buckingham Palace, by satellite.'

Gray's cup overranneth. 'Most kind,' was all he could blurt out. He could imagine the royal hand putting down the Spode cup, the corgi's eyes obediently following its mistress's to the screen. At such moments a man might be excused his dreams. What would his thought be, he wondered, when the call came from the Palace? He imagined himself sitting in the Rolls-Royce as it purred down the Mall, a sprinkling of sightseers craning forward as the sentries saluted and he sailed through the gates. 'Will you form a government, Mr Gray?' 'Of course, Ma'am.' The first of many meetings, perhaps culminating in the moment when his knee sank towards the damask cushion and there was a slight tap on his shoulder. 'Arise, Sir Frederick.' Sir Frederick Gray. The three words that formed a poem more lovely than any Shakespeare Sonnet.

'We're getting something!' A technician spoke out excitedly from his position beside a large monitor screen and Gray elbowed aside the general. The camera crew closed in. A cueman had his arm raised. This was the moment. Gray craned forward so that the world could see the tears of pride in his eyes as he welcomed back his protégé. His eyes opened in wonder as he took in the scene and then, very slowly, little by little, he began to edge back behind the general.

'The Shoshones used to make love after battle to give thanks for still being alive,' said Holly.

Bond kissed her naked shoulder and watched a flimsy

undergarment drifting by. 'Say not the struggle nought availeth,' he murmured. 'What a pity they couldn't do it when they were weightless.'

'I expect they found other compensations.' Holly kissed Bond on the mouth and spread her arms wide. 'Oh James, this is heaven.'

Bond raised his head to glance out of an imaginary port-hole. 'Already?'

Holly hugged him to her. 'You're a fool, James.'

'I must be,' said Bond. 'Making love in zero-gravity in my condition. I should be in hospital.'

'Nonsense. You're in beautiful condition. I like my men slightly burnt at the edges.'

'Gruesome girl!' Bond kissed her hard on the mouth. 'We should have saved all this till Venice.'

Holly pulled back her head. 'Are you going to take me back to Venice, James?'

'I think our respective employers will both turn a favour-able eye on a period of convalescence.'

'You don't think we could convalesce up here?'

'Food presents a problem.'

'Who needs food?' Holly took Bond's cheeks between her fingers and kissed him greedily.

Bond enjoyed the kiss and floated away a few inches to enjoy the sight of her naked body. Something on the cabin wall attracted his attention. Something that was moving. A small television monitor. In the heart of the lens a small red light glowed lubriciously. Bond winced.

'What's the matter?' Holly floated towards him like a solicitous mother.

'Nothing too serious.' Bond received her in his arms and reached surreptitiously over her shoulder to pluck the cable from the monitor. It stopped moving and the light went out. 'Nevertheless, I think we ought to think about getting back. I have a feeling people will be worrying about us.'

Holly's lips started to stitch a pattern of kisses down Bond's chest. 'Please, James. Take me once more round the world.'

THE WORLD'S GREATEST THRILLER WRITERS – NOW IN GRANADA PAPERBACKS

Robert Ludlum

The Gemini Contenders	95p	☐
The Rhinemann Exchange	£1.00	☐
The Matlock Paper	85p	☐
The Osterman Weekend	85p	☐
The Scarlatti Inheritance	95p	☐
Ludlum Super-Thrillers Gift Set	£3.95	☐

Ian Fleming

Dr No	85p	☐
From Russia, with Love	85p	☐
Diamonds are Forever	85p	☐
On Her Majesty's Secret Service	85p	☐
Goldfinger	85p	☐
You Only Live Twice	75p	☐
Live and Let Die	75p	☐
The Man with the Golden Gun	75p	☐

Alan Williams

Shah-Mak	75p	☐
Gentleman Traitor	60p	☐
The Beria Papers	75p	☐
Barbouze	85p	☐
Long Run South	85p	☐
Snake Water	85p	☐
The Purity League	85p	☐
The Tale of the Lazy Dog	85p	☐

Gerald A Browne

Slide	75p	☐
11 Harrowhouse	75p	☐
Hazard	75p	☐

Trevanian

The Loo Sanction	95p	☐
The Eiger Sanction	85p	☐

THE WORLD'S GREATEST THRILLER WRITERS –
NOW AVAILABLE IN GRANADA PAPERBACKS

Len Deighton

Yesterday's Spy	60p	☐
Spy Story	75p	☐
Horse Under Water	85p	☐
Billion Dollar Brain	85p	☐
The Ipcress File	85p	☐
An Expensive Place to Die	85p	☐
Declarations of War	60p	☐
The Best of Len Deighton Gift Set	£4.25	☐

Peter Van Greenaway

Doppelganger	60p	☐
The Medusa Touch	85p	☐
Take the War to Washington	75p	☐
Judas!	75p	☐

Ted Allbeury

Snowball	50p	☐
A Choice of Enemies	60p	☐
Palomino Blonde	50p	☐
The Special Collection	60p	☐
The Only Good German	75p	☐

All these book are available at your local bookshop or newsagent, or can be ordered direct from the publisher. Just tick the titles you want and fill in the form below.

Name ....

Address ....

....

Write to Panther Cash Sales, PO Box 11, Falmouth, Cornwall TR10 9EN.
Please enclose remittance to the value of the cover price plus:
UK: 22p for the first book plus 10p per copy for each additional book ordered to a maximum charge of 82p.
BFPO and EIRE: 22p for the first book plus 10p per copy for the next 6 books, thereafter 3p per book.
OVERSEAS: 30p for the first book and 10p for each additional book.
Granada Publishing reserve the right to show new retail prices on covers, which may differ from those previously advertised in the text or elsewhere.